I0652440

The Shadow of Frankenstein
(*The Empire of the Necromancers 1*)

The Shadow of Frankenstein

(*The Empire of the Necromancers 1*)

by

Brian Stableford

A Black Coat Press Book

"The Grey Men" previously appeared in *Tales of the Shadowmen* No. 2 (2006) and "The Child-Stealers" in *Tales of the Shadowmen* No. 3 (2007).

The Shadow of Frankenstein (The Empire of the Necromancers 1) Copyright © 2006, 2007 by Brian Stableford.
Cover illustration Copyright © 2008 by Daniele Serra.

Visit our website at www.blackcoatpress.com

ISBN 978-1-934543-63-4. First Printing December 2008. Published by Black Coat Press, an imprint of Hollywood Comics.com, LLC, P.O. Box 17270, Encino, CA 91416. All rights reserved. Except for review purposes, no part of this book may be reproduced or transmitted in any form or by any means, electronic or mechanical, including photocopying, recording or by any information storage and retrieval system, without permission in writing from the publisher. The stories and characters depicted in this book are entirely fictional. Printed in the United States of America.

Introduction

The Empire of the Necromancers is a sequel to Paul
Féval's *John Devil*.[1] More precisely, it is the prologue to
a vaguely-conceived but hopefully extensive series of
sequels to my translation of *John Devil*—which is not
exactly Féval's version, because it includes a long supplementary essay pointing out the inconsistencies in the
novel's plot and making some suggestions as to how
those inconsistencies might be resolved. *The Empire of
the Necromancers* assumes that my interpretation of
what "really" happened in *John Devil* is correct.

Forty years ago, Kyril Bonfiglioli (the editor of *Sci-
ence-Fantasy*) rejected an early story of mine on the
grounds that it was "too recherché"—which was a polite
way of saying that the vast majority of readers would be
unable to figure out what it was supposed to be about.
Earlier this year, a publisher's reader killed off a much
more recent book with the brutal judgment that "Nobody
is interested in this stuff...there is no point in publishing
it"—which proves that I have not changed my ways in
the interim. One could certainly argue that no one but a
lunatic would bother to write a sequel to a novel that
practically no one has read in the last 100 years and

---

[1] Available from Black Coat Press, 2005, ISBN 978-1-
932983-15-9.

practically no one is likely to read in the next 100, but I've done it anyway, because the whim took me.

Anyone who wants to read *John Devil*—together with my analysis of its enigmas—is very welcome to do so. It is, in my opinion, a very interesting and historically significant book, but I must confess that my own particular fascination with it arises from the fact that I kept such close company with its slowly-unfolding narrative for several months while translating it—an experience that is mine alone. It was a strange thing to stand in Féval's shoes, as it were, following the course of a story that he was making up as he went along (under some external pressure from the editor who was serializing it, it seems, and the readers to whom the editor was pandering), using narrative techniques that he was also improvising anew, in his capacity as one of the exploratory pioneers of popular fiction. Such an experience gives one a whole new perspective on the craft and business of writing—but no one else is likely to care about that, so the point of this introduction is to provide some prefatory information that will make *The Empire of the Necromancers* easier for its potential readers to understand.

John Devil is the story of a long and complicated duel of wits between its eponymous anti-hero and an English police detective named Gregory Temple. John Devil is a legendary figure, whose name is assumed during the story by a remarkable person who might, in fact, be two people. Its primary wearer is certainly Comte Henri de Belcamp, the son of a French aristocrat and an English thief named Helen Brown; in my interpretation, Henri is also Tom Brown, Helen's notoriously villainous son, although he claims that Tom Brown is actually his half-brother—a claim to which various other characters, including Gregory Temple, eventually lend their support. Comte Henri's objective in John Devil—which is set in 1817—is to build a powerful steamship with which to rescue Napoleon from exile in St. Helena and spearhead the building of a French empire in India.

Although he contrives to negotiate an amazing series of obstacles—some of which seem curiously self-imposed—Henri de Belcamp fails to bring his plan to completion (as known history requires him to) and he shoots himself in the head, apparently fatally, although he is such a master of disguise and deception that one is free to doubt the result. Along the way, he frames Temple's assistant and prospective son-in-law, Richard Thompson, for murder, but then contrives to take his place in his cell in Newgate—shortly before Temple arrives with the intention of working the same trick, thus bringing about a highly dramatic confrontation, in which Henri drives Temple to the brink of madness.

John Devil cries out for a sequel, and I suspect that, if Féval had ever managed to work out to his own satisfaction who had actually done what in the interstices of his plot, and exactly why, he might have attempted one. He would have been faced, however, with one intractable narrative problem: John Devil is simply too accomplished, and his plans too grandiose, to be hidden away in a secret history. In Féval's day, the genre of alternative history had not yet been invented, and it would have seemed inconceivable to him that his character might return with a plan worthy of his talents and ambition, which really could change the face of the world. Fortunately, I have no such inhibition. I can do what Féval could not, and give John Devil an opportunity worthy of his talent and élan—thus providing his mortal adversary, Gregory Temple, with a corollary challenge worthy of his.

I ought, perhaps, to mention one more observation I was able to make while standing in Paul Féval's shoes as his translator, and that is his astonishing ability (which must, I think, have astonished him too) to identify with whichever of his characters happens to be occupying center-stage at any particular point in his story. It seems extremely probable that when he began *John Devil*, he intended Gregory Temple to be its hero and Henri de Belcamp its villain, but things did not work out that way. When he brought Temple to center-stage, Féval inserted himself wholeheartedly into Temple's character—but he did exactly the same with Henri, so the contrast between them became utterly confused, first morally and then logically. More than that: when the author had occasion to bring other characters temporarily to center-stage, he identified so forcefully with them that they too became forceful and heroic, even if—like the vertically-challenged petty criminal Ned Knob—they had initially been designed to provide comic relief. I liked that, so much that I decided that Ned Knob must continue on his accidentally-destined road, and become more heroic still—perhaps even more heroic than either of his sup-posed masters (who are, at the end of the day, a little too deeply embedded in the history of their time to welcome the kinds of changes to which it might be subject if something really big were to upset it).

Now, as they used to say in the days of serial fiction, read on...

Brian Stableford

PART ONE: THE GREY MEN

Chapter One
In Jenny Paddock's Parlor

Ned Knob was sitting opposite Sam Hopkey in one of the new booths in the parlor of Jenny Paddock's Cabaret Theater when the grey man walked in.

Sam was on the upholstered bench, with Jeanie Bird at his side. Ned was on a stool with his back to the door, so he did not see the grey man immediately. The first he knew of the miracle was the expression on Jack Hanrahan's face.

Hanrahan had just sidled over to the booth, reaching out a hand to support himself against the post while he leant down to mutter in Ned Knob's ear. He had got as far as "I'd very much like a word with you if I may, Master..." when his eyes—which were flickering from side to side, as was their habit—were arrested by the sight of something that made all the color drain instantly from his face. He stopped in mid-sentence, as if his throat had been cut.

Ned knew that the sight that could do that to Jack Hanrahan must be an exceptional one. Jack Hanrahan was a burker, whose business it was to haunt mortuaries and churchyards, seizing the dead from their slabs or hauling them out of their graves so that they might serve the ends of medical science on the dissecting table. A sight that could make Jack Hanrahan blanch was a sight indeed, and Ned was as anxious to see it as he was to score a point off the body-snatcher by conserving the color in his own cheeks. He just had time to see Sam Hopkey turn white in his turn, and Jeanie Bird arrive on the brink of a fainting fit, before he glanced over his shoulder to see what had occasioned such dread.

He had to admit, when he found himself looking straight into a monochrome image of Sawney's face, that there was reason enough for a certain amount of mental disturbance.

Sawney had been hanged not quite six weeks before, despite all that his friends could do for him. When a man is charged with being the most prolific supplier of false witnesses that London has ever known, there is little that can be done by way of mounting a convincing defense with the aid of false witnesses, even if his professional shoes have been filled by as clever and articulate as Gentleman Ned Knob.

Had Sawney returned from the dead, Ned wondered, or was this some kind of strange doppelganger?

Ned knew that he would need all his famed articulacy if he were to rise to such an unexpected occasion, but he was never daunted by a challenge. He spun around on his stool, glad for once that his legs were not long enough to reach the ground when he was thus seated. He leapt to the floor, throwing his arms wide as he went to greet his old friend.

"Sawney! What a joy it is to see you!" he cried—although he would have been clearly audible had he spoken in a whisper, so profound was the silence that had fallen on the Saturday-night multitude. The crowds packed Jenny's establishment every night now, from newly-whitewashed wall to wall, but Saturday always whitewashed wall to wall, but Saturday always attracted a surplus.

Sawney's grey face showed no sign of immediate recognition, so Ned went on. "We thought you dead, you know," he said, "and it has to be said that, save for your evident ambulatory capability, you certainly have the look of a corpse."

Ned heard a chorus of sharply intaken breaths, but the simulacrum of Sawney did not seem offended. The shade of grey that now possessed the old man's face—and his hands too—was somewhere between the color of clay and the color of slate, but it did not have the glutinous sheen of freshly-dug clay or the leaden glimmer of freshly-cut slate. It was, as Ned had frankly observed, a dead grey. What was more distressing still was that the eyes slowly scanning the room had no color in their irises, nor any tiny red blood vessels in their whites; the pupils were like black points set upon on two billiard-balls.

Sawney's hair had been greying before he went before the judge, but it was a paler shade now. If the suit he was wearing was the one he'd been buried in, though, it had certainly sustained a deal of wear in the coffin.

"Don't you know me, Sawney?" Ned asked, taking the old man by the arm. "It's Gentleman Ned—or Republican Ned, as they're as likely to call me nowadays. Here's Sam, do you see, to whom you've been a second father—and Jeanie, his lovely leading lady. Sit down and have a drink with us, old chap. Jenny! A brandy for Sawney—it's raw outside and the cold has got into his bones."

Sawney reacted at last. He looked Ned in the face, and his lips moved. The sound that came out was not his old acting voice, with which he had been able to reach every last corner of an auditorium, but it was clearly audible. "Ned," he croaked, his voice as dry and grey as his face. "In the parlor. And Sam. Wanted to see Sam. Jeanie too. Cold in my bones."

"That's all right, Sawney," Ned said, pulling him toward the booth. "We'll soon have you warm. Take my stool. Do you know Jack Hanrahan, Sawney?" It was mostly mischief that made him ask that question, because he had gathered from Jack Hanrahan's reaction that the two had met before. He was curious to know whether Sawney would recognize the burker, assuming that they had met for the first time after the hanging.

Sawney did not look at Jack Hanrahan—for which mercy the burker seemed relieved. Hanrahan beat a hasty retreat, his expression readable as blind terror. Sawney, meanwhile, continued to look at Sam Hopkey and Jeanie Bird. "My friends," the grey man said, in a strangely tender manner, given the neutrality of his tone. "Wanted to see you."

Sam and Jeanie, to their credit, were actors enough to mask their own superstitious dread as Sawney took Ned's stool. Ned fetched another from a neighboring table.

"Not on stage, Sam?" Sawney murmured, as if making conversation.

"Tonight's performance is over, Sawney," Ned told him, as he hopped up on to his new seat. "You're late, I fear—but you'd be a good few days late for All Soul's Eve, if you really were a ghost. You're not a ghost, are you, Sawney? How did you cheat the hangman, old friend?"

Sawney's papery brow furrowed slightly at that, as if he were puzzled, or searching for a lost memory.

Jenny Paddock arrived with a jug of brandy, four glasses on a tray. It was not her habit to wait at tables, but she was not a woman to hang back when something extraordinary needed to be done.

"Thank you, Mistress Paddock," Ned said, politely. "You may pour, if you don't mind."

"You can pour yourself—and I'll take the money now, if you don't mind," was Jenny Paddock's retort. Ned thought the demand a trifle rude—and quite unnecessary, given his status in the establishment and the fact that Sawney showed not the least sign of running amok or strangling anyone. He handed over threepence, and then poured brandy into all four glasses. He glanced sideways to see how far Jack Hanrahan had retreated.

The burker had paused a dozen paces away; he had his own glass in his hand, having just taken a liberal gulp of gin. Hanrahan was staring at Ned now, not at Sawney. Ned liked that; he always gloried in the admiration of tall men.

Sawney had still not replied to Ned's last question, and Sam seemed uncharacteristically tongue-tied, so Ned decided that it was up to him to keep the conversation going. "We miss you, Sawney," Ned assured him, "but we're keeping things going, exactly as you would have wished. Jenny Paddock's Cabaret Theater is the talk of the town, always packed out. We're a success, and we owe it all to you." He thought it best not to add that the publicity given to Sawney's hanging had done the troupe no harm.

After a pause—while Sawney continued staring at Sam and Jeanie, with what might have been affection in his grey features and disconcerting eyes—Ned went on. "Perhaps that's as well, given that the witness racket hasn't picked up at all. Business is bad all around, I fear—except for burking, where there's said to be a boom. There's hardly a grave from Highgate to Dulwich that hasn't been raided these last three weeks, if you believe the gossip—which we don't, of course. I wish you'd tell me though, that you aren't dead at all, and never were. I think there's many a mind hereabouts would be set at rest by that assurance."

Sawney lifted his glass to his colorless lips, and sipped the brandy. Having tested it, he drained the glass and put it down, obviously hopeful of another.

Ned poured.

"How did you escape, Sawney?" Sam Hopkey whispered.

"And where have you been these last forty days?" added Jeanie.

"Forty days," Sawney echoed, as if slightly surprised by the figure. "Forty days and forty nights, in the wilderness. Wanted to see my friends."

"If you've been fasting," Ned said, "we'd best get you something to eat—if there's anything left, that is." He raised his voice to shout: "Jenny, my love! Have you some mashed potato and gravy?" He took the absence of a rude reply as an affirmative.

"How did you get away, Sawney?" Sam repeated. "I couldn't bear to go myself, you know, but there are people in this crowd who went to your hanging, and saw it done. Are you a ghost? Tell us, I beg of you."

"Ghost?" Sawney repeated, quizzically. "Am I a ghost?"

"No!" said Ned. "Let's not have superstitious talk at this table! You're as solid as you ever were, Sawney, although you seem a trifle thinner. I've seen you play a ghost, mind, up there on that stage Mistress Paddock built for you. That's what you're doing now, isn't it?

You're playing games with us, because you knew we thought you dead. You've made yourself up as a ghost, and you're playing the part to the hilt, as ever. Bravo, Sawney, bravo! But Sam's right, you know—it would be a kindness if you'd explain to us exactly how the hanging failed to kill you."

While he was speaking, the door opened again—but Ned's back was still to the door, and he did not turn around immediately. Sam and Jeanie did not react as they had to the sight of Sawney, with awe and terror, but they did react. Ned realized that the dramatis personae in the unfolding drama was not yet fully assembled. He turned to look at the newcomers—and Sawney turned too.

This time, only one of the two men who had come in was grey enough to seem dead, and he was no one that Ned Knob had ever met. This grey man was so tall as almost to qualify as a giant, and powerfully built. His head seemed slightly out of proportion to his body, but that might have been a trick of the light cast by the lantern he was carrying—which he was still holding up at head height, even though Jenny Paddock's was reasonably well supplied with candlesticks.

The grey giant had the same white-irises eyes as Sawney. Their strange gaze picked Jeanie Bird's face out of the crowd, but there did not seem to be any menace or recognition in them. Ned's stare, by contrast, was drawn by a similar magnetism to the other new arrival.

The giant's companion was as wondrously short as the giant was tall, and seemed as vividly alive as the giant seemed dully dead. Had the short man been 25 years younger, Ned Knob might have felt that he was looking at a long-lost brother. Age aside, he and the shorter newcomer were very similar in their physique. The newcomer's good suit was a better quality than Ned's, even though Ned tried as hard to live up to his first-chosen nickname as to his second, but that only served to emphasize that here were two dandies in miniature. The shorter newcomer was carrying a large suitcase in his gloved left hand, sturdier than any bag Ned had ever needed to carry his own meager portables. He was presumably a well-traveled man.

The smaller newcomers was looking at Sawney, having quickly scanned the room. It seemed that the exotic pair had come looking for Sawney—but the small man hesitated before coming forward to claim him. He was evidently wary of a place so crowded, into which he had never stepped before.

Ned spun around again and hopped down to the ground. He went directly to the shorter of the two men, and marveled at the fact that he could look the fellow straight in the eye without tilting his head at all. "Welcome to Paddock's Cabaret, my friends," he said. "You're a little late for the performance, I fear, but I hope you'll have a drink with us. Would you care to join my party? I'm Ned Knob, by the way. May I know who you are?"

The short man only hesitated for a moment before setting down his suitcase, pulling off his brown glove and reaching into an inner pocket. He took out a silver card-case, drew out a visiting card, and handed it to Ned without saying a word.

"Germain Patou," Ned read, aloud. "A physician—from Paris, I see.[2] Well, Monsieur Patou, if you're the man responsible for our friend's uncanny state of health,

_____

[2] Germain Patou was introduced in Paul Féval's *The Vampire Countess*, Black Coat Press, 2003, ISBN 978-0-9740711-5-2.

you're doubly welcome." Then, on an impulse, he leaned forward, and whispered in the other's ear, so softly that he could not be overheard even in the general hush: "*A l'avantage, mon ami!*"

Patou's eyes gave him away, although he tried to hide his surprise. "I am pleased to make your acquaintance, Monsieur Knob," he said, his pronunciation very precise despite his French accent, "and I am sure that everything is indeed for the best. I am your friend's doctor, as you have deduced—and he is not yet fully recovered from his ordeal, as you can plainly see. We have come to take him back to the ward, if you will kindly permit it."

"Sawney doesn't need my permission to go where he will, Monsieur Patou," Ned said. "You'll forgive my familiarity, I hope, but I don't meet many men whose stature is similar to my own, and never one from Paris. You're a man of 40, I suppose—tell me, is it true that the Emperor Napoleon was no taller than you or I?"

Again he heard a chorus of gasps, but none of them was Patou's. Patou smiled before replying: "I had the honor of meeting the Emperor on more than one occasion, when he was the First Consul," he said. "I had a dear friend who knew him very well. Alas, he was taller than I—and therefore taller than you—by twice the width of my thumb." He held up his hand as he said it, by way of illustration.

"Alas," Ned echoed. "Will you have a drink with me, Monsieur Patou—and your friend too, of course. I have just ordered a meal for my old friend, who seems a trifle thinner than when we saw him last. What is your companion's name, by the way? Has he too passed through the hangman's noose and survived to tell the tale?"

"John," said Patou—addressing the giant rather than answering Ned's question, although the name provided one item of the information for which Ned had gone fishing, "will you take your fellow patient by the arm and guide him to the door. I'm sorry, Monsieur Knob, but I am fearful for the well-being of both my patients. No one should be wandering abroad on a night so cold, even to see his old friends. He will come again when he is fully recovered—you may be sure of that."

"I'd dearly like to know the hospital in which he's lodged at present," Ned was quick to retort as the giant moved forward. "We'd all like to visit him, wouldn't we, Sam? With your permission, doctor, of course. Is he in Guy's, perhaps, or St. Thomas's?"

"You may be sure that I shall send word to you when that is possible," Patou said, his voice still purringly polite, although there was a slight edge of steel in it now. "Mine is a private sanatorium. As you can see, your friend has been very seriously ill, and he is far from himself at present. When he is well enough, I shall be very glad to admit visitors to see him."

"But where?" Ned retorted. "Your card has only a Paris address."

Patou bowed, and reached out his ungloved hand to take back the card. Then he produced the stub of a pencil from the pocket of his trousers, and scribbled on the back of the card. "You may reach me via that address," he said.

Ned glanced down. The address was in Stepney; Ned did not know the street, but he did not know of anything in that neighborhood that could pass for a private sanatorium. He had taken note of the fact that the Frenchman had not said that he was actually in residence there. Ned wondered how many men it would require to immobilize the giant. There would be no shortage of volunteers if he called for help on Sawney's behalf, and the two newcomers could not possibly stand off a multitude. On the other hand, Ned did not want to start a fight in which Sawney might get hurt. The old man's condition was obviously very delicate. If this physician really had revived him after a hanging, even if the executioner had been careless, it was the next best thing to a miracle—and it would be a great pity were the work to be carelessly undone.

"You're very kind," Ned said, insincerely. "Are you sure that Sawney would not be better if he were fed before he braves the night again?"

"Quite sure," Germain Patou replied. "But I hope that you'll permit me to pay for the wasted supper." He rummaged in his trouser pocket again, and this time hauled out a sixpence. He threw it on the table, saying: "Please let me buy you a drink, Monsieur Knob—and your friends too. Are you ready, John?"

"Won't you stay a little longer, Sawney?" said Jeanie Bird, courageously. The giant was still staring at her; there was no hostility in the stare, but it was intimidating nevertheless.

Patou moved around Ned with surprising agility, and laid his hand on Sawney's shoulder. "We must go back, now," he said. "You will see your friends again, I promise."

Sawney stood up. "Wanted to see you," he said, regretfully. "Must go back now." His voice had faded to a broken whisper, and his grey brow was deeply furrowed, as if the memories he had been trying to recover were proving perversely evasive.

The Frenchman guided Sawney back to the giant named John, who took Sawney by the arm. Sawney looked up at the giant, trustfully. "Wanted to see..." he repeated—but this time his voiced drained away to nothing, and he seemed to be on the point of collapse. The giant took firmer hold of him, supporting him as he took a step towards the door. Ned did not imagine that there would be many in the hall who would be sorry to see him go. He did, however, observe that the giant cast a long backward look at Jeanie Bird.

"You must come back and see us again, Monsieur Patou," Ned said, softly. "You have our undying gratitude, for what you have done for dear Sawney. Do you hear me, Sawney—we love this man, for what he has done for you, as we have always loved you. Send for us when you can, I beg you."

Sawney roused himself in response to this speech. "Ned," he said, weakly. "Gentleman Ned. Wanted to see..."

"You shall see us all, old friend, when you're well," Ned assured him. "Depend on it."

The giant was already guiding Sawney through the door. Patou bowed and tipped his hat before picking up his suitcase and following them.

Ned was so confounded by the event that he did not even try to prevent Jenny Paddock from scooping up the sixpence as she laid down the unnecessary mashed potatoes, or complain when she did not offer him any change. "Stay here, Sam," he said—although Sam had not given the slightest sign of getting up. "I'll follow them all the way to Paris, if I must. I'll meet you here tomorrow, as usual." He paused just long enough to make sure that Patou's visiting card was safely stowed in his breast pocket before setting off for the door. By the time he got to it, the hubbub of conversation had risen behind him to twice its normal volume.

The night was very dark, and there was enough fog to stifle the meager lamplight that shone at either end of Low Lane. That was not to Ned's disadvantage, though, for it made the giant's lantern that much easier to see, and to follow. The exotic company made slow progress, for the giant was still supporting Sawney and was by no means light on his feet himself.

Ned had followed better men than these and gone undetected. He was on his home ground, and knew how to hide himself away whenever Germain Patou glanced behind—which he did quite often. Ned had hoped that they might turn north but they went south, towards the Thames, and then turned east. They went under Black-friars Bridge and continued along the embankment towards Southwark Bridge.

If they had a boat waiting for them, Ned knew, his boast that he would follow them to Paris would be so much wasted breath.

The route that the three men followed was not a safe one for a man dressed as Patou was dressed, even if he had not been carrying a bag, but they went unmolested. If the giant's size were not deterrent enough, the lantern-light still displayed the corpse-like pallor of the Frenchman's two companions. The hawks patrolling the rookery and the shore were very prone to superstition, and there had been all kinds of eerie rumors abroad since the recent epidemic of burking had begun. No one imagined that the surplus of snatched bodies was merely being piled up in some cellar beneath St Thomas' Hospital, and everyone had his own hypothesis as to the use to which they might have been put.

So far as Ned knew, there had been not an atom of evidence available within the bounds of the city to support any of those hypotheses—until now.

Despite its slowness, the journey was not a long one—but the three men did have a boat waiting. Nor was the ferryman's skiff the craft that would take them all the way to their destination—in which case Ned might have been able to follow it along the bank. The ferryman took them no more than 30 yards out into the watercourse and 100 yards downstream, where a two-master was waiting on the far side of Southwark Bridge, on the edge of the navigation channel. There were men waiting too, to haul Patou's two companions up to the deck—ordinary men, so far as Ned could judge, not grey ones. The lantern in the stern cast just enough light for the vessel's name to be read: *Prometheus*.

The giant passed his own lamp down to Patou before climbing up, and Ned hoped that Patou might keep it lit, but the short man snuffed it out before he was lifted in his turn. Ned was doubly annoyed when someone else came out on to the bridge to look down at the new arrivals. Ned's heart began to pound within his breast, and not because of his exertions in following the three strangers from Jenny Paddock's. It was pounding because the man on the bridge was wearing a Quaker hat.

Ordinarily, Ned would have remained deep in the shadows, anxious not to be seen by the men he had been following, even though that no longer mattered. The sight of the Quaker hat changed his mind. He stepped forward on to the quay, deliberately setting himself beneath an oil-lamp, where he knew that he would be seen—and having done that, he raised his arm, as if in a salute.

The man in the Quaker hat did not return his gesture—not, at least, before a blanket was suddenly thrown over Ned's head from behind, and he was grabbed by at least two pairs of hands.

Throwing a blanket over someone's head to cushion the cudgel-blow that would lay them out was a burker's trick. Ned just had time to curse the name of Jack Hanrahan before the anticipated blow landed on the back of his head and knocked him insensible.

Chapter Two
A Cell in Newgate

Ned knew that he must have stirred and tried to sit up
before becoming fully conscious, because the first thing
of which he became fully aware—apart from the thun-
dering pain in his head—was someone pressing a cup to
his lips and bidding him drink.

It was laudanum, but diluted to a concentration that
would do him more good than harm. Once he was sure
of that, Ned drank meekly. He wanted his headache gone
as soon as possible; wherever he was, he was in trouble,
and would need his wits about him.

"Lie down!" a voice urged him. "Wait just a little a
while, and you'll be well enough to talk."

Ned managed to open his eyes a little, in spite of the
pain—but the light, such as it was, made the speaker a
mere silhouette. He was tall, though not as tall as the
grey giant, and he was not wearing a hat. Ned did not
recognize the voice.

Ned did as he was told and lay back, keeping as still
as possible to aid the relief of his sore head—but he kept
his eyes open by the merest crack, so that he could study
his surroundings. It was difficult to concentrate, but he
knew that he had to try.

He was in a bare-walled cell whose walls had been
recently whitewashed—although some of the old graffiti
still showed through as a series of enigmatic blurs. It had
no window but it did have a small ventilation-shaft let

into one of the corners and a grille in the sturdy door. The wooden pallet on which Ned was lying was obviously intended as a bed although it had no mattress. The only other furnishings the cell boasted were a rickety table and two chairs. The table bore a medicine-bottle, a jug of water and a freshly-lit candle in a cheap tin tray.

The silhouette drew away, and resolved itself into the form of a man. He was better-dressed than Ned—though not so well as Germain Patou—but there was nothing of the dandy about the cut of his black jacket or his burgundy cravat. If this was a gentleman, true or feigned, he wore his status casually.

It was not until his captor finally sat down at the table that Ned saw his face, in profile. For a moment, he failed to recognize the face just as he had failed to recognize the voice, but then he realized who it was.

"Well," he said to himself, silently, "I must be in Hell or Bedlam, and it may not matter which. If the dead are walking abroad tonight, they have come out in full force." He had to make an effort to pronounce the words clearly inside his agonized skull, and was proud of himself for holding on until the end of the sentence.

Ned was doubly resolved, now that he knew who had power over him, to do exactly as he had been instructed, and lie as still as he possibly could until the laudanum calmed his raging headache. While he did so, he tried to calculate exactly how much trouble he might be in, and of exactly what sort.

He could not do it; events had moved too rapidly, and had taken too many strange turns.

"But I am Republican Ned Knob," he reminded himself. "I have more wits about me than any common enemy of the crown. If I do not appear on stage with Sam and Jeanie, it is only because I would be taken for a clown by virtue of my size. I can act as well as Sam, though not as well as Sawney could. If this man is determined to send me after Sawney, I must best him by cunning. It can be done. It has been done!"

A few minutes later, he sat up, and made a show of dusting himself down. "Well, Mr. Temple," he said, "I'm very glad to see you. I thought I'd been attacked by an eager burker, adapting to the excess of demand over supply as any orthodox political economist would. Perhaps I was, and you came to my rescue? Where am I, by the way?"

"Newgate," Gregory Temple replied, brutally. "Where you've long belonged, Master Knob—and where you'll likely stay, if you do not give me satisfaction."

"Newgate," Ned echoed, trying to sound no more than pensive. "My memory is at fault, then, for I do not remember being arrested, let alone charged, tried, convicted and sentenced—or has the law lost sight of such niceties, now that it must cope with determined radicals as well as the rabble?"

"You've not been charged with any crime as yet," Gregory Temple told him. "You should not congratulate yourself on that score, though, for I can think of half a dozen if I need to, and make every one of them stick."

Ned was annoyed by that. "You are addressing me with naked contempt, Mr. Temple," he said, getting off the bed and coming to sit at the table, opposite his captor. His head reeled but he took himself firmly in hand and resolved to sit very still while he faced his adversary. "I do not deserve that. If either of us has any cause for resentment against the other, it is me. You did me a very bad turn once, by means of shabby trickery—but that was a long time ago and I'm not a man to hold grudges. I've forgiven you, for your lovely daughter's sake. If you wanted news of her, you did not need to have me kidnapped—you had only to seek me out and ask."

He realized immediately that he had made a mistake in mentioning Temple's daughter. His captor's face had been quite bland until then, considering that he was reputed to be a madman prone to apoplectic fits, but it became exceedingly furious now. "My daughter!" Temple cried, explosively. "What would a foul worm like you know of my daughter?"

Ned was taken aback, and honestly puzzled. "Did you not know that I know your daughter?" he asked, in frank surprise. "I have not seen her as often lately as I did in the wake of... the unpleasantness, but I spent three months at the chateau this summer. I know that you have not visited her there for years, but I assumed that as you are now up and about..." He broke off, frightened in spite of himself by the way that Gregory Temple was staring at him. "I appear to have misunderstood," he murmured, "I apologize."

Temple seemed to be fighting his own anger, with more than a little difficulty; it was his turn to be silent, and to wait until he was better able to speak. Eventually, he said: "How was she?" Evidently, he had cut off all communication with his offspring, although Suzanne Temple had been too proud to confess that to Ned.

"She is well," Ned said. "Richard, too—both Richards. The Comtesse is also well... and her son. You do know that the Comtesse has a son?"

"That I knew," Temple said. "What I do not know is how and why you have been her guest."

"Ah," Ned said. "I'm sorry—your reputation as a detective led me to assume that you would know everything. I carried a message to the new chateau on the night of the Comte's acquittal. Many of the guests awaiting him there thought it politic to withdraw in a hurry, but I stayed with Lady Frances—Countess Boehm, as she became, or Sarah O'Brien, as you knew her—to be of what service I could. As things turned out, there was a great deal I could do... not so much for Lady Frances, but for Jeanne Balcomb, whose position as the Comtesse de Belcamp needed to be proved, and regularized. I was Mr. Wood's clerk once, you know. There were a great many documents to sort through, a great many commissions to carry out, necessitating a great many trips back and forth across the channel. I'm quite the seasoned traveler now, Mr. Temple." He stopped, anxious now because he did not know exactly how far Temple's ignorance extended.

Temple was silent for a few moments before he said: "I see. But that's not the reason you're here, Master Knob—not directly, at least. You're here to answer questions about Jack Hanrahan and Alexander Ross."

"Hanrahan!" Ned exclaimed. "What do I know about Jack Hanrahan? And who on Earth..." He broke off again, cursing himself for not having remembered soon enough that Alexander Ross was the name Sawney had been given at birth—and the name under which he had recently been hanged.

"You were seen talking confidentially to Hanrahan last night at Sharper's," Temple stated, baldly, "just before your friend Ross came in—startling you as much as everyone else. I understand."

"Hanrahan said that there was something he wanted to talk to me about," Ned admitted, remembering the fact belatedly, "but I never found out what it was because

Sawney came in just then—and Hanrahan backed away, like a frightened rabbit."

"But you do know Hanrahan—and you know his profession."

"I know him as well as any of the regulars at Jenny's—which no one calls Sharper's any longer, by the way, though the old plaque still hangs outside the door. He, I dare say, knows me a little better, since I'm now in charge of Sawney's old troupe—his actors, I mean, lest you should think I mean something else. I can't replace him on stage, of course—no audience could take a man of my status seriously in the kinds of roles he used to play—but I can write and direct, and ever since Sawney persuaded Jenny to take down Tom's old boxing ring and make a stage instead, we've gone from success to success. You should come and see my boys and girls perform, Mr. Temple—although it might be as well to come as Solomon Green. Some of the old hands are better by far at holding grudges than I am. What are you doing nowadays, by the way? I never really believed the rumor that said you were in Bedlam, let alone the one that said you were dead—although I think Suzanne might be very grateful for some proof of their falsity, if she really has none."

"That's not what you were brought here to talk about," Temple said, sharply. "And so far, you've told me nothing at all. How did Ross cheat the rope?"

"A very interesting question, Mr. Temple," Ned said, "And another I might have the answer to, if only I hadn't been interrupted. He seemed confused when I asked him, and I was trying to help him remember when his physician arrived to take him away. I fear that Sawney's memory isn't what it used to be, since he doesn't seem to remember that my poor Pretty Molly is long dead. I could have detained him, of course, but when a friend you took for dead shows unexpected signs of life, it's hard to be vexed with his physician."

Gregory Temple produced something from his waistcoat pocket and threw it on the table. It was Germain Patou's visiting card. "Who is he?" the former head of Scotland Yard demanded, as if he still had every right to do so.

"If you've read the card," Ned said, "you know exactly as much as I do. If you had a spy in Jenny's last night, who saw Jack Hanrahan come to talk to me, he must have heard every word that was spoken between us."

"Every word except one," Temple retorted, as if he had caught Ned out in a tremendous lie.

"Oh, that," said Ned, disdainfully. "I merely said à l'avantage. That's what the Knights of the Deliverance used to say in France, you know, instead of the for the best they whispered when they met in London. Patou did not give the customary reply—but he probably thought it unnecessary, given that the Emperor is dead and the Deliverance disbanded."

"That being the case," Temple said, coldly, "Why did you say it?"

"Because he is French, and because I've found it a very useful way to ingratiate myself with a certain kind of Frenchman. I told you just a few minutes ago, if you recall, that I carried a vital message to the Brotherhood at the new chateau. They have cause to be grateful to me, even though their cause is lost, and I'm a man who knows the value of gratitude. I can admit that safely, can I not, Mr. Temple? You cannot have me hanged merely for knowing a defunct password, and using it a trifle promiscuously."

"And this Patou recognized the Deliverance's watchword?" Temple queried, "Even though he did not make the approved reply?"

"He admitted openly to having met Bonaparte before he was Emperor, and to having a dear friend in common," Ned pointed out. "As to who that friend might have been, your guess is as good as mine."

Temple stood up, as if he wanted to pace around the room, but he thought better of it. He sat down again, but he held himself upright so that he could look down on Ned in spite of the fact that they were both seated. "Don't play games with me, Master Knob," he said, apparently trying to sound menacing. "As yet, you have not given me a single item of useful information."

"I'm aware of that, Mr. Temple," Ned agreed, wondering what the times were coming to when a man like Gregory Temple had to make an effort to sound menacing, and could not be entirely convincing in the role. "Just as I'm aware that you haven't told me why I should. The truth is, alas, that I have no such information to give you, and I'm not playing games with you at all. I'm as curious to get to the bottom of this matter of the grey men as you are, and would be glad to trade facts with you, if you had information to give me in exchange—but I'm an honest man, and will not try to trick you into telling me what you know without having anything to offer in return. I'm sorry that my knowing your daughter seems to offend you, but I'm not ashamed of being her friend, any more than I'm ashamed of being a radical and a man of some reputation at Jenny Paddock's. You may try to terrify me with your power and authority if you wish, but I repeat that I do not deserve your contempt, and you have no right to hold me here without charge."

Gregory Temple stared at him in open amazement, astonished to be addressed in such a manner by a man like Ned Knob. Ned felt that it was time to seize the initiative.

"I think I can guess, now," Ned aid, "why I was knocked on the head last night—it was last night, I presume? Your spy wanted to take possession of the card that Patou gave me, to discover what he had written on the back. You're ready to move against the body-snatchers whose increased activity has begun to cause alarm in Westminster—but I'm not part of that conspiracy. I'm an innocent bystander, who merely happens to be a friend of one of the men this Germain Patou seems to have brought back from the grave."

"You're a rogue and a liar, Master Knob," Temple said, his snarl still unconvincing. "Who was the man you saluted from the quay near London Bridge?"

Ned's head had been quiet for some little time now, thanks to the laudanum and the care he had taken to be still, and he felt that he had learned more from his present situation than Gregory Temple had learned from him. He felt that he was a step ahead of his captor now—which was exactly where he liked to be, in every situation.

"Ah!" he said softly. "So that is what this is really about. That is why we are here à deux, I suppose. No subordinates, no superiors—just poor Ned Knob and the once-great Gregory Temple. You should have lied to me, Mr. Temple, and told me that I had indeed been seized by burkers, and that you really had dashed to my rescue. I might have believed you, at least for a second or two. These are dark days for men of your kind, are they not? The government is direly anxious, since the gagging acts have made things worse instead of better. This is London, of course, not Paris—we are more careful to keep the existence of our secret police as secret as their names. You were the top man at Scotland Yard, I know, but that was before your supposed madness and public disgrace. You take orders now, I dare say, but you're not the sort of man to follow them to the letter, and if personal matters should intrude on your inquiries... well, once again you know as much as I do, Mr. Temple. The man wore a Quaker hat, as I'm sure you've been told. I saluted the hat, for old time's sake, although I could not see who wore it. Your guess is as good as mine."

Temple clearly had not liked this speech, but he had a tight rein on his temper at present. "And what is your guess, Master Knob?" he asked, with feigned politeness.

"If it is him," Ned replied, without hesitation, "then I suppose he too might have been brought back from the dead. Indeed, I can hardly suppose otherwise, since I know for a fact that he has not been in contact with his beloved Jeanne since the day he was reported to have shot himself in the head."

"You're teasing me, Master Knob. Why do you not name him?"

"Because I hardly know what name to give him. Should I call him Comte Henri de Belcamp, or James Davy, or Tom Brown... or simply John Devil the Quaker?"

"I had to carry a message to his father that another Tom Brown had been captured and hanged," Temple said, stonily, "having confessed to the murders of Maurice O'Brien and Constance Bartolozzi."

"I know," Ned replied, unable to stop himself although he knew that it might be unwise. "I sent that message."

Temple scowled. "You flatter yourself a little, Master Knob," he replied, almost calmly. "Ross was still the puppet master then, I think. Ross persuaded the boy to do it, and coached him in his speech."

"And I persuaded Sawney to persuade him," Ned replied. "Would you like to know why?"

Temple hesitated, but eventually said: "Ross refused to tell me the reason. I would have done better to ask him before he was condemned to hang, rather than afterwards, but I had no suitable opportunity."

"He would not have told you no matter how much force or cunning you exerted," Ned said, "but I will tell you, if you wish. Then I shall have told you something you did not know, and you'll have no more reason to be annoyed with me."

Temple did not like that, but he nodded his head. "Touché," he conceded. "Why did you do it, Master Knob?"

"Because your daughter asked me to—oh, don't be angry! She didn't do it on her own behalf, let alone to strike a blow at you. She did it for the Marquis, and for Jeanne. They had such a fervent desire to believe—such a fervent need to believe—that Henri was not the assassin of Maurice O'Brien and Constance Bartolozzi that Suzanne asked me to help them in that, just as I was helping them in other ways. It was a small thing—there's no shortage of men who are to be hanged, alas, and the lad would have done it merely for the jest and the notoriety, even if we hadn't been able to offer help to his mother. He loved his mother, that boy—who was not Helen Brown, of course, no matter what he said in his little speech. You always knew that, I suppose... and yet you carried the message anyway, and offered it without comment. You're right; I did take a little of someone

34

else's credit—not Sawney's, but yours. If you had called the lie a lie... but you loved the old Marquis too, didn't you? So you see, Mr. Temple, that we were allies once, even though you're now a member of Lord Liverpool's secret police, while I'm a steadfast reader of the Black Dwarf."

"Don't play games with me, Master Knob," Temple said, stiffly. "The Marquis is dead now, and if John Devil really has returned from the dead, he's your fast friend and my deadly enemy. I can keep you here, you know, for all that you haven't been charged with any crime. You might not be a man to bear grudges, but you have never been subject to the pressure that was put on me. Believe me, Master Knob, I would not hesitate to kill you here and now if I thought that it would bring me one step closer to the real Tom Brown."

"But it wouldn't," Ned pointed out, disdainfully. "And when you say that you can keep me here, you mean that you have the power, not the right. I am no longer the kind of man who bows down to power, Mr. Temple, but only to right. There was a time, I believe, when you were that kind of man yourself, and I hope that you still are. I have done nothing wrong, Mr. Temple. It is not a crime to stand on a quay and salute a Quaker hat, no matter what you might think of the man who might have been wearing it."

"No, it isn't," Temple conceded. "But if I let you go, you'll try to seek him out—and that will surely lead you into wrongdoing."

"I am interested to know what has become of my friend Sawney," Ned Knob said. "I am interested to know how he cheated the hangman, and how many other grey men there are in London just now. If Monsieur de Belcamp is responsible for Sawney's rescue or resurrection, I shall be very pleased to make his reacquaintance—but I'm my own man now, Mr. Temple. I follow right, not power."

"I'm interested to know how Ross cheated the noose myself," Temple admitted. "Hanrahan and his sinister brotherhood have been far too busty of late, and the situation is getting out of hand. When rumors of the living dead reach the palace of Westminster, even the Luddites seem mere scarecrows. You might be useful to me, Master Knob. Will you work for me, if I let you go—until we discover the secret of the grey men?"

Ned had expected this, and had known for some time exactly what he ought to say, but when he opened his mouth to speak, he found that he could not do it. "No, Mr. Temple," he said, as honesty got the better of him. "I won't work for the police, secret or otherwise, in this or any other matter. If all men were equal before the law, I could respect it—but until they are, I'll not assist it."

Temple clicked his tongue. "All you had to do," he said, resentfully, "was lie. I'd have expected you to betray me."

"I'm sorry to have disappointed you," Ned said, sarcastically. "But if you let me go, you'll have to do it for the right reason, not because I've provided you with a sly excuse. If you want to connect Jack Hanrahan to Sawney, and prove that Germain Patou is the buyer for all the corpses ripped from their graves these last few weeks, you'll have to do it yourself. And if you want to neglect your actual orders to go chasing after your old employee James Davy, who crushed your career and broke your system—and left you here in Newgate to explain why Richard Thompson had gone missing, even though you hadn't had the privilege of freeing him—you'll have to do that by yourself as well. I won't report 'll have to do that by yourself as well. I won't report to you, Mr. Temple, and I won't make false promises to you."

Temple was no longer holding himself stiffly. Indeed, he had slumped so far down in his seat that he seemed little taller than Ned Knob—who had drawn himself up under the pressure of his bombast. Silence fell, and Ned moved his head from side to side to stretch the muscles in his neck. If the worst came to the worst, he thought, at least he'd be able to lie down until his headache was completely gone. If Temple released him, he'd not be able to allow himself to rest.

"If I were you," Temple said, bitterly. "I'd be wondering why John Devil the Quaker has come to London without sending for his favorite messenger-boy. Perhaps he's heard that you are now a man of principle, and is too delicate to offend you with a new offer of employment."

"I know that you only mean to insult us both," Ned replied, proudly, "but I could believe that. The Comte de Belcamp was always honorable in his dealings with me. I tried to blackmail him once, and he struck back at me as I deserved, but afterwards, he treated me as a man—and that was not the way I was accustomed to be treated, in those days."

"His name," Gregory Temple said, dourly, "if he really is still alive, is Tom Brown. He lost the moral right to be the Comte de Belcamp long before he pretended to shoot himself in the head in his father's presence. You might have provided another Tom Brown to take the blame for some few of his crimes, but that was mere sham. If he really is alive, he is—as he has always been—a common criminal nurtured and raised by Helen Brown."

"He is far more complicated than that," Ned riposted, "and always was. That was his gift—whereas other men played parts, while remaining the same in secret, he lived all his roles wholeheartedly. When he was playing the assassin, he was the ultimate assassin; when he was playing the cavalier, he was the bravest and most chivalrous knight there ever was. Jeanne would not understand, of course—she could not begin to comprehend how such a perfect lover could vanish from her life completely, if he were not actually dead—but I am a wholehearted man myself, Mr. Temple, and I have a very good understanding of stagecraft, thanks to Sawney. I understand how plays are made, and how they ought to grip their audience. I understand how this scene is supposed to go. given your character and mine. You should let me go, Mr. Temple. Tell yourself, if you must, that you will always be able to find me again, if and when you think further interrogation might be valuable. In the meantime, you can go after Jack Hanrahan, or investigate Germain Patou's address in Stepney, as you please."

"This is no more a play than it's a game," Temple told him.

"All the world's a stage, Mr. Temple." Ned replied. "Now that we've each said our piece, it's time for us to move back into the wings. I don't doubt that we'll have other scenes to play, in later acts, but this one is surely done. Am I free to go?" He got down from his chair as he spoke, and as glad to find that he could stand upright without feeling dizzy.

Gregory Temple stood up too, not too proud to take full advantage of his height in looking down upon his insolent prisoner. He needed every inch to make himself convincing, as he said: "I can find you when I need to,

Master Knob—and I can bring you back here at the snap of my fingers. I can put a noose around your neck, if the whim takes me. Next time we have occasion to talk, you really ought to be ready and willing to answer my questions."

"Yes, Mr. Temple," Ned said, content to be meek now that he had made his point. "I know all of that—and I think we understand one another. Will you take me to the turnkey now, and instruct him to let me go free, so that I may go about my business?"

Chapter Three
The Burking Business

Ned did not know whether to be glad that he was released into broad daylight, or annoyed that he had been
kept all night in prison. He consoled himself with the
thought that it was not the first night he had spent in a
cell, and was highly unlikely to be the last, given that he
had declared himself an enemy of the Crown and all in-
justice. He bought himself a good breakfast and a mug
of beer—which seemed to clear away the drowsiness
imparted by the laudanum without bringing his headache
back in full force—and then he went to the public baths
to wash himself.

Afterwards, he went to the market in Covent Garden, and asked for news of Jack Hanrahan. No one knew
where he was, but there were plenty who could give him
the names of people who might. The burker's trail was
not an easy one to follow, but Ned was a persistent
hound, and he finally tracked his quarry to the Sunday
afternoon market in St. Paul's Yard. Hanrahan was
wearing his good suit, but Ned was not convinced that
he had been to church. He had already been busy,
though; he was carrying a large haversack stuffed with
what seemed to be tattered sheets and remnants from a
textile mill.

"Hunting for a good book, Jack?" Ned said, as he
came upon the burker loitering near a stall selling tracts
and almanacs.

"Not here, Master Knob," Hanrahan replied, making a show of his contempt. "There's a far better stall further along, as you presumably know, where a man can buy The Rights of Man if he knows the right password."

"You wanted a word with me last night, Jack," Ned reminded him, drawing him into a gap between a heap of rugs and a rack of second-hand suits. "I've come to collect the message."

Hanrahan's wariness was leavened with slight surprise. "When I tried to deliver the message," he said, "I had no idea that the gentleman would come to you himself. Did he not write what he wanted on the card he gave you?"

Ned did his best to hide his own surprise. "Ah," he said, as if he had half-expected it. "When Patou gave you the message to pass on, he obviously had no idea that he would soon have occasion to set foot in Jenny's himself. I've been slow on the uptake I fear—I should have gone straight to the address he scribbled on the card, instead of looking for you. I'm sorry, Jack."

"No trouble," the body-snatcher replied. "I hadn't realized that the gentleman wasn't known to you. Perhaps he was working on behalf of someone else?" Ned had been wondering whether it might be polite to mention that Gregory Temple was keenly interested in the burking business, and Hanrahan's business in particular, but he decided that since Hanrahan was prepared to fish for information so blatantly, he might as well take the opportunity to do likewise.

"I imagine that he was," Ned agreed. "He's a physician, it seems, and must be in charge of the grey men in that capacity, but he's not the mastermind behind the scheme. How did Sawney give him the slip, do you suppose?"

"I couldn't say," Hanrahan replied, dropping his load and making a show of searching through the suits on the rack while the tailor peered at him from the other side. "As you must have guessed from my expression, Master Knob, last night was the first time I clapped eyes on one of them. I've heard talk, mind—but you know the kind of fancies that spring up whenever rumors fly. I'm just an honest tradesman, trying to make a living. What happens to the goods after I deliver them isn't my business—but I tell you straight, Master Knob, I'd far rather imagine that someone might breathe new life into them than know that they'd only be cut up and thrown away."

"I'm with you on that, Jack," Ned agreed. "I know that you're just a cog in the machine, collecting the goods and passing them on to the physician, with no questions asked—that's just as it should be. But you're an honest radical, as I am, and I know how glad you must be to know that you're doing good as well as making a living. If the dead are being brought back to life, Jack, then those who take them from their graves are saints, working in the great cause of progress. You have my congratulations—and my sincere thanks, for what you've done for Sawney."

"I was startled to see him, that's all," Hanrahan said, gruffly. "I wasn't scared. I was as glad as any of you to see him walking and talking." He hauled his cargo back on to his shoulder and moved off abruptly, in the direction of the bookstall where one could purchase banned books, if one knew the password.

Ned followed him. "You weren't as startled as I was, I can tell you," he said, companionably. "At least you knew that he wasn't safely tucked up in his pauper's grave. Are you perfectly certain that he wasn't still alive when you sold him? You know your business far better than I do, of course, but one hears much nowadays about catalepsy and premature burial, and one hears plenty of tales of half-hanged men revived by their friends when the law has been careless."

Hanrahan did not pause at the bookstall but pushed on until he was clear of the market, obviously reluctant to say more while they might be overheard. He set off northwards, towards the old wall, striding energetically in spite of his burden. Ned glided effortlessly by his side.

"You're right, Master Knob," the burker conceded, when he was sure that no one else was in earshot. "I've opened coffins that have been torn up inside, to find men who were supposed dead with their fingernails bloody and torn. I've seen men snatched early from the rope at Tyburn and carried off, with the stewards unable to interfere, or even turning a blind eye. Not everyone's dead who's supposed to be, it's true. But Sawney... I was certainly convinced that he was gone, else I'd have handled him a good deal more tenderly than I did. You followed him, didn't you? Do you know where they took him?"

"I followed Patou and the grey men down to the quay," Ned admitted, knowing that he would have to share his own information if he were to get a full return from the burker. "He took a ferry out to a ship in midstream—the *Prometheus*, as I said—where his master was waiting. I showed myself, so that they could come and pick me up if they wanted to, but someone threw a blanket over my head and smacked me hard on the back of my skull. To tell the truth, Jack, I thought for an instant it might be you, intent on making a delivery."

Hanrahan seemed genuinely offended. "I know they call me a burker," he said, "but I'm no common murderer, however fresh the Frenchies might want their goods. I have my methods, Master Knob, and I can lay my hands on the genuine article easily enough. I'd have sworn on St. Paul's, St. Giles' and St. Luke's that Sawney was the genuine article when I bought him from the undertaker's cart for half a crown—and you can be sure the undertaker thought so too, else he'd never have sold him to me. His neck wasn't broke, or I'd have got him for two shillings, but I never saw a tongue so black or a throat so deeply grooved on a man who still had breath in him. Anyway, if I'd taken it into my head to collect you, you wouldn't be walking about today as bright as a button. How did you get away? Fought them off single-handed, did you?"

"Oh, it wasn't burkers—nor even common cutthroats. When the fellow in charge found out that he's got the wrong man, he apologized."

"Wrong man?" Hanrahan repeated, incredulously, as he came abreast of a small high-sided cart with a horse between its hafts that would not have fetched a shilling to be boiled down for glue. The back of the cart was generously furnished with rags too filthy to attract even the meanest thief,

Ned turned his nose away, saying: "I hope you're not going to render the new ones as foul as that, Jack."

"No fear," said Hanrahan, as he threw his latest purchases into the back of the cart. "I've got my good clothes on. I'll take them down the cesspit another day, when I've sorted out the pieces that'll make good winding-sheets. These will do for this afternoon's job."

"Right," said Ned. "You're working. I didn't answer your question, did I? Yes, they got the wrong man.

They were after Patou, of course. An easy mistake to make, in the poor light. I must say, though, that they seemed a far better class of nighthawk than one normally meets south of Covent Garden at midnight on a Saturday. I don't know what the physician had in his bag, but I imagine that's what they were after. Do you mind if I ride a little way with you? I won't come into the graveyard, mind—that's the kind of work best done in private."

"I'll not be doing any digging today, Master Knob," Hanrahan replied, rather scornfully. "I know people think that I spend every night digging down through freshly-turned soil, when I'm not out cutting throats, but that's not how the business works. I have dig down on occasion, it's true, but I prefer to get the bodies before they're laid to rest, if I can. I like to purchase them fair and square—from the next of kin, if that can be arranged, although I'm not excessively particular. These days, it can be arranged more often than you might think. Dissenting's been a boon to the business, and no mistake—except for Methodists, of course. The Clapham sect's the worst of all. Give me Unitarianism any day—godlessness that likes to keep up appearances. Better hop up smartly—that's the half-hour chiming and I'm due at St. Luke's in less than 30 minutes. Mustn't be late, or the little girl might end up underground regardless. Can't entirely trust the grieving, you know, if things don't go exactly to plan.

Ned did as he was bid, hoping that he would get used to the stink soon enough. His head had started to ache again, and he felt a pang of regret at not having purchased a phial of laudanum from the market while he had the chance.

45

Hanrahan untethered the horse, got up on to the bench beside Ned, and took up the rein and the whip. There was no need for the whip, though——the horse moved off obediently in response to a twitch of the rein.

Once they had made their way out into the traffic, Ned said: "It's possible, of course, that they weren't out to rob Patou at all, Jack. Maybe he has enemies, who want to do him harm—or who want to claim his services for a rival master. I ought to warn him, ought I not? Would you carry a message for me?"

"The Frenchie already knows that he has enemies, Master Knob," Hanrahan told him. "He lies very low, except when circumstances force him out—as they must have done yestereve. I never saw his master at all... although I've heard the name John Devil muttered abroad, as it always seems to be when anything remarkable is going on. You'd probably know more about than I would."

Ned shook his head wearily. "I never had the pleasure of knowing Mistress Paddock's husband," he said, with a sigh. "That was before my time."

"Not that John Devil," the burker said, giving his nag a flick of the whip for amusement's sake. "The Quaker, Tom Brown—the one who murdered Noll Green and Lochaber Dick in Paris. I heard tell you were there, and saw the whole thing."

"Pretty Molly used to put the story about when she was in her cups," Ned admitted, "but I fear that she was only trying to make me out a better man than I am. I did know Mr. Wood, though, who was Tom's solicitor, and he always said that Tom wasn't near a bad a boy as gossip painted him. Always loved his mother, you know."

"So did everyone else, the way I heard it," Hanrahan observed. "Many a tear shed when she shipped out for Botany Bay. She was married to a Frenchie once, wasn't she?"

"Yes, she was," Ned said. "I knew her husband slightly, although I know the present Comtesse much better. I've been in Paris a fair bit these last three years—but I never heard of a doctor named Germain Patou."

"I'll wager there's hundreds of doctors in London you never heard of," Hanrahan observed. "He's a doctor all right, and no mistake, if he brought Sawney back from the dead—and that giant too. I wish he'd warned me that I might bump into the goods again walking and talking."

"I don't suppose he intended you that you should," Ned opined. "Sawney wasn't supposed to wander off on his own, whatever he was doing on the boat. Was the giant one of yours, by any chance?"

"No. You'd need a big heap of foul rags to hide a body like his—have to fold him up, see, or his feet'd stick out of the cart. Ever tried to fold a body when rigor's set in, Master Knob?"

"Can't say I have, Jack. Is that St. Luke's off to the right, along Fann Street?

"Yes it is—and we're still in good time." Hanrahan paused for just a moment before saying: "I suppose he might've been alive—old Sawney? The dead can't really be brought back, can they, Master Knob? This is all some kind of mummery, isn't it?" His voice was level enough, but Ned knew that there must be a deep anxiety as well as an honest uncertainty in the burker's words. He was glad to think that such a tall man was unashamed to seek reassurance on such a weighty matter from Gentleman Ned Knob.

"Well," Ned said, carefully, "There's a story—which is in print, not just idle chatter, so it might be true—about a gentleman scholar in Switzerland who found a way to reimpart the vital spark to a patchwork of dead flesh. Electricity is said to be the key—and now that men like Benjamin Franklin and Humphry Davy have begun to bring the fire of lightning down to Earth, who knows where it'll end?"

"Not the Methodists, that's for sure," Hanrahan muttered, as he turned the horse and maneuvered the cart into Fann Street. "Before your time, I know, Master Knob, but did you ever hear tell of a doctor named James Graham?"

"As a matter of fact, Jack, I did," Ned said, taken completely by surprise by the question, and wondering whether he might be getting somewhere at last. "He had a connection to Helen Brown too, you know, when she was taken up by the Duchess of Devonshire back in the '80s. Graham was the Duchess's pet quack—ran a so-called Temple of Health and Hymen in Mayfair, with an electric throne and a celestial bed and all manner of silly gadgetry. Would have been as famous as Mesmer, they say, if he hadn't got himself thrown in jail in Edinburgh. Why do you ask?"

"I happened to run across some of the equipment sold off when the Temple went bust," Hanrahan replied. "No sort of bed, mind—baths, they were. Do you know who he called his Goddess of Health? That woman who was Horatio Nelson's mistress—Emma Hamilton."

"I didn't know that," Ned lied. "That's amazing, Jack—to think that Graham's old equipment is still in use. Mr. Davy and Mr. Faraday would certainly be interested to know that—and I'll wager they'd be able to put

48

it to very good use, in the cause of Radical Enlighten-ment. Where is it, if I might ask?"

"Shipped down river," Hanrahan told him. "It was on a quay near Southwark Bridge when I saw it, about to be loaded up—probably on to the same vessel you saw last night."

"Downriver," Ned repeated, thoughtfully. "But they bring the ship upriver at regular intervals, to collect all kinds of cargoes. Sawney must have slipped ashore last night, and made his way back to his old home-from-home. What was he doing on the ship in the first place, I wonder?"

Hanrahan had no answer to that, and tried to signify as much by shrugging his shoulders as he jumped down from the cart, which he had driven round to the vestry door of St. Luke's Church. Ned could see a funeral party wending its slow way to the northernmost part of the churchyard, into the shade of a clump of wych-elms. There was a coffin at the head of the procession, shoul-dered by four pall-bearers, but Ned had a strong suspi-cion that the corpse had been removed before the lid had been screwed down.

The vestry door opened, and a black-clad man came out, wearing a polished top hat and carrying a small bundle tightly wound about by a dirty sheet. Hanrahan handed over a few coins and accepted the bundle into his own arms. Then he slid it gingerly into the back on the cart, using a pole and a pair of tongs to cover it with the filthy rags that no one would be eager to displace. Ned estimated that it weighed no more than four stones; it was the body of a child, no more than ten or twelve years old.

The man retired into the church. "That was no grieving next-of-kin," Ned observed. "That was the undertaker, or one of his mutes."

"I only said what I preferred, Master Knob," the burker said, defensively. "I can let you ride as far as Fleet Street, if you want, but I can't take you all the way. Guarantees given, you understand—but I'll deliver your message to Patou. He has enemies, who thumped you on the noggin thinking you were him, and apologized when they found you weren't. That's good, in a way. If a man has to have enemies, best to have civilized enemies."

"Very kind of you, Jack," Ned said, "Fleet Street will be ideal, and I thank you wholeheartedly. If Monsieur Patou asks after me, will you tell him that my success at Jenny's doesn't prevent me from taking other commissions, provided that they're lucrative enough. I'm a versatile man, and a good friend to have when a man is a stranger in the city and finds himself beset by enemies."

"I'll tell him that too," Hanrahan promised. He was silent until he turned back on to the North Road at the end of Fann Street, and then he said: "Do you suppose this one will be back too, Master Knob? She's only a kid—can't be as much as eleven. Never had a chance to live a life, although I dare say she did her fair share of skivvying."

"I don't know, Jack," Ned said, soothingly. "But if Patou can give her a second chance, you're surely doing a hero's work. If there's an alternative, anything's better than leaving a little girl to rot in a grave."

"You're right, Ned," Hanrahan said. "You've a good head on your shoulders, and a good heart too. There's not many men who've asked to ride with me on my cart, you know. You're no Methodist, that's for sure—but then, you're a satirist. I'm a radical myself, you know, in my heart, and I used to be more ardent than I am now. I was there when they pilloried Dan Eaton back in 1812, ready to defend him—not that he needed any defending, as it turned out."

"Why, Jack, we're practically twin souls," Ned said, brimming over with camaraderie. "I was in court to see Tom Wooler argue the toss with Sam Shepherd—the Attorney General himself. And what a fine fist he made of it! These are great times, Jack, for revolutionaries like us. The aristocrats have their past and their tradition, but we have our future and our hope... and a better hope for the resurrection, it seems, than the Clapham crowd. Not that I've anything against Wilberforce, you understand. He'll have slavery abolished in England before the decade's out, and that's a great thing... but they say that there are islands in the Caribbean where the dead serve as slaves. Slow of wit, I've heard, but very docile, and never need to sleep. Now then, what do they call them?"

"Zombies," said Jack Hanrahan, promptly. A man in his trade would be bound to pay attention to such tales, Ned knew, and Limehouse had more than its fair share of sailors who'd seen the Americas, even though Liverpool and Southampton were the ports of choice for the Atlantic trade.

"That's right," Ned agreed. "But they don't use electricity there, so rumor has it. It's all done with magic and the power of the will."

"They call it *voudun*," Hanrahan supplied. "African magic, Frenchified."

"That's right," Ned said. "Toussaint l'Ouverture led the slaves of Haiti to revolt against Bonaparte himself when he tried to bring slavery back after the Jacobins abolished it. I wonder if Germain Patou has ever been to the Caribbean?"

"More likely to have been in Paris while Mesmer was there," Hanrahan opined, "given what I saw on the docks that day."

"Or both," Ned said, thoughtfully. "Ben Franklin was on the committee appointed to evaluate Mesmer's claims, as I recall—and Antoine Lavoisier too. Humphry Davy knew them both—I've heard him say so—and he was well received in Paris when he visited with Faraday. I wonder if Mr. Davy knows Germain Patou."

"That's not the kind of question I can ask Patou," Hanrahan said, perhaps fearful of being asked to carry yet another message. "If you know Humphry Davy, you'd best ask him. Do you know Davy?"

"Only slightly," Ned admitted. "I was a regular at the Royal Institution's open lectures at one time, although I've grown a little lax of late. So was Tom Brown, I understand, before he was transported—but that, of course, was before my time. Perhaps I should have tried a little harder to understand the lectures, but I went there as a good radical, to show my support for Jacobin science, never thinking that I could fully understand the wonders of electrolysis..."

"They brought him water, you know, and food," Hanrahan said, nostalgically. "Dan Eaton, I mean... when he was in the pillory, for printing The Rights of Man. Now, if Patou could bring Tom Paine back to life—what a triumph that would be!"

"So it would, Jack," Ned agreed. "So it would."

Chapter Four
The House in Purfleet

When Jack Hanrahan let Ned Knob down from his cart in Fleet Street, Ned made a considerable show of going away, because he knew that the burker would be wary of being followed. Given that he had a strong suspicion as to where the cart was headed, though, he did not need to trot along behind it. He merely had to take up a convenient point of vantage once or twice along the way, to make sure that Hanrahan was still headed for the river.

He was not unduly surprised when the burker went around the Tower on the north side and made his way to the St. Katherine Dock. Patou was bound to be more careful now, having been seen at Jenny's and the quay near Southwark Bridge, in company with two grey men.

The cart skirted the docks and made its way to the edge of the Thames, to a jetty not far west of Tower Hill. Ned ran on ahead, as fast as he could go, to the Hermitage Stairs. There he found a ferryman whose boat was twice the size of a common skiff, and was fitted with a sail.

"Can you slip across to Cherry Garden Pier and wait in its shadow?" Ned asked. "There'll be a ship along in a matter of minutes—an hour at the most—riding the stream and the outbound tide. She's a two-master, but she won't be carrying much sail, given the flow. If you can keep pace with her till she docks again, without her master knowing he's being followed, there's half a guinea in it."

"There's six shillings now and another six when we get there," the ferryman relied, "provided that we go no further than Gallion's Reach."

"Six now, six then and another six if we have to go further than Hornchurch Marshes," Ned said, showing the ferryman a generous handful of coins that he had pulled from his trouser pocket.

"You're a gentleman, and no doubt," said the ferryman, only a little sarcastically—but he did as he was asked, and waited under Cherry Garden Pier on the south bank until Ned nudged him and showed him the vessel he was to follow.

"Right," said the ferryman, unenthusiastically. "Should've known it'd be her. If it weren't broad daylight, sir, I'd hand your money back—but it's only at night that she's said to be haunted. I'll follow her for you, but you needn't fear that I'll get too close. "

"If you know for certain where she's headed," Ned said. "You can take me there at your leisure. Do you know her regular berth?"

"Not far this side of Hell, I'd imagine," the ferryman opined. "I don't want to know—but I'll do as I promised, provided that I can keep my distance, and darkness doesn't fall."

"Why do you say that she's haunted?" Ned asked. "She seems very ordinary to me."

"You don't ply your trade between the Tower and Westminster after dark, sir," the ferryman said. "I've seen strange things in my time, and learned to keep my eyes averted from all kinds of skullduggery... but those eyes! If you'd seen those eyes looking out over the water..."

"Does her master have those eyes?" Ned wanted to know.

"I don't know," the ferryman admitted. "He shields them with that Quaker hat he wears—but when a ship is carrying the souls of the damned, its master is bound to be a demon. That's just common sense."

More common than sense, Ned thought, but he held his tongue.

They eased into the stream when the *Prometheus* had passed by. There was plenty of traffic on the river, and Ned did not think that anyone aboard John Devil's craft would think their sail suspicious, but he fretted nevertheless as they negotiated Woolwich Reach and Gallion's Reach, and kept on going past Crossness and the Erith Marshes.

Ned wondered, as they went, whether Gregory Temple had discovered anything at Germain Patou's Stepney address. He suspected not. Whatever message had been waiting there for Ned Knob would not be given to anyone else—and now, it would not need to be given to Ned Knob either. If Temple had drawn a blank, he would presumably redirect his attention to Jack Hanrahan, but that wouldn't matter either, now that Ned had satisfied himself that Hanrahan was on the very periphery of the affair. In time, Temple was certain to find out where Patou was, and where the grey men were normally kept, but for the time being, Ned had at least a day's start on the secret police.

He wondered, too, how many other people were of the opinion that a vessel crewed by monsters and captained by a demon was making daily trips up river into the Port of London. Ferrymen were not known for keeping close counsel, and they carried a great many passengers by day and night—even in the heart of the city, where there were bridges a-plenty—but there had been so many other stories of a fanciful sort abroad in the last 20 years that no one paid any of them serious heed. The Thames would be choked with ghostly pirate ships and rotting sea-serpents had all the tales been true.

The ferryman was beginning to grumble that he could not possibly go any further than the bend at Grays when the vessel they were tracking finally put in to Purfleet. Ned handed over the last of the promised coin, and begged the ferryman to set him down as quickly as he could. The ferryman was glad to oblige, and Ned set off at a sprint to catch up with Germain Patou's landing-party.

Half a dozen seamen—none of them grey-skinned—were loading up a cart far sturdier and more capacious than Jack Hanrahan's. Although the transferred cargo contained ordinary supplies as well as corpses, the number of parcels packaged in dirty winding-sheets told Ned that Jack Hanrahan was far from being the only supplier to this particular buyer. It occurred to him that when people spoke of a burking "epidemic," they were only referring to bodies that had been reported missing. Who knew how many more there might be like the little girl from St. Luke's, whose posthumous disappearance would never attract the slightest attention?

Ned did not know how far he might have to go when the cart set off and he set off in pursuit. He hoped that it would be no more than a few hundred yards, given that the masters of the grey men seemed to find the river so convenient for their purposes. So it transpired; on the eastern edge of Purfleet, there was a three-story house with two stubby swings and a hectic multitude of gables, set in high-walled grounds. The only obvious means of access was a sturdy steel gate that was locked as soon as the cart had vanished inside, but Ned wasn't in the least worried by that.

He made a tour of the walls, looking for the most convenient point of entry. There was ivy on the walls to the rear, but the bulk of it was inside and would not lend him much support. Fortunately, the wall was old and the mortar between the stones was crumbling. With the aid of his clasp-knife—which he plied with great care, not wanting to blunt the sharpness of the blade as well as the point—he was able to hollow out a sequence of foot-holds that would take him to the top. Once he was there, the ivy made the descent much easier.

There were birch-trees within the wall that hid his descent from the windows of the house, so he did not think that there was any possibility of his having been seen as he slid over the wall. He felt entirely confident of his invisibility as he crept through the undergrowth towards the house.

The ground was lower at the back of the house than at the front, so the rear door gave access to a basement whose floor was considerably lower than the floor of the front hallway. There was no one in the kitchen garden, but Ned saw movement in several of the windows on the floor above the basement and the floor above that. The house seemed to be abundantly tenanted—and he understood very quickly what the ferryman had meant by those eyes looking out. Grey faces were continually appearing at one window or another, merely in order to look out. They were not keeping watch as sentries might: they were simply staring into the garden, as if they had nothing better to do than contemplate the tawdry wilderness.

Sawney might be the best of them rather than the worst, Ned thought, for all that he could not seem to string his thoughts together. *Whatever has been done to these people, it has let them weak in body and in mind*—but Patou seemed genuinely concerned for Sawney's wellbeing, and he a physician, not some Caribbean slave-holder.

Ned rested for some little while when he reached the extremity of the useful cover, wondering whether he ought to wait for darkness—which would come soon enough, given that All Souls was more than a week past. If he intended to play the spy and make his escape without his presence ever being suspected, that was undoubtedly the wisest course—but how much could he learn by peering in through windows? The weather was cold, and it would get a good deal colder when night fell—and what would he do when he went back over the wall, given that he was so far from London?

In the end, the fact that Gregory Temple could not be very far behind him was the deciding factor. There was only one way that he could stay ahead of Temple— and only one way to put the mystery beyond Temple's reach, if that seemed to be the right thing to do.

"I'm a gentleman, after all," he murmured, dusting his sleeves, "and I'm an old friend of the family. Why should I be shy?"

Even so, he hesitated for five more minutes before he marched out of the copse, strode resolutely to the kitchen door and knocked.

When the door opened, he tensed himself, expecting to find himself face to face with a grey man, but the woman who answered was ruddy in the cheeks and bloodshot in the eyes. She was wearing a cook's apron.

"Who are you?" she demanded, in a tone more worthy of a fishwife. "What do you want?"

"Forgive me for coming to the tradesmen's entrance, Ma'am, if I should have presented myself at the front door," Ned said, cheerily, "but I have not been a gentleman all my life, and I am still at something of a loss when it comes to country house etiquette. My name is Ned Knob, and I'm here at the invitation of Monsieur Germain Patou, physician. I wonder if you could send a message to say that I'm here. He knows me, and is expecting me—though not, I confess, precisely at this hour."

"Wait!" commanded the cook—and slammed the door in his face. Five more minutes passed. When the door opened again, there was no sign of the cook; a footman had been sent to welcome him in.

"Would you come this way, sir?" the footman asked.

"Certainly," said Ned—and followed the manservant through the kitchens and up a dozen steps to the ground floor, then up two more flights of carpeted stairs to the very top of the house. The candles had not yet been lit, and the corridors were very gloomy; all the doors ere carefully closed, and he met no grey men on the way.

He was shown into a room that seemed to him the very image of what a scholar's study should be. Germain Patou was there, but it was not Germain Patou's study. The blond-haired man sitting behind the desk was younger than Patou, and slimmer. He looked very well, and very much alive—which was a little odd, considering that he was supposed to have blown his brains out in the summer of 1817, but not odd enough to astonish Ned Knob.

59

"Ned," said Comte Henri de Belcamp, alias Tom Brown, alias John Devil the Quaker. "It's good to see you again—I'm glad you got our message in spite of all the confusion, and were able to respond despite your mishap on the quay. Do sit down. May we offer you something to drink?"

"Cognac, if you have it," Ned said, taking the seat he had been offered, across the desk from the Comte. Patou went to a cabinet, poured brandy from a decanter and meekly brought it to him.

Ned raised his glass, and said "*A l'avantage!*" as if it were a toast.

"We no longer need all that," the Comte said, affably. "The Knights of the Deliverance would have served their purpose, had things gone well—but things did not go well. Indeed, I do not think I ever had a day in my life when things when so awry as the day when I thought it politic to die—and that was not for want of healthy competition."

The cognac was good—far better, at any rate, than Jenny Paddock's *eau-de-vie*. "Why did you not call for me sooner, old friend?" Ned asked. "I am quite offended. Was I not your most trusted lieutenant in England?"

"We only knew one another for a few weeks, Ned," the Comte reminded him. "It was a significant passage in your life, I know—and I am very grateful for all that you have done for my grieving widow—but you should not overestimate the extent of our actual acquaintance. Even so, you're absolutely right. I should have called for you sooner, and I was very disappointed to see you seized so rudely when you waved to me from the quay. I sent the boat back, of course, to see if there was anything to be done, but the blackguards had carried you off into the dark streets. I'm very glad to see that you're all right. Germain says that you told Hanrahan to tell him that he has enemies, but we already know that. Would you mind telling us how you got away from them?" His voice seemed light enough, but the suspicion behind the question was palpable.

"I pointed out that he had no right to hold me," Ned said. "He accepted the justice of my case, and let me go."

"Indeed?" the Comte said. "It seems that his moral progress is as rapid as his intellectual progress. He would not have been so gentle had he actually managed to capture Germain... although I had not thought him likely to make such a silly mistake, give that we were clearly visible from the shore. Was it living men who took you, or grey men?"

"I fear that we're talking at cross-purposes," Ned told him, apologetically. "I misled Hanrahan slightly when I said that my captors were after Monsieur Patou. They were only after the address he wrote on the card. I imagine they have investigated it by now. I did not go there once I knew that it had been compromised—I followed the *Prometheus*. I could not see anyone else doing likewise, but you might not have much time. Gregory Temple isn't a man to underestimate."

Ned had seen Comte Henri de Belcamp astonished before, and had even had the honor of causing such astonishment himself, but he still thought it a feat worthy of congratulation—and so he congratulated himself, albeit a trifle reluctantly, when he saw the expression on the other man's face.

"Temple!" exclaimed the Comte, running his fingers through his blond hair. "I thought that I had put him in Bedlam for once and for all. Is he on my trail, then?"

"He is now," Ned told him, moving on swiftly to add: "Not my doing, I assure you—but his men saw your hat, just as I did, and he drew the same conclusion. Prior to that, he was only on Hanrahan's trail, trying to follow it back to the buyer who had created such a busy market in dead bodies. If you desire to work in secret, you really shouldn't advertise yourself. There are Quakers by the thousand in London, but they don't sneak up and down the Thames in a ship that every ferryman on the water believes to be haunted."

"That was bound to happen," Patou put in. "We should never have taken any of the grey men aboard the ship."

"How shall we—or they—ever find out what their capabilities are, if we do not try them?" the Comte complained, allowing his attention to be distracted. "How will they ever recover their old selves, if we keep them cooped up here with nothing to look at but unfamiliar walls and a mediocre garden? They need stimulation, Doctor, as you yourself have aid a hundred times. If we're to beat Mortdieu, we need to accelerate our progress. It was a mistake to send Ross, I'll admit... but in all fairness, he made more progress in the hour that he was gone than he'd done in the previous month, despite all your efforts. That's what they need if they're to recover their memories completely: to see familiar faces in familiar places, to converse with people they loved. How else can they recall themselves, or be themselves?"

"There was one who had no trouble," Patou said, grimly—but the Comte was already looking at Ned Knob again, his troubled eyes questioning.

"Until last night," Ned went on, "Temple had no idea of your involvement. He's with the secret police now, chasing radicals... especially radical burkers. He knows now, though—thanks to a stroke of mischance. Hanrahan came to deliver the doctor's message to me just as Sawney made his grand entrance, and Temple had a spy in the parlor, who jumped to the conclusion that I knew far more than I did. Temple still knows nothing, except that I saluted a Quaker hat—but that's all he'll need, given that he has no trouble with his own memory, and his burning desire for retribution. But I must know, before we decide how to deal with Gregory Temple— did you really bring Sawney back from the dead, or was the hangman careless?"

His urgency was in vain; he got no immediate answer. Instead, the blond man turned to Patou again. "If Ned could follow the ship, Temple won't be far behind," he said. "We have two sets of enemies now, Doctor, and they're both too close for comfort. I'm not sure which of them is more to be feared at present." He turned back to Ned. "The secret police, you say? England has secret police now, and Gregory Temple is working for them? I do not know which is the greater scandal... but I suppose I must take some of the blame. I left him ruined as well as broken in that Newgate cell, and I dare say that he had little choice in matter of employment, once he was released. Damnation! You've changed, Ned. You were little more than a boy back in '17, so I suppose it's only to be expected... I should have reckoned on that, and come to you much sooner."

"I had a good teacher," Ned said, "if only for a matter of weeks. I'm here now—who is after us, apart from Mr. Temple?"

Again, the Comte did not reply immediately. Ned let loose a little sigh. It seemed that Helen Brown's son had not changed at all; he still fancied himself the master manipulator, who used everyone, trusted no one and never under any circumstances told anyone the whole truth, or anything at all until he had to.

"We'll have to move again," Germain Patou said. "There's been no sign yet of Mortdieu, and he's less capable than we are of moving unobtrusively, even though he probably has as many living men in his employ as we have. The secret police are a different matter. I'm as reluctant as you are to cut the experiments short again, but what choice do we have? The setback to our work will be far greater if they find us now."

" The *Prometheus* can't carry all the materials we've gathered here," the Comte said. "We'll need a bigger ship—one that can carry us across the ocean, to some quiet island in the Caribbean. Do you have money, Ned? Money enough to charter a clipper?"

Ned laughed. "I had enough to charter a vessel from the Hermitage Stairs to Purfleet," he said, "but not enough to take me much beyond Grays. The cabaret at Jenny Paddock's is a great success, but the bulk of the profit is Jenny's. Your widow..."

"I cannot go to Jeanne," the Comte said, flatly. "To her, I am dead, and so it must remain. If you see her again, Ned, you must not tell her that you have seen her husband. In fact, you have not seen her husband. Jeanne's son is the Marquis de Belcamp now; until he has a son, there is no Comte de Belcamp."

"Sawney and I killed Tom Brown," Ned observed, "who died with his conscience clear. Mr. Wood and I had already disposed of the phantom Percy Balcomb once and for all. So who are you now, my friend? I cannot imagine that James Davy or George Palmer is a suitable candidate for resurrection."

"In Purfleet," said the ci-devant Comte Henri de Belcamp, "I am Arthur Pevensey, a Cornishman—but I can't say that I like the name as a permanent fixture. My adversary, as you heard just now, has taken the name of Mortdieu, although I call him ungrateful Lazarus... but we have no time to waste on such fancies. If the secret police are on to us, and have Gregory Temple for their bloodhound, we must move quickly. If we cannot buy or charter a better ship, we must do what we can with the one we have."

"I asked you a question a little while ago," Ned reminded him. "Are you really raising the dead?"

This time, the ci-devant Comte condescended to reply. "Yes," he said. "We are. Nor are we the only ones, for our monopoly was cut short far sooner than we'd planned. Of the first dozen we brought back from the dead, eleven were doltish—and most of them still are—but one was not. If only he had been as docile as the rest! He stole the secret from me... although I have to confess that it was not actually mine by right of discovery. Now he is our rival—our enemy. We've clashed a time or two already, but he seems to grow stronger every time, while our progress is frustratingly slow. Your friend Ross is now our most promising pupil, having overtaken John— although John had the finer mind while he was still alive, and may yet surpass him again." He stopped suddenly. "You're having difficulty believing this, aren't you, Ned?"

"A little," Ned confessed. "Jack Hanrahan couldn't quite believe it, even though he saw Sawney dead and resurrected. I told him that electricity must hold the key—and I suppose it must, since you have bought James Graham's magical electric baths."

"Well done," said the ci-devant Comte. "I used to attend Humphry Davy's lectures at the Royal Institution, you know, when I was Tom Brown—I called myself after him, in one of my many impostures. I could have made the discovery myself, if only I'd dedicated myself to such work... but I had to go to Australia as you know. How's your mother, Ned?"

"Quite well," Ned said. "I've heard Mr. Davy myself, although Faraday is the man of the moment now. I don't have your intellect, but I'm a great admirer of what the Tories call Jacobin science. You ought to be aware, Monsieur, that I'm a radical now, and a man of conscience. I'm all in favor of slaying the dragon of death, but there's a...."

The ci-devant Comte cut him off. "Would you like to see Monsieur Patou raise the dead with your own eyes, Ned?" the blond man asked. "Would you like to make certain of the truth of what we're doing?"

"Is that wise?" Patou objected, twisting his lips into a frown. The physician pulled out his watch and looked at it. "Is it even time?"

"Yes," said the ci-devant Comte, rising decisively to his feet. "It is wise, and it is time. Ned has been sent to us by Providence, in our hour of need, and he needs to know what we are about if he is to commit himself to our plan and bring us more recruits. As for the time, we have no leisure left to let them simmer, and we have a new batch ready to bathe. Lead the way, my friend."

Patou put his watch away, and went to the door. Ned stood up and followed him, with the former Comte bringing up the rear. The candles still had not been lit on the top floor, but the corridors below were illuminated. There was a murmur of noise from most of the rooms they passed, but no one came out as they passed by, and the only other people Ned saw were servants, of every common hue but grey.

They went down from the ground floor to the level where the kitchens were, but Ned discovered then that there was a further set of cellars even further below ground, sealed by a heavy door with a massive iron lock. Patou did not have the key, and had to let the blond man pass him by to open it.

There was a glimmer of light within the vault, but it was rather distant, and Ned waited on the threshold until Patou had lit a lamp. When the physician had done that, he led the way again, into the bowels of the Earth.

The cellars were damp, and had the reek of the salt-marshes that confused both shores of the estuary from Rainham to the Isle of Grain. They were not cold, however. There was a massive fireplace at one end of the chamber into which they had come, where a fire was burning behind an iron grille. It vigorous flames provided the light that Ned had glimpsed from the corridor outside the doorway, but it was only Patou's lamp that showed him the other contents of the room.

Forewarned by Jack Hanrahan, Ned was not entirely surprised to see six capacious bathtubs, each one equipped at one end with a fearsome mass of supplementary equipment. Ned cast his mind back to the demonstrations he had seen at the Royal Institution, but the Voltaic cells and Leyden jars he had seen there bore little enough resemblance to the lumpen masses gathered here; only the wires that sprang from their earthenware crowns assured him that they must be generating powerful electrical currents, which were being fed into the fluid in the baths.

The fluid was not water; it was far more viscous, and far more active. It bore some slight resemblance, in its texture and transparency, to frogspawn—but instead of tiny huddled tadpoles, it held human bodies. The bodies must once have been white, or brown, or black, but they were now the same shade of grey that Ned had seen the night before, in Sawney's exposed flesh and that of the giant.

Ned barely noticed that there were more bodies heaped up in an unseemly fashion in the corner of the room most distant from the fire, presumably awaiting their turn in the baths. He was far more interested in the corpses floating beneath the surface of the uncanny fluid, as if suspended between Heaven and Earth, mortality and eternity.

Patou handed the lantern to his taller companion, then rolled up his sleeves. He went to the first bath. The physician carefully pushed his right hand into the fluid, and touched the neck of the thin man who lay there, naked and seemingly asleep. "No pulse," he reported. "No revitalization of the skin. Irrecoverable, I fear."

Patou moved on to the second bath. This too was a man—only one of the six vessels held a female—but one of sturdier build. The Frenchman did not seem optimistic as he began his examination, but his face brightened almost immediately. "Yes!" he said. "The fluid is flowing in his veins, and his flesh has recovered its consistency. He'll be ready..."

"Wake him now!" his master commanded.

Patou pursed his lips, but he did not complain. Nor did he delay. He plunged both arms into the slimy mass, and took the floating man by the shoulders, slowly but firmly altering his attitude. After ten or twelve seconds, the man's feet were on the floor of the bath, and Patou pulled the head free from the fluid. The stuff clung to the grey man's face, but Patou immediately set about brushing it away, exposing the strange skin to the air.

The man who had been lying peacefully asleep in the bath spluttered and coughed, and fluid vomited from his mouth—although Ned guessed that it was coming from his lungs rather than his stomach. Patou tried to force the man to lean slightly forward, while making sure that he could not slip and fall, but he was too short to carry out the task effectively. The lantern was abruptly thrust into Ned's hands, and the man who had once been Tom Brown lent his own height and his own hands to the work of waking the man who had been dead.

More than a minute passed, but the grey man's eyes eventually opened. All the color had gone from their irises; the pupil was set in a globe unreddened by the least blood vessel. Ned inferred that the resurrected dead no longer had red blood in their veins but something else—something gifted to them by the fluid that had revivified their necrotic flesh.

While Ned struggled to hold the lantern steady, the ci-devant Comte looked the living dead man straight in the eye, and said: "What is your name? Can you remember your name?"

The man returned from the dead did not look around, as a man waking from an ordinary sleep would surely have done. He did not say: "Where am I?" or "Who the Devil are you?" He looked back at the man who had been Comte Henri de Belcamp and John Devil the Quaker, and he furrowed his colorless brow, trying to do as he had been told, and remember his own name.

Time went by; the question was repeated.

In the end, the former dead man spoke. "John," he said, in a voice thick with the effects of the fluid still clogging his mouth. The syllable was clear enough, though.

His interlocutor did not seem entirely pleased with the answer. "John," He repeated, scornfully. "Can no one find a way back from the Underworld but men named John? Can all the burkers in London not find me a Theophilus or a Walter? Or is there some infection spreading from brain to brain, which fills them all with the same false identity? What surname, dolt? What is your family name?"

The man raised from the dead made no protest at the abuse heaped upon him—quite unfairly, Ned thought—but only tried meekly to do as he was bid. Alas, it seemed that the task was too much for him, at present.

Germain Patou reached out to take his friend's arm. "Relax, *mon ami*," he said. "Best to wash and clothe him while he's still as tractable as a new-born. Your old friend has seen what he needs to see—he might be more use to us talking to Ross, continuing the good work he began last night. Ross has been asking incessantly for his old friends Sam and Jeanie, and that's a healthy sign, although it's become a trifle tiresome. If we only had time..."

Perhaps that was tempting fate too far, Ned thought, as the footman who had taken him upstairs came hurrying through the door in great agitation.

"You must come at once, sir—there's trouble at the dock, aboard the *Prometheus*. Someone's trying to seize the ship!"

Chapter Five
The Battle for the Prometheus

Minutes later, Ned was bundled on to the back of a cart with a dozen other men—none of them grey—while weapons were brought from the house and handed out. Patou had been instructed to stay behind, but the footman had climbed aboard. Ned was offered a brace of pistols, but refused—pistols, he knew, made very inefficient clubs once they had been discharged. He refused a saber too, for being too unwieldy for a man of his height, but he accepted a cutlass whose blade was no longer than the length of his forearm.

What he wanted to know, however, was against whom he might be wielding it. He asked, but only received a single word by way of an answer: Mortdieu.

Even when the cart moved off into the gathering darkness, its two horses having been whipped to a rapid trot, there was too much confusion about him for Ned to do anything profitable—except to keep his head down, lest he take an accidental blow from a cudgel. Once the hubbub calmed, however, and a sense of purpose overcame the mob, he was able to make his way to his commander's side.

The streets of Purfleet were poorly lit, even by comparison with Low Lane, and the sky was cloudy, but there was no fog hereabouts and the air seemed crisp and clean.

"This is more than I bargained for," Ned said, candidly. "I'm a good messenger, but a terrible soldier. Stealth is my forte, not swordplay—and to be honest, I don't know enough as yet to know what cause I'm supposed to be fighting for. Why is this Mortdieu attempting to steal your ship?"

"I told you—he's my ungrateful Lazarus," said the ci-devant Comte. "Germain's greatest triumph, and bitterest defeat. You've seen enough to know that the brain is not as easy to revitalize as the body. It seems that the flow of the mind is much harder to regenerate than the flow of the blood. Patou has brought 50 men and women back to life in those baths of his—more here than in Portugal, though three in every five we buy are too far gone even now. Of those 50, barely half can construct a coherent sentence, and only a dozen seem able to remember who and what they were in life. Germain is gaining in skill with every day that passes, and he has worked more miracles than you have so far seen, but there is a very great deal to be learned, and his successes have been as unpredictable as his failures. Mortdieu is the only one, so far, who was capable of understanding what we have done for him—but instead of being grateful, he tried to steal our secret for himself, to make his own grey army."

"I see," Ned said. "You have stolen the fire of Heaven in order to make an army of angels, but you have spawned a rebel Satan who is amassing a demonic army of his own."

"Don't mock me, Ned," whispered the ci-devant Comte de Belcamp, with a quality of menace in his tone that Ned had savored before. "You must fight for me now, if you're with me still—but if you prefer to cut and run, I'll understand. I should have come to you earlier if

I wanted time enough to explain my cause and my plan. There is no time now, alas—but I'd dearly like your help, if you're willing to offer it. Not as a fighting-man, for you don't have the stature for that kind of work, but as a trusted aide."

"I have a good life now, Monsieur," Ned murmured, after a moment's thought. "I'm as curious as a cat, it's true, and not without ambition—but I need to know what your purpose is, mon ami. To free Bonaparte from St. Helena and build an empire in the Indies, that I understood... but I'm a radical now—a red republican in my heart of hearts—and I'm no longer prepared to sell my conscience as easily as I once was."

"This is no mere matter of empire-building," said the former John Devil, his voice so slight now that Ned was sure that none but he could hear it. "This is greater still, and will change the world forever, if it is not nipped in the bud by foul treachery. It's immortality, Ned, if we only have time to master its evolution. It's the end of the empire of death and the empire of fear. Tell Gregory Temple that, if and when he questions you again. Tell him that I'm the least of his enemies now, and can save him from the worst if I can only win the necessary time and he can put the past behind him. Tell him that I can help him live forever, if only I can overcome my nemesis, and he can overcome his bitter heart. Tell him that Mortdieu's the one who needs to be stopped, if he can do it..."

The man who had been John Devil the Quaker—and still kept up the pose, on occasion—allowed his voice to trail off. The cart was already drawing to a halt on the quay, which was only slightly better lit than the street. Ordinarily the docks would still have been at work at this hour, but *Prometheus* was the only sizeable ship

73

at the dock tonight. If she had the same reputation here as she had among the watermen of the city, that was not at all surprising.

The living men jumped down one by one, lifting up their weapons. The ci-devant Comte de Belcamp leapt over the side of the cart and landed like a predatory cat, ready to lead them. There was little or no time to evaluate the situation. Ned stood up, and craned his neck in order to see what he could of the brawl that was taking place on the deck of the *Prometheus*. It was mostly a play of shadows, but there were lanterns attached to each mast. He could not tell whether the white, brown and black faces on deck were outnumbered by grey ones, but there was a considerable struggle going on. Having counted heads, though, Ned concluded that the recently-arrived reinforcements would be more than enough to win the fight in a mater of minutes. It seemed that Mortdieu's raiders had been held at bay long enough.

The reinforcements in question did not hesitate in their charge. They were met on the gangplank, and had to fight their way aboard, but Ned could see that the resistance was weak, and that the would-be pirates knew that they cold not win. The erstwhile attackers were retreating now, scattering as best they could. One or two contrived to leap ashore, and Ned heard a sequence of splashes as others tumbled into the water—perhaps including some of the ship's defenders as well as its attackers. He squinted into the gloom, trying to identify grey faces among those of more vivid color, but the light was too poor.

Ned wondered how hard it might be to kill the resurrected dead for a second time, given that they no longer had red blood to bleed—but he deduced that it could not be as hard as all that, given that they still had beating hearts to stop, and throats to cut. The might be grey, but they breathed air, and must take in sustenance. They could not be immortal.

Could they, he wondered, produce children of their own? Could they produce grey children of their own? That question might, in the long run, be the key to their potential relationship with humankind.

Ned dropped his cutlass, and jumped down from the cart in his turn. He poised himself on his toes to run off into the streets of Purfleet, asking himself how much it would cost him to hire a fiacre to take him all the way to Covent Garden—but he could not hold that thought. Instead, he climbed back on to the cart and craned his neck again, anxious to know how the fight was going.

He picked up the cutlass absent-mindedly, simply because it was there—but he was glad that he had when he felt the cart lurch as someone stepped up behind him.

He turned to face the new arrival, perversely relieved to discover that the grey man was not a giant, nor even a man of average height. Ned realized that he had not the slightest idea whether this was one of the resurrected dead from the house in Purfleet or one of the others, raised from the grave by his own sinister kind. He was, however, somewhat reassured by the fact that the grey man was not carrying a weapon.

"I don't suppose, by any chance, that you know your name, mon ami," he said, as lightly as he could.

"I have not forgotten it," the grey man said, speaking far more coherently than Sawney had, "but I have discarded it. Do you know yours?"

"I do," Ned confirmed. "Have I, then, the honor of addressing Monsieur Mortdieu, the general of the great army of the dead?"

"I have not forgotten sarcasm either," the grey man said, apparently lacking nothing in intelligence or articulacy, "but I no longer find much use for it. Would you like to be raised from the dead, mon ami, when your time comes?"

"I'd rather it didn't come for a while yet," Ned replied. "And if the occasion should arise sooner than I hope and expect, I think I'd rather be among friends."

"You might find," the grey man observed, "that the friends you had before are no longer your friends, and that it will be to your advantage to make new ones."

"I might," Ned agreed. "You don't seem to be afraid of me, even though I have a sword, while your height and reach are almost as meager as my own. Would you care to tell me why that is?"

"You did not charge with the others," the grey man pointed out. "You're evidently a man of extreme discretion."

"So much for having no further use for sarcasm," Ned said. "You're evidently a man of discretion yourself. Your army might stand a greater chance of victory if you were at their head, leading by example."

"Do you think so, mon ami?" the grey man said. "That would depend, would it not, on exactly what their objective is?"

As the grey man pronounced the last two words, as neatly as any living man could have done, Ned was deafened by a mighty bang. He was hurled forward by the blast-wave that spread out along the quay from the *Prometheus*. He sprawled face-down on the floor of the cart, and felt the cutlass plucked from his hand. The two horses reared and neighed, but they could not break the tether that had secured them to a windlass, and were thus unable to bolt. The cart continued to rattle and jolt, but the grey man was not thrown out of it.

Ned tried to get up, but a heavy boot came down on the back of his right hand and pinned him.

The grey man knelt down beside him, but did not cut his throat. "The house is mine, now, mon ami," he said, "as it should be. The dead-alive imprisoned there are mine, now, as they should be. Fear not—I've a ship of my own at Tilbury, and I'll be gone in less than 48 hours, as soon I've gathered everything I need. You won't see me again, if you have no wish to do so—but you ought to remember what I tell you, and mark it well. I have nothing against the living, if they do not seek to rule the dead-alive. Indeed, I love the living, for they are the seeds of my own kind. If the living will only let me alone, and leave me to my work, I and my kind will let the living alone, but if your kind takes up arms against me, or tries again to usurp the privilege that is mine, I shall be an enemy more terrible than any you have ever faced before. I have no wish to harass the living, and every hope that your kind and mine will be able to share this world in amity, but I have observed the reactions of your kind to the sight of mine, and I thin it politic, for the time being, to be a man of extreme discretion. If anyone should ask you what took place this evening, tell them that the dead-alive have won the liberty that is their right as human beings, and hope to use it peacefully and productively. Tell them that we have no wish to go to war—but that if we are forced to do so again, as we have in the past, we shall do so with all the might we can muster. Can you remember all that?"

"I can remember the gist of it," Ned told him, resentfully. "I've the mind of a living man, and have no need to be taught to think all over again—but if you want your message to be heeded, you would probably have done better to confide it to a taller man. People of our humble stature are rarely taken seriously, as you may well remember."

"I remember everything," Mortdieu assured him. "I never had the slightest difficulty in being taken seriously, and I beg you not to underestimate your own potential. I'm truly sorry to have lured so many of your friends aboard the doomed ship, and to have left them without the slightest help of resurrection, but you can be sure that I'll treat Germain Patou far more gently, for old time's sake. Please don't return to the house, tonight or any time tomorrow. Go back to London, and retire to your bed for a while. It will be better for both of us if I am gone before you tell your tale."

The cart lurched drunkenly as the grey man jumped down, and then continued to vibrate as the horses twitched and fretted.

Ned got down himself as soon as he felt able, nursing his bruised hand. He raced to the water's edge, where the gangplank leading to the *Prometheus* had been. The gangplank had been blown apart, and one of the two hawsers securing the ship to the dock had been severed. The one at the bow had held, though, so the ship had merely changed its attitude as the stern drifted away from the quay. The upper deck was ablaze, although the furled canvas had not yet caught alight. The hull had been holed at the waterline, and the cargo-holds were filling up with water, but the ship was going down slowly.

There were men still on deck—living men, not grey ones—and two of them were howling for help. Ned found a rope and threw it to them, but could do no more. He found a lifebelt, though, and hurled that into the dark water, where there were heads bobbing amid all manner of debris. He hunted for more ropes to let down the side of the dock. He called for help too, but none came from the shoreward side.

There was no sign of the ci-devant Comte de Belcamp. Three men had gained the base of a flight of stone steps leading up to the quay, but there the fight broke out again, although none of them was grey. The one who was beset by two was hurled back into the water, but he seemed well able to swim, and struck out towards another place where he might climb up. Not everyone in the water was as fortunate—several were injured, and were having difficulty keeping afloat, let alone striking out for the dock.

There was a mighty gout of steam as the weight of the water in the *Prometheus'* holds pulled the upper deck level with the water. The fire died, and the best of the light with it. There was a man directly below Ned, who had grabbed one of the ropes he had let down, but his arm was injured and he could not climb. Ned set his legs and began to pull hard, calling down to the man to set his good hand and his feet in whatever nooks and crannies he could find, so as to take as much of his own weight as he possibly could. Ned was small, but he was strong. After five minutes of struggling, the man grasped the rim of the dock with his good hand, and Ned caught hold of him while he scrambled for footholds, eventually wriggling over the edge on to the apron.

"Thanks, mate!" the sailor said, spitting out a quid of tobacco and a mouthful of river-water. "Never thought I'd make it."

"Some didn't," Ned said, regretfully, peering over the edge to see if there was anyone else who might benefit from his immediate assistance.

"Tricked and bested by a handful of men—and half of them walking corpses, by God!" the sailor went on. "I wish I could be sorrier to see her go, but she's been about the Devil's work since we shipped out of Lisbon. If I'd had any sense, I'd never have signed back on—but I've always been a fool for money."

The sailor was looking back at his ship as he spoke. The *Prometheus* was sinking into the harbor now, although she hit bottom long before her masts were fully submerged. The arms carrying the topsails were level with the waterline, and Ned saw two swimmers grasp them gratefully, desperate to rest.

"They've a ship of their own at Tilbury, if Mortdieu wasn't lying," Ned said. "If Henri can regroup his forces, there might be time for a counter-attack."

"Who's Henri?" the sailor demanded, as he came to his feet, wringing wet.

"The erstwhile master of the *Prometheus*. Pevensey, is he calling himself now? The pretended Cornishman."

"He's not my master any more," was the sailor's curt reply. "I've lost my ship and must find another. This time, I'll stick to the tea trade if I can. If I must, I'll ship convicts to Botany Bay—but I'll have no more of demonkind, that's for sure."

"Best of luck to you, then," said Ned, sincerely. "What chance would we have, do you think, of finding a boat to carry us upriver, if we walk westwards?"

"Little or none," the sailor opined, hugging his wounded arm to his chest. "Far more chance of getting stuck in a bog. We'd best seek shelter for the night—I need to dry my clothes by a roasting fire and find out if my forearm's broken. I know an inn, if you'd like to come with me—I don't think they'll turn us away, even though they know we've been trafficking with the Devil, if we plead our innocence loudly enough."

"No," said Ned, with a sigh. "I'm dry, and there's always the road. But you might pass the message along, if you see any of Master Pevensey's servants, or the man himself. Mortdieu says that he has a ship at Tilbury, waiting to carry him away, once he's seized Patou and plundered the house. If he's lying, then his ship is somewhere else—but he certainly intends to be gone as soon as he can. Once he's at sea, Henri will never catch him, and probably won't find it easy to locate him again."

"I'll pass the word along," the sailor agreed, "If I have the chance. I owe you that much."

"Thanks," Ned aid, sincerely. "Good luck to you."

As it turned out, he had more than one opportunity to pass his message on himself before he quit the quay. He gave the same intelligence to the footman who'd brought the deadly warning to the cellar, and to another soaking wet sailor from the *Prometheus*. Ned formed the impression, however, that the footman and the second sailor were of much the same mind as the first, firmly resolved to be done with the Devil's work forever.

"Perhaps it's for the best," he murmured to himself, as he went in search of a hirer's or a coaching stop. "If Mortdieu withdraws from England, and takes Patou with him, it'll put an end to the burking epidemic and things will soon return to normal."

By the time he was fortunate enough to find a stop with a mail-coach expected imminently, however, Ned had changed his mind about that final judgment. Things would never return to normal. How could they? However slowly matters might evolve, a crucial bridge had been crossed that had delivered the human race into a new era. The greatest of all the old certainties had fallen by the wayside. Death was no longer the end—not, at least, for everyone. Whether Mortdieu contrived to hoard the secret or not, it had been discovered and would be again. Science was a method, after all; what one scientist could do, another could repeat—and another and another, ad infinitum. The day of the grey men had come, and there was no way to turn back the clock.

"Have you come from the docks?" asked one of the businessmen waiting to board the London-bound coach. "I heard an explosion over that way, not half-an-hour ago, and saw flames in the sky."

"Nothing to worry about," Ned assured the tall man, looking upwards to meet his eye. "Just the living and the dead-alive fighting over the dubious privilege of controlling the process of transition, while it's still esoteric. The *Prometheus* was blown up, but there were at least a dozen survivors, probably more. I don't know how many were killed, but probably not as many."

The man, inevitably, looked down at him as if he were mad. When the coach eventually came, the man and his fellows climbed up inside, while Ned was forced by the leanness of his resources to take a place on top, where stouter men than he had frozen to death on journeys not much longer. By the time he dismounted—in Fleet Street yet again—he was chilled to the bone. He jogged all the way to Jenny Paddock's.

Because it was Sunday there had been no performance that evening, and the parlor was half empty. There was no sign of Jack Hanrahan, but Sam Hopkey and Jeanie Bird were snuggled together in their favorite booth.

"Buy me a brandy, Sam, for God's sake," Ned croaked, as he sat down on the bench beside Jeanie, forcing her to move into even closer proximity with her leading man, until he jumped up to obey his director's command.

"Did you find Sawney?" Jeanie asked, eagerly, while Sam was at the counter.

"I found the place where he was, an hour ago," Ned told her, glumly, "but how long he'll be there I don't know. He's among his own kind now—I doubt that we'll be seeing him again, although I'm sure we could have done him a power of good, between the three of us."

"And what is his own kind?" Jeanie asked, fearfully.

"I believe they like to style themselves the dead-alive," Ned said. "It wasn't the hangman's carelessness that spared Sawney, or a miracle that brought him back to life. It was science, like Mr. Davy's and Mr. Faraday's."

"Science?" echoed Sam, as he set a generous brandy down in front of Ned and took the stool where Ned would normally have sat. "What kind of science can bring the dead back from beyond the grave?"

"I've see it done," Ned told him, before swilling the brandy down. "It'll cause trouble, I don't doubt, but in a hundred years' time, it will be the destiny of every living soul—and I, for one, will welcome it."

"You've seen it done by the Frenchman who was here last night?" Sam said, just to make certain.

"The very same," Ned said. This time, he did not have his back to the door, so he knew as soon as anyone else what was happening as the Constables and Town Sergeants poured through it with their truncheons at the ready. There were a dozen in all. They had not come to start a fight, though, but merely to make sure that no one else would. A single man strode in behind them, with his head held high and the air of a man who had just recovered something that was rightly his. Given that he could not have been reappointed Chief Superintendent of Scotland Yard, Ned had to assume that it was his dignity, or his sense of purpose, or both.

Gregory Temple marched straight to the booth, where Ned Knob only seemed to be cowering because his limbs were so infernally cold.

"Edward Knob," Temple said, taking less relish in the pronouncement than Ned might have anticipated, "I arrest you in the name of the law, on the grounds that in St. Luke's Churchyard, at three o'clock this afternoon, in company with John Hanrahan, you purchased the dead body of a young girl for use in unspeakable practices."

Ned heard the chorus of gasps that greeted this announcement, and could imagine the whispers that would follow it. Ned Knob a burker! Ned Knob a necrophile! Who would ever have thought it? Well, what can you expect from a miserable dwarf?

"Mr. Temple," he said, unable to suppress a shiver as he stood up to meet his fate, "you don't know the half of it, or even the tenth. Jack Hanrahan is a hero, and not only because he went to see Dan Eaton pilloried, in order to defend him against anyone wishing to do him harm, but because he gave that little girl a second chance to live—exactly as he did for Sawney Ross. You'll not find a man or woman in here willing to chide him for that."

A silence fell then, as profound as the one that had greeted the sight of Sawney's grey face, but Ned knew that it would not last.

"And before you take me away," Ned went on, striking the best leading man's pose that he could contrive, without the benefit of Sam's or Sawney's height,

"I have a message for the world from General Mortdieu of the Necromantic Empire, which is this: He has nothing against the living, provided that they do not take up arms against the dead-alive. Indeed, he loves the living, for we are the seed of his own good folk. Nor should we hate or fear him, since he offers us the hope and expectation of a better resurrection—a radical resurrection. Down with King George, and long live the Republic!"

The audience was too dumbstruck to cheer him, but he knew that they would remember what he had said for a long time to come. They were living people, after all; they needed no help to learn to think for a second time.

Chapter Six
The Interrogation Cell at Bow Street

This time, Ned was not taken to some secret covert in Newgate Prison, but to Bow Street Police Station, where he was immediately lodged in an official interrogation cell. This one was better furnished than the one in which he had been entertained the previous evening, although it had neither bed nor window. Its table was much sturdier, it was far better lit, and it had two uniformed constables in attendance. On the other hand, the chair in which Ned was placed could not be described as well-upholstered or comfortable. Gregory Temple remained standing, obviously feeling that no height was too great from which to look down on a man like Ned Knob.

"You should not have arrested me, Mr. Temple," Ned complained. "I was not a accomplice to Jack Hanrahan's crime—if it can still be reckoned a crime, now that we know what we know. Had you let me at liberty, I'd have got to the bottom of this mystery in no time at all, and you may be sure that I'd have told you everything."

"You will forgive me if I doubt you," Temple said, curtly. "You will be doubtless be glad to know, since you say that you are innocent of any crime, that I have been seconded to Scotland Yard, and am able once again openly to wear the title detective. You may be less delighted to know that Jack Hanrahan has agreed to testify for the Crown against all his old associates, including yourself and Germain Patou. He has told us everything."

"And a great deal more, I don't doubt," Ned said, with a wry smile. "You couldn't possibly order me a cup of tea, by any chance? I'm still cold, having been forced to sit on top of a mail-coach in highly unsuitable weather, with the wind blowing in my face all the way from Purfleet to Fleet Street. A bite to eat would be nice, if it wouldn't overburden or hospitality. I was just about to order supper at Jenny's when you burst in with your guard of honor."

Temple turned to one of the Constables. "Fresh tea for the four of us," he said, "and find something tooth-some for this man to eat."

The Constable's moustache twitched, but he dared not let the scowl spread across his features. He left without uttering a word of protest.

"You know as well as I do, Mr. Temple," Ned went on, "that I never spent more than a few minutes in Jack Hanrahan's company until this afternoon, when I ingra-tiated with him purely and simply to obtain informa-tion—information which will be of just as much interest to you as it was to me, and which I'm perfectly willing to share, in spite of the ungrateful and insulting manner in which I've been treated. I can now give you a more accurate sketch of the causes of the burking epidemic than can possibly be contained in Jack's fancies and fabulations—although I repeat that I could have given you a far more complete account had you only let me pursue my inquiries further."

"That's as may be, Master Knob," Temple said. "But Hanrahan has got in first, and he's given us enough to pack you off to Australia—and enough to hang Germain Patou, if his own people do not want him for the guillotine."

"This is all very silly," Ned told him. "Sit down, Mr. Temple and listen. I've seen him, and he asked me to give you a message. I've also seen his new arch-enemy, who was equally enthusiastic to find a reliable messenger. There's a great deal I still don't know, but if you want to hear what I do know, you'd do better to talk to me man-to-man than continue this charade of bullying."

"Did I not hear one of your messages just now, in Sharper's?" Temple parried.

"Only part of it—you seemed to be in a hurry, and I didn't want to be cut off in mid-speech. That would have been poor stagecraft, and Sawney would never have forgiven me. But you're right—that was the core of the message given to me by Patou's ungrateful Lazarus, who seems to be trying to reserve the privilege of restoring the dead-alive entirely to himself, at least for the time being. It was intended for the whole world, so I proclaimed it as loudly as I could. The message I was given by the man you once knew as James Davy, on the other hand, is for your ears alone, which I shall be glad to pass on in exactly that fashion, if you would care to ask the other Constable to leave us alone for a minute or two."

Temple shook his head. "This is an official interrogation, Master Knob," he said, "which must be conducted under formal rules of guidance." Ned realized, a trifle belatedly, that Temple's manner was not entirely of his own choosing. The produce of Jack Hanrahan's squealing had obviously made its way higher up the chain of command. Temple was still constrained by circumstance, even though he had been seconded to Scotland Yard.

"Ah," Ned said. "I see. My apologies to you, Mr. Temple—although you really did seem to be enjoying yourself just a little, back at Jenny's. I had forgotten how good you are at playing a part, once you have the determination to do so. Very well—within the framework of an official interrogation, what would you like to know?"

The first Constable came back in then, carrying a tin tray. It bore a teapot and four mugs, with a sugarbowl and a jug of milk. There was also a plate bearing some day-old bread and a few slices of ham. Ned sighed, but he was hungry enough to attack the meager meal with some enthusiasm. Temple poured the tea, and passed two of the mugs to the Constables, who nodded in acknowledgement of his generosity. Temple asked all three of them whether they required sugar. The Constables requested two spoonfuls each, so Ned asked for three, calculating that his tour of duty must have been a good deal more laborious than theirs. Temple contented himself with one, but heaped it more generously than he had heaped any of the others, apparently unaware of the insight he was providing into the essential perversity of his character.

Temple sat down, and waited until Ned had finished the bread and ham. "Where was the girl's body taken, Master Knob, and by what means?" the detective asked, formally.

"Purfleet," Ned said, unhesitatingly. "Aboard a vessel named *Prometheus*, which sank in Purfleet harbor not three hours ago. You'll be getting your own reports of that very shortly, I dare say, but it won't make the Morning Post until the day after tomorrow."

"The ship sank?" Temple echoed, already forced to deviate from his planned agenda, though not from his formal manner. "How did it come to sink?"

"It was attacked by a party of raiders, including both living and dead-alive," Ned told him. "To begin with, the crew thought it was an attempt to seize the ship, but it wasn't. The fighting was a mere diversion, to distract attention from a petard placed at the water-line. The intention was to sink the vessel, in order to prevent its further use."

"Its further use in the stealing of corpses?"

"No—its use as a means of escape. When the master of the *Prometheus* found out that you were on his trail, Mr. Temple, he immediately decided to pack up and leave. No matter how great his need for an abundant supply of dead people was, I doubt that he would ever have come within 50 miles of London had he not assumed that you were a broken man, incapable of taking any further interest in him."

"Who are you talking about?" Temple demanded, bluntly.

"I told you—the man you once knew as James Davy. The viper you nursed in your bosom, who extracted all your secrets by stealth and turned them against you. The man also known as the bandit Tom Brown and as Comte Henri de Belcamp—being fully entitled to both names, by reason of his rather remarkable birth and upbringing, although he appears to have renounced them forever. I believe that he was calling himself Arthur Pevensey at the time of his probable death, masquerading as a Cornishman."

"What do you mean by at the time of his probable death?" Temple asked.

"He was lured aboard the *Prometheus* two or three minutes before it blew up. There were survivors, but I didn't see him among them."

"Did you see his corpse, then?"

"No—but I doubt that General Mortdieu will consent to revive him, even if it is still in good condition. General Mortdieu does not seem to me to be the kind of person likely to repeat his predecessor's worst mistake."

"And who is this General Mortdieu to whom you refer?"

"The cleverest and most ambitious of the dead-alive, resurrected by Germain Patou and Arthur Pevensey in Portugal, probably not far from Lisbon. He had another name when he was alive, of course, and claims to know what it was. I have a suspicion of my own regarding that item of information, but I doubt that it matters any longer. Now he is General Mortdieu, hero of the Revolution against Death and Emperor of the Dead-Alive. He says that he has no wish to make war on England, or on any nation of the living, and I am inclined to believe him, for now. As to the future... I have given that matter some thought while I was en route to London, in spite of being frozen half to death, and it seems to me that it depends on whether the dead-alive can breed. I did not have the opportunity to consult Monsieur Patou on that question."

"I don't understand what you mean," Temple said.

"You will, when you've had time to think about it. Point one: the dead can now be brought back to life—not all of them, but some. Point two: the dead-alive have trouble remembering who they were before they died, and most seem in need of considerable re-education—but at least some can recover all of their memories and the power of their will. Point three: in consequence of points one and two, the world has changed, utterly and irrevocably. Point four: at present the so-called Arthur Pevensey and the so-called General Mortdieu are squabbling over the secret of reviving the dead, evidently having different views as to how the advent of different views as to how the advent of the new race should be managed. I do not know what either of them intends, but I know that it is a matter of small importance. Point five: if the dead-alive can reproduce their own kind, they are a new species, potentially capable of replacing humankind as overlords of the Earth. If not, then we are the larvae from whose corpses they must hatch as flies—in which case, they must continue to indefinitely cherish us as we cherish our children, if ever they do wrest political control of civilization from our hands. Point six: for the moment, you probably think that I am mad, and may even wish that I were—but that does not matter in the least. Whether you believe me or not, the world has changed, absolutely and forever."

There was a brief silence, while Ned and Gregory Temple each took several sips of sweet tea.

"You are perfectly certain that the dead can be resurrected?" Temple said, with only the slightest inquisitive inflection.

"I have not seen the process from beginning to end," Ned admitted, "but I did see the factory in which the dead are prepared for their return to life, and I witnessed a key stage in the resurrection process. I am far more certain now that it can be done, and has already been done a hundred times over, than I was last night after seeing Sawney Ross turned grey." As he finished this speech, Ned felt his breath catch in his throat, and he coughed to clear it.

Temple shook his head. "If you were to repeat this story in court tomorrow, you'd be presumed to be a madman," he observed.

"Tomorrow," Ned agreed, "denial will still be possible. In the longer term, it will not. More than a hundred people saw Sawney come into Jenny Paddock's last night, some of whom had seen him hanged. There are ferrymen sheltering beneath London Bridge and Blackfriars Bridge who'll be glad to tell you about the passengers the *Prometheus* sometimes used to carry after darkness fell. There'll be crewmen from the *Prometheus* herself trying to find new berths tomorrow morning, who'll be more than pleased to explain why. And even if all of those people should happen to be more anxious than I am to avoid being called a liar for telling the truth, we may be certain that General Mortdieu does not intend to hide his Empire of the Dead-Alive forever. If nothing else, they will want... well, I suppose I ought not to call it new blood, since the dead-alive have something other than blood in their veins, but I dare say that you can follow the logic of my argument now that I've set it out for you."

"It sounds impossible," Temple said, flatly.

"Yes, Mr. Temple," Ned replied. "It does. Indeed, it was impossible just a little while ago, but it is impossible no longer. We stand on the threshold of a new era, and all the firepower in the British Empire cannot hold it at bay. Ours will be a century of multitudinous resurrections, and we might as well try be proud of the fact."

Temple hesitated again, then said: "Where exactly, in Purfleet, was the girl's body taken?"

"To a house on the east of the town, standing in its own grounds and surrounded by a high wall. It has three stories at the front, four at the back, because the ground falls away so steeply. It also has a further set of vaults beneath the basement, where Germain Patou's equipment was sited until this evening. You will recognize the equipment easily enough if you can get there in time; as Jack Hanrahan has probably told you, it once belonged to James Graham's Temple of Hymen and Health. Not that I'm endorsing anything else he may have told you, mind."

"What do you mean by if you can get there in time?"

"Mortdieu is stripping the place as we speak, of anything useful to his campaign," Ned told him. "He has a ship of his own—at Tilbury, he said, although I would not put it past him to tell a fib or two in the interests of putting his adversaries off his trail. I have no idea where he will steer his ship once it sets sail, but he said he would be gone within 48 hours, of which at least five must now have elapsed."

"You seem to take a remarkable relish in all this, Master Knob," Temple observed, perhaps speaking entirely for himself for once.

"Do I?" Ned riposted. "Well, perhaps I do. I am a radical, you see, Mr. Temple, and a great enthusiast for Jacobin science and the philosophy of progress. I like to think of the order of things being upset, in the hope that it might make way for something better. Is that really such a crime, even in the eyes of a loyal lackey of the state?"

"If the reawakened dead really were stalking our streets last night," Temple said, leadenly, "and are about to overrun the world in years to come, I could not call that progress."

"That is because you are an old man, Mr. Temple," Ned said, cruelly, "and a man of the old order. I, on the other hand, am a young man of the new order. Perhaps our positions will be reversed in a short while, if you should choose to join the ranks of the dead-alive, or are rudely press-ganged into their company. Perhaps you will be able to think of it as progress then."

Temple shook his head, as if to clear it of unwelcome ideas. "You really are serious, aren't you?" he said, wonderingly. "I never had a moment's doubt that Hanrahan was lying through his teeth, but you actually mean what you say. Either you are mad, or you're telling the truth."

"I'm an honest man, Mr. Temple," Ned told him, regretfully. "Too honest for my own good, on occasion. He promised that he would bring you back from the dead, if you can put the past behind you and make a new start. That was the message he asked me to give you."

"Mortdieu?"

"The man who once posed as John Devil the Quaker, and still takes some pride in wearing the badge of that office. He might be able to fulfil the promise—Germain Patou may have been a vital element of the partnership to begin with, and Mortdieu will presumably take the opportunity to capture him, but he must know more than enough to set up in business again, provided that he still alive."

By now, Temple had ceased to make any pretence that this as still a formal interrogation, conducted under official rules of guidance. "You cannot possibly know how difficult it would be," the old man whispered. "To put the past behind me, I mean. You do not know what that man tried to do to me."

"Yes, I do," Ned assured him. "I don't know exactly how he set about it, but I know he did whatever he could to leave you in Newgate a broken man. You were too strong for him, though. You came back from the dead, just as he did, without the necessity of Germain Patou's magical fluid and electric shocks. He's a different man now—and I think you know as well as I do how utterly he can change, when he steps from one role into another. It wasn't you who defeated him, remember—it was the burning of his steamship by riotous natives in Africa. That, and love."

"Love!" Temple spat out the word as if it were an oath.

"Yes, love. If he had not loved Jeanne, and wanted so much to be worthy of her love... he really did want to change history, you know, so that he might be innocent of the murders of Maurice O'Brien and Constance Bartolozzi—not for his own sake, but for hers. He really did want to annihilate Tom Brown: not to be him any longer, and never to have been him at all. He really is a man who can put the past behind him and make new starts—but then, he's a younger man than you, and one who believes in progress. Perhaps his belief is not yet as strong as it might be, but I think I might be able to help him in that respect, if I were given the chance."

Gregory Temple closed his eyes. The expression on his face was impossible to fathom, but it was not that of a man who could yet begin to believe in progress.

"What did you find at the address in Stepney?" Ned ventured to ask.

"Enough to tie Patou into half a dozen burkers," Temple told him, willingly enough. "But we didn't find the address of the house in Purfleet—you did better there."

"I probably did better with Jack Hanrahan too," Ned said. "I persuaded him that I was his friend, so he talked to me as honestly as he talks to anyone. I still won't be your spy, Mr. Temple, but that doesn't mean that I can't be useful to your inquiries. I haven't joined forces with John Devil either—I'm still my own man, and I'm more curious than ever to know more about the world that is to come. If you release me, I'll do what I can to find out more about Mortdieu's plans—and John Devil's too, if ever I see him again."

Gregory Temple shook his head again, this time very tiredly. "The interview is over," he said to the two silent Constables. "Take Master Knob down to the overnight cells—he looks as if he's in dire need of a good night's sleep."

"I'd be a deal more comfortable in my own bed, Mr. Temple," Ned opined.

"I doubt it," Temple said. "I know where you live—but I don't doubt that Hanrahan was lying about your involvement in his crimes, trying to reduce his own guilt by imparting it recklessly to others. I'll try to persuade my superiors that you're too useful to lock away. With luck, I'll be able to release you in the morning. In the meantime, you probably do need that good night's sleep. I hope the cells won't be too noisy for you."

"Mr. Temple," Ned said, "you're a gentleman, and a wise one too. I always thought so. That's why he admires you so."

"He tried to destroy me with a series of lies," the detective murmured, "and very nearly succeeded."

"The extent to which a man will go to wreak destruction," Ned said, soberly, "is the most accurate measure of his fear. Oddly enough, no one ever tries to destroy me—their first instinct is always to give me messages to carry. I wish I could be proud of that, as well as glad."

Chapter Seven
The Road to Greenhithe

The beds in the cells at Bow Street Police Station were by no means famous for their softness, and the cell block was even noisier than the street where Ned Knob lived, but Ned was not a man used to a thickly-padded mattress, silken sheets or silence. He slept tolerably well.

The establishment was not famous for its breakfasts, either, but Ned was quite satisfied by the hot sugared porridge he was brought at 6 a.m., and the tea that came with it was perfectly drinkable, even though it had only one spoonful of sugar in it—and not one that had been heaped by Gregory Temple.

Ned also made full use of the bowl of hot water and the brick of soap that the turnkey brought him—he was, after all, still Gentleman Ned Knob as well as Red Republican Ned, and he was determined not to conduct himself like any common jailbird.

He would have slept somewhat later than usual if he had been given the chance, having had an unusually exhausting Sunday, but his jailers had a routine to observe. When he had finished washing, however, he lay back down on the bed and dozed, fully expecting Gregory Temple to come to his rescue at any moment.

As things transpired, the moments dragged by while Bow Bells chimed seven, eight and nine, and Ned had almost begun to suspect that he had been cheated when the lock finally turned in his door and the great detective came in.

"Get up, Master Knob," the detective said. "We've no time to lose, and this is no time to be lazing in bed till mid-morning."

"I would have been glad to turn my hand and my head to more profitable occupations, Mr. Temple," Ned said, in an aggrieved manner, as he was hustled up the stone steps and out into the yard where the armored wagons waited to carry prisoners to the court, "had you only seen fit to make such provision. I've been on tenterhooks for hours, eager to be off."

The carriage into which they climbed was no court-ferry, nor did it bear any official insignia. Evidently, Gregory Temple's re-recruitment to the not-so-secret police did not inhibit him from traveling incognito. The bench inside was a good deal better upholstered than the bed on which Ned had been lying, and the cab was closed against the biting wind, so the journey promised to be a comfortable one.

"To Purfleet, I suppose?" Ned murmured, as they headed down Kin William Street towards London Bridge.

"Greenhithe," Temple told him.

"Not even Tilbury," Ned said, pensively. "I suspected that Mortdieu was lying about that. Strange, is it not, that one can sense a lie even in a man who has come back from the dead?"

"You're a veritable genius, Master Knob," Temple said, sarcastically. "Events have moved on, by the way, since we spoke last night. I sent men to investigate the house at Purfleet, but they arrived too late to prevent its destruction."

"Destruction!" Ned echoed. "John Devil survived the blast, then, and wasted no time in striking back at his ungrateful Lazarus?"

"Not so far as my men could tell. The sinking of the *Prometheus* sparked another reaction, it seems. The harbormaster at Purfleet had been unhappy for some time, it seems, and all the dock-workers too. Business had declined sharply since certain rumors began to run along the shore regarding the cargoes brought into port by the unlucky vessel, and considerable resentment had built up against her master. No one, of course, saw fit to involve higher authorities in their anxieties—these are men used to taking care of their own problems. The explosion in the harbor was the last straw. In the old days, mobs used to give notice of their intentions with a few hours of rough music, but we live in precipitate times. The house in Purfleet was visited by an armed gang whose only purpose was to burn the owners out, and they did so with remarkable precision. The house—all of it, at least, that stood above ground level at the front—is now a blackened shell."

Ned considered this for a few moments. "Well," he said, eventually, "if General Mortdieu had nothing against the living when he spoke to me, he has something against them now. Did he manage to get Germain Patou's equipment out of the cellars, and the dead-alive out of their rooms, before the fire took hold?"

"It seems so," Temple told him. "My men found nothing in the cellars but a few dead bodies that were by no means fresh, and there were no obvious skeletons among the rubble of the main body of the house."

"And you think they took their plunder to Greenhithe?"

"My agents were unable to determine where any material removed from the house might have been taken. Fortunately, my former colleagues had maintained their own surveillance at Sharper's."

"What was fortunate about that?" Ned asked. "Jenny's customers must have melted away like snow in June after your grand entrance. No one of interest to you could possibly have remained there."

"Indeed not," Temple agreed. "Even your friend Sam Hopkey and his doxy decided to go home, though their lodgings are even less salubrious than your own. They did not even get as far as the end of Low Lane. There was a carriage waiting at the corner, and they were persuaded to get in."

Thus far, the porridge he had eaten for breakfast had sat in Ned's stomach in a very satisfied manner, but now he felt suddenly queasy. "What do you mean, persuaded?" he demanded. "How? By whom? Why?"

"Don't alarm yourself unduly, Master Knob," Temple said. "By persuaded, I only meant to reassure you that they were not treated violently. They got into the carriage willingly, after a brief conversation with their former employer, Alexander Ross. How many people might have been waiting in the carriage the watcher could not tell—it was a capacious vehicle, and the curtains were drawn—but one other person got down: the large man who was with Germain Patou when he came to collect Ross on the previous night. Patou might have been inside, of course, but he was not seen. I had already been transferred, as you know, but the orders I had given before I was moved were still in force. The agent followed the carriage, which made slow enough progress to enable him to do so, until it was nearly to Deptford. He lost sight of it there, but found it again at Deptford

Creek. There, for once in his life, he found witnesses ready and willing to talk—it's not only the inhabitants of Purfleet who have taken alarm these last few days. The grey men and their companions went aboard a launch; the steamship to which it belongs is moored at Greenhithe."

"A steamship! It wouldn't be the *Deliverance*, by any chance?"

"No, it wouldn't—but I'm not in a position to judge whether it might have borne that name in the past. Steamships are becoming a familiar sight on the Thames, but they still attract attention, especially if they are French. This one is called the *Outremort*. John Devil still has his sense of humor, you see."

Ned thought hard about that for more than a minute before saying: "No, Mr. Temple, it makes no sense. This carriage of which you speak arrived at Jenny's after you had taken me into custody. You say that it was a slow vehicle, but I had to wait at the coach-stop for more than an hour before I could even begin my homeward journey. I did not see Sawney or the giant while I was in the house at Purfleet, but Patou was there, and I do not believe that he would have sent them out without his guardianship after what had happened on the previous night.

"The carriage must have left the house after I spoke to Mortdieu—and it cannot have done so on John Devil's orders. I can believe that Patou might have made his escape when the house was besieged by Mortdieu's dead-alive, and that he would surely have taken Sawney and the giant with him if he could, but I cannot believe that he would have driven to Low Lane to see Sam Hopkey. Sawney might well have done that of his own accord, just as he had the previous eve, but if he acted under orders, those orders can only have come from..."

He stopped, suddenly confused. When he resumed, it was to say: "No, surely that makes no better sense. Perhaps you're right, after all, Mr. Temple, and the *Outremort* is John Devil's. He always has more depth to his plans than he permits others to see, and it must be the Deliverance renamed... although it is hard to imagine how he reclaimed the vessel from his widow without exciting her suspicions. No matter... the real issue is that if Sawney has taken Sam and Jeanie there, it's more like to be on John Devil's business than Mortdieu's. I wish I had a clearer idea of what each of them desires and intends to do with their secret, while it still remains secret."

"It had crossed my mind," Gregory Temple observed, "that your friends might have been taken in order to exert pressure on you, once it was known that you had been arrested—to inhibit you from telling what you knew."

"If so, I was far too much of a blabbermouth to be so easily dissuaded," Ned said. "I doubt it. Mortdieu intended me to speak, and the Comte was unworried by the knowledge that I would have to talk to you again. Had ether wished to silence me, he could have done so very easily. If Sawney came for Sam, it was likely for his own reasons—he came to Jenny's of his own accord the previous night, although he seemed very uncertain of what he wanted to say and do once he was there. I tried as hard as I could to jog his memory—I must have succeeded better than I thought."

"Perhaps it was as well that I arrested you," Temple observed, "or he'd have collected you too."

"Sam and Jeanie went with him voluntarily," Ned pointed out, "and I'd have done the same, even knowing that he really had been brought back from the dead. He's neither a vampire nor a ghoul, but a walking miracle of science. Whatever he wants Sam and Jeanie for, it's not to murder them."

"Are you certain about that, Master Knob?" Temple asked, with sudden intensity. "If he belongs to the ranks of the dead-alive now, he might be urgently desirous of sharing his condition with his old friends. He is no longer human, you must admit."

"I admit no such thing," Ned retorted, fiercely. "Though he has something other than blood in his veins, he is as human as you or I. This is the Age of Enlightenment, Mr. Temple; we should no longer fear demonic possession, and need no longer assume that anyone returned from the grave must be a thirsty vampire eager to suck the blood of those he once loved. We must put superstition behind us now that we live in an age of vital electricity and mutable species. If only we would open our eyes wider, and clear away the fog of ancient childish terrors, we would understand that every living creature is engaged in a ceaseless quest for improvement. I have been to the Jardin des Plantes, you see, as well as the Royal Institution. I have heard Monsieur Lamarck speak. Even though he is old and blind, he is more clearsighted than any other man alive, for he knows that our humankind was a long time in the making, and is not yet complete. Sawney is not a monster, Mr. Temple—he is Sawney still, with a second lease of life. We must understand that, if we are to serve the ends of progress in this matter."

"And this Mortdieu?" Temple challenged him. "Is he too an angel of progress rather than a demon of destruction?"

"Yes," said Ned, firmly. "He has nothing against the living, he says, and he will be tolerant of their misunderstandings, at least for a little while."

"He is fortunate to have chosen such a willing messenger," Temple observed, "although he cannot understand the living very well if he thought that they might listen to a worm like you."

"I remind you once again that you should not call me that, Mr. Temple," Ned told him, flatly. "I am a man like you, though short of stature and born to poverty. I have committed crimes in the past, I admit—but I did so because I was not content to live as I was, and wanted to be better. And you should not insult worms either—in Monsieur Lamarck's great scheme, every worm is striving to evolve, just as every man and woman is striving, in opposition to every obstacle. Every insect and spider, every slug and snail, every scorpion and serpent is on the path of progress. A man as clever as you should know that, Mr. Temple, in spite of the fact that you have lately been employed to set such obstacles in the course of your own kind, exerting all your might to oppose a change that will prove irresistible in the end. Perhaps I think better of you than you think of yourself, but I cannot believe that a man like you would have fired on the crowd at Peterloo had you been on duty that day, or delivered a false verdict against Tom Wooler had you served on his jury. Or are we going to Greenhithe merely to raise a mob to burn out the grey men wherever they might be hiding, in houses or on steamships, lest they pollute our glorious lives by bringing us back from the dead when our need arises?"

"You do not have the right to criticize me, Master Knob," Temple said, flatly.

"I do," Ned informed him, stoutly. "Why should I not?"

"Sam Hopkey and Janie Bird gave false evidence in the trial of Richard Thompson," Temple said, spitting out the words as if they were venom. "Recruited by Alexander Ross and paid by you, on behalf of the real murderer. You all did your level best to hang a honest man, and were all so proud of what you did that the doxy even kept the name in which you baptized her for her court appearance."

"And you fed liquor to my pretty Molly in order to trick her into telling you what happened in Paris on the night that Noll Green and Lochaber Dick turned on one another," Ned retorted, "and were only too anxious to believe what she said, in spite of her maudlin condition. But Richard Thompson did not hang for the crime he did not commit, did he? Are you really bitter because he was convicted on false evidence, or because he had already been liberated when you arrived to save him? If you value him as a friend and a son-in-law, why have you not visited him for four years? Perhaps you're angry with me because I have—because I've sat your grandson on my knee, and laughed in delight with his mother and father."

Gregory Temple hammered on the partition with the head of his stick, and cried; "Stop the carriage! This ungrateful whelp is getting down here, in order to make his own way to Greenhithe, London or the Devil!"

The carriage stopped, but Temple did not throw the door open. Ned sat where he was, waiting—but he could not resist peeping out of the window to see where they were. He did not know the south shore of the Thames at all well, but he did not think that they could be any further away from the point opposite Tower Hill than the region across from Greenwich. They still had a long way to go to Greenhithe.

In the end, Temple rapped on the pane again, and told the driver to move on.

"You do not know what that man said to me that night," he murmured. "You do not know how he tried to drive me mad."

"I know how wholeheartedly he plays his roles," Ned said. "I know what he can do, when he sets his mind."

"Can you guess, then, how he intends to use the secret of resurrection, if he can retain control of it against opposition from his own creations?" Temple demanded. "Can you guess what kind of empire he dreams of building this time?"

"Not exactly," Ned admitted, "but I think he has had his fill of Napoleonic dreams. He did say that this was a more important matter than empire-building in India. I suspect that his plans are still ill-formed, because he does not know as yet what capabilities the dead-alive might have."

"And this Mortdieu?" Temple countered. "What sort of dreams do you suppose he entertains?"

"I don't know," Ned admitted, "but I suspect that his situation is exactly the same. He does not know, as yet, exactly what he is, or what he might make of himself. What he and his rival both desire, for the time being, is time. Each, in his unwisdom, wants to retain control of his research for himself—what each wants is to be the new Prometheus, the titan and the demigod. However young they may be, each of them is still bound to the assumptions of the old order. Patou might be different, given the chance, but he has been working thus far in their shadow. As I said before, it does not matter how hard they strive for selfish monopoly; they cannot keep it. What the scientific method produces once, it will produce again and again. Mr. Davy understands that, if they do not—I mean Humphry Davy, of course, not the false James Davy who cheated you."

"But what if either or them does harbor dreams of world domination, and of the enslavement of the living to the dead-alive?" Temple demanded. "You spoke in those terms yourself, while you were listing your points—indeed, you spoke as if the dead-alive are certain, in the end, to become the world's rulers. If that is their ambition, what should we humans do, little man? Should we stand aside, in the holy name of progress, and wish the *Outremort* and her master—whoever he might be—bon voyage and the best of luck?"

"I know that we should not act like superstitious fools," Ned said. "We are not children to panic at the idea of the bogey-man. We must use our heads, Mr. Temple, and calm our rough-hewn instincts. If humans have found the secret of resurrection, we should be ready and willing to employ it—just as Jesus was, and did, if the scriptures are to be believed. Jesus was selfish in the end, rising from the dead himself but leaving his fellow to wait in vain for a different redemption, but we might be better than that, Mr. Temple, if only we were prepared to try."

"That's blasphemy!" was Temple's response

"Indeed it is," was Ned Knob's calm reply. "Time has moved on, Mr. Temple—we are no longer living in the mythic past. Perhaps the dead-alive will be better fitted to rule the world than the living, if only they can recover the wisdom of their first lives to add to the wisdom of their second. Perhaps they will be kinder to my kind than your kind ever were. You fear enslavement, as fervently as any slavemaster must, but it is not such a bugbear to those whose servitude has ever been immiseration and degradation. I would rather hope for a Republic, even in a world ruled by the dead-alive—but no, Mr. Temple, I do not think we should stand aside. I think we should do exactly what we are doing now. We should try to find out the truth of the matter, so that we can make a reasoned decision as to how to act."

"I thought you might be useful to me," Temple said, "because I thought you would be anxious to rescue your friends. You are forcing me to doubt my judgment."

"I am anxious to discover whether my friends are in need of rescue," Ned replied. "If that turns out to be the case, I shall be glad to do what I can in that cause—but as for being useful to you, that I cannot and will not guarantee. I see no need for us to be enemies, but in matters political, we are not allies and I shall make no pretense that we are."

Ned remembered, as he concluded this speech, that the ci-devant Comte Henri de Belcamp had commented on the fact that he had changed. He complimented himself on the fact that the renegade aristocrat had spoken more truthfully than he knew.

"Be careful," Temple advised him gruffly. "You might easily end up in jail again."

"As poor Tom Wooler did, even though Shepherd could not pervert a second jury. I could doubtless end up in the pillory just as easily, like valiant Dan Eaton, or be cut down by a saber wielded from horseback like so many innocents in St. Peter's Fields. You cannot frighten us in that fashion any more, Mr. Temple. We are too many, and too fervent in the business of making progress. We are poorly armed as yet, but science, the new Prometheus, is stealing new fire even as we speak. You cannot hold back that tide."

Temple did not answer that. Instead, he lifted the curtain to look out. "Bexley," he said. "We'll be in Greenhithe in a matter of minutes. We'll need a plan of action, if the *Outremort* is still at her berth."

"Action would not be to our advantage," Ned pointed out, "given that we have no army far our back— or have you mustered one to follow us at the gallop?"

"I've summoned agents of two sorts," Temple admitted, "but I have not the authority to mobilize men by the dozen, let alone the hundred. The show of strength in Sharper's relied on local men whose commander had his own reasons for making his presence felt there. By noon, I should have nine or ten at hand—but if I can send the right message back to Scotland Yard and Whitehall, I can gather a much larger force by dusk."

"But you and your men will need to see with your own eyes what kind of crew the *Outremort* has, and gather firm proof that there are honest citizens in danger... although I dare say you'll settle for Sam and Jeanie if there's no one else, no matter how much resentment you've stored against them. If only Germain Patou were a Napoleonic spy... but fat George and Louis XVIII are better friends now, are they not, and their secret police forces are presumably hand-in-glove? The Brotherhood of the Deliverance is no more, and even the *Deliverance* may have become the *Outremort*..."

"A plan, Master Knob," Temple reminded him. "I had hoped simply to be able to tell you what I wanted you to do, but I see now that we cannot proceed on that basis. Would you care to tell me what you would like to do?"

"The first thing I would like to do," Ned told him, "is to find out who the master of the *Outremort* is. I should also like to know whether Sam and Jeanie are aboard—and, if so, under what terms. What I do not want to do is to instigate any violence of any kind, aimed at anyone. I think we should both be discreet, Mr. Temple, and learn what we can by stealth before we reveal our presence. So, for the time being, I am ready to stay discreetly by your side, and do my best to help you in any covert enterprise that will improve our understanding of the situation."

Temple shook his head slowly. "You're a true marvel, Master Knob," he said. "I apologize for calling you a worm."

"Thank you, Mr. Temple," Ned replied, judging that the time had come, at last, to be magnanimous.

Chapter Eight
Aboard the Outremort

The docks at Greenhithe were a good deal busier than those at Purfleet had been, and the *Outremort*'s mooring was a relatively quiet spot in a hive of activity—so much so, in fact, that the activity to either side had encroached somewhat upon working-space than ought to have been hers. The warehouses along the waterfront provided an abundance of coverts from which observers could keep watch, so Ned Knob and Gregory Temple had no trouble approaching a very convenient position at the entrance to a narrow alleyway running between two such store-houses. A cargo was in the process of being unloaded into one to their left, so the quay in front of it was strewn with tea-chests and various bales, but the traffic from the one to their right was in the other direction, casks of wine being loaded on to a series of carts to be hauled away.

There was no one visible on the deck of the steam-ship, but there was a carriage standing on the quayside with its horses still in harnessed, tether to a trough. The animals had been given feed-bags, but they seemed to have consumed the oats therein.

"Waiting for passengers," Temple opined. "Perhaps to return your friends to Covent Garden."

"Perhaps," Ned agreed.

Temple took a small naval telescope from his great-coat and extended it to its full length. The steam ship was no more than 40 paces away, but he evidently wanted to magnify the portholes in the hope of being able to glimpse something within.

"I can make out a grey head in one of the spaces aft of the engines," he reported. "There's another—but it's impossible to tell whether either is Ross or the giant. A human head might be easier to identify. Judging by the conformation of the ship, there must be at least one cargo-hold in the stern, but whether the port-hole where the head is visible is in a separate section or lighting the hold I can't tell."

"Her fire is burning low," Ned observed, studying the smoke drifting from the two funnels. "They'd be stoking her up by now if they intended a swift departure. They're lying very low, though—if they're not waiting to put anyone ashore, they must be waiting for others to come aboard."

"Her launch is missing," Temple said. "There's no way of knowing whether your friends really were brought here, although it's not unlikely that it set out on some other ferrying mission once it had deposited them."

Ned nodded his head. If this was Mortdieu's vessel rather than John Devil's, and the dead-alive had contrived to extract James Graham's magical baths from the cellars before the house in Purfleet was torched, along with their electric batteries, the salvagers would have had to ferry them across the river for want of a convenient bridge. That would have required several journeys in a launch. Greenhithe was a good deal closer to Purfleet than Tilbury, but it would not have been the work of a mere hour—even by night, when the traffic was far less heavy than it was now. On the other hand...

113

"Here's someone," Temple muttered, cutting into Ned's speculations. Two men had emerged from below the steamship's decks into the bow, where the gangplank was situated. They were not grey men, but perfectly ordinary sailors; they were dark-skinned, but Ned could not identify their country of origin. They seemed to be arguing as they crossed the gangplank, but not angrily. They untethered the two horses from the trough, but did not bother to climb up into the driver's seat before leading the animals away along the quay.

"Not going far," Temple opined. "Probably collecting supplies. No need to leave the quayside, if they know where to go. It'll take time, though, if they've a complex shopping list."

"Here's more of them," Ned said, as a second cart drew up at the spot from which the first had departed. This one was laden with various goods packed in boxes, bales and barrels. The job of unloading it would have been completed very quickly had half a dozen men come out from the steamship, but it would not have been a diplomatic move for the grey heads Temple had glimpsed through the aft portholes to show themselves on such a busy quay in broad daylight. The only man who emerged from hiding was a ship's officer, obviously a European, who set about issuing instructions to the two sailors aboard the cart. They complained, but he ordered them to get on with the work.

Temple and Ned watched intently, hoping that someone else might come out, if only for a moment. They were watching far too intently, as it turned out, for they did not hear the man who crept up on them from the far end of the alleyway until he was close enough to put a pistol to Gregory Temple's head.

"Forgive me, Mr. Temple," the ci-devant Comte de Belcamp said. "I have no wish to harm you, but I feared your reaction to the sight of me."

Temple stared into the barrel of the weapon as though it were a cobra poised to strike.

Ned, by contrast, looked John Devil up and down, astonished to find him not in the least damp or bedraggled—although he was not wearing his Quaker hat. "You have a remarkable immunity to fire and flood, my friend," he said.

"I hope you are my friend, Ned," the blond man replied, "For I lost a fair few last night—more to desertion and kidnap than death, thank God—and can spare no more. I need to take my old ship back, and I need to rescue Germain Patou, who I believe to be a prisoner on board. You can imagine the insult I felt when I found out what vessel it was that Mortdieu had obtained in order to hunt me down. The ship is stolen, by the way, and illicitly renamed, so I have perfect right to reclaim it."

"Given that you are legally dead, Monsieur de Belcamp," Gregory Temple said, acidly, "even this radical scoundrel could not claim any such right on your behalf. According to Ned, your wife still thinks herself a widow, and you cannot pretend to be working on her behalf."

John Devil sighed. "You're as tiresome as ever, Mr. Temple," he said, holding the pistol very steady. "According to our mutual friend, your daughter still thinks herself no better than an orphan, but we have no time to trade insults of that sort. How many men does Mr. Temple have nearby, Ned?"

"He is hoping to have nine assembled by noon," Ned told him, "but he has not made contact with any as yet."

"And does he intend to try to seize the ship from Mortdieu?"

"His plan is not yet developed," Ned replied. "For the moment, we are simply gathering intelligence—but I doubt that he will let the vessel depart, if he can prevent it, and he probably has the authority and the means if he can get a message back to Westminster."

"Then it's as well I happened along, for I have more intelligence than the pair of you could gather in a fortnight, even with the aid of a trawler. Will you get down on your knees, Mr. Temple."

"No," said Gregory Temple. "Blow my brains out if you must, but I will never kneel to you."

"I'm not asking for worship," John Devil replied. "I'm asking for you to take up a position in which Ned can conveniently tie your wrists to your ankles, to keep you out of harm's way."

"I will not," Temple said, stubbornly. "Blow my brains out, if you so desire."

The ci-devant Comte shook his head wearily. "Tiresome as ever," he repeated. "Suit yourself." Then he put his fingers to his lips, and whistled the old signal, which Ned Knob had first heard in Jenny Paddock's in March 1817.

Had Ned had the chance, he would have demanded that John Devil hold off for a discussion, and he was sure that he could have convinced his former master not to do anything stupid—but John Devil really was laboring under the delusion that he was a man of fine intelligence, and was determined to act the idiot as only a vain man could.

Events unfolded in a tremendous hurry. The two men who had been unloading the cart in to the *Outremort*'s deck were both on the quay, each burdened by a bundle taken from the back of the cart. There were a dozen other men within five paces, stacking up goods that were being unshipped from the neighboring vessel—but eight of the dozen, it seemed, were John Devil's men, for two of them immediately leapt on the *Outremort*'s sailors, while two more went or the officer on the deck. The other four swarmed aboard, armed with billhooks and cudgels. More men were already converging on the gangplank from the other side, where the work of loading up carts at the second warehouse had also served as a cover for the infiltration of the ci-devant Comte's remaining followers.

"Who loves me, follow me," John Devil muttered, as he joined his crew. Ned opened his mouth to protest, but he could see that it would do no good, so he rocked back on his heels fully prepared to watch and wait. He realized too late that Gregory Temple was not so wisely hesitant. The detective brought a metal whistle from his own pocket, and blew the long shrill blast upon it that the policemen of London used to summon help. Now more men came running, from both ends of the quay— but only four of them that Ned could count.

Temple did not pause to shout out any orders before he hurled himself after his nemesis, avid to grab him from behind now that the pistol was no longer pointed at his head.

"Imbecile," Ned muttered. "You had only to do nothing for a little while, and you could have taken control of the situation once your men were fully gathered— but perhaps it will work out for the best."

The bandit was too quick for the policeman; by the time Gregory Temple had gained the deck, John Devil had disappeared below decks, into the narrower half of the vessel, where the crew-quarters were probably located. The noise of shots was immediately audible.

All along the dock, work stopped as honest laborers paused in honest wonderment. When the four policemen arrived at the end of the gangplank, though, they paused, having no idea who their appointed adversaries might be.

Gregory Temple was already embroiled in a brawl on the deck—although no one there seemed to know which side he might be on, and he was therefore not subject to any immediate or deadly attack. He tried to push the wrestling sailors out of the way in order to follow his quarry, but there simply was not room. He called to his subordinates for help, and they rushed to his aid, evidently forming the opinion that, since all the men on deck was in their commander's way, every one of them must be a heinous criminal. The policemen started laying about them with their truncheons, to the left and to the right, hitting anyone and everyone save for their master—with the inevitable result that anyone and everyone began hitting them and their master.

"Things will be much better ordered under the Republic," Ned observed, sadly. "If the dead-alive can conduct themselves more seriously than this, I shall be glad to cast my vote for their election to the National Assembly."

The combined efforts of the two sets of combatants and the policemen had already resulted in four men being knocked down, three more thrown overboard, and a small group of defenders retreating to the doorway that gave access to the bow of the ship. There was now a considerable quantity of empty space on the deck now, and the gangplank itself was clear.

Ned scurried forward, crossed the gangplank, and made his way aft to the part of the deck that had not yet seen any movement at all. There he searched or a second means of ingress to the spaces below deck—and having found a hatch, made his descent into a well flanked by two big doors. He tested one at random, found it to be unlocked, and opened it.

He stepped into a capacious cargo-hold—or, at least, into a space that had been designed as a cargo-hold, although it had evidently been pressed into service as passenger accommodation. By the yellow light of two oil-lamps, he saw 16 grey men and one man who had not yet died sitting meekly on the floor, all awake and somewhat agitated.

The man who had not yet died was Germain Patou. His hands were tied behind his back, and his ankles bound together. Ned whipped out his knife, and sawed through the bonds as quickly as he could.

"The deck's clear, at present, Monsieur Patou," he said. "You may make your escape in safety."

"I cannot leave them!" Patou retorted, indicating his companions with a brief turn of the head. "What is happening, Monsieur Knob? Is it Arthur?"

"I fear that Arthur Pevensey may have gone the way of all his other aliases," Ned said. "He is in a piratical mood, I fear. Do you know if my friends are aboard?"

"In the port hold, twin to this one," Patou said. "Please go—I need to calm these people."

The dead-alive had not menaced Ned in any way; their disturbance was fear and anxiety, not anger. He nodded, and closed the door behind him as he went to its mirror-image. The second door was similarly un-locked, and the second space was a duplicate of the first—except that there were two humans sheltered there as well as a similar company of grey men, and three people standing: Sam Hopkey, Jeanie Bird and Sawney. None of them was tied up, so Ned folded up his knife and put it away.

"Ned!" cried Sam. "Come in and shut the door— there's a battle royal raging beyond the engine-room, it seems. You might get hurt."

Ned did as he was bid. "I only came aboard because I feared that you might be hurt," he explained. "I think we might be able to get out if we made a run for it—but Sawney would have to stay behind, for there's a crowd on the dock, and I don't know how they'd react to the sight of a grey man."

He watched Sam and Jeanie turn inquisitive eyes to the man who had been their dearest friend and second father, and knew that there was no question here of any kidnap or evil seduction. In all of this confusion, one thing at least was perfectly plain. When Sawney had said that he had come to Jenny Paddock's because he wanted to see the people who had meant most to him in his previous life, he'd told the simple truth—and he'd come back for exactly the same reason, evidently with Mortdieu's permission, if not his actual encouragement. Sam and Jeanie must have come with Sawney to say goodbye, before he went away on a sea voyage from which he might not return for many years.

Sawney's grey lips twisted into a faint parody of a wry smile. "Best go, Sam," he said, softly. "Don't fear for me—I have my mind back now, and my feelings too. I have what I need, thanks to you, and what these others need in me. I can play the man, now, as the part deserves to be played."

"Sawney, old friend..." Ned began—but then the door that he had closed behind him burst open again, smashing into his back, and sent him tumbling upon the planks that formed the floor of the hold.

Ned twisted as he fell to look back over his shoulder, and saw that it was John Devil who had come tumbling after him—but he had to wait a second more to see who had shoved John Devil, and was following closely behind, apparently intent on killing the man who seemed so very hard to kill.

It was neither Gregory Temple not Mortdieu; it was the giant named John, wielding a club in one hand and a machete in the other.

The giant had been meek when Ned had seen him last, but he was not meek now. The black dots in his strange eyes seemed unnaturally sharp, perhaps because the eyes were protruded slightly by wrath. His face was scored along one side where a bullet had ploughed through his exotic flesh, tearing a groove into which Jeanie Bird might have been able to insert a slender forefinger. The wound was leaking viscous fluid, which foamed as it bubbled out, as unlike blood as anything that could conceivably surge in any creature's veins, driven by a human heart.

John Devil's pistol was empty now, and it made a very feeble club. Even so, the ci-devant Comte de Belcamp was determined to come to his feet and face his pursuer—to die hard, if he had to die at all.

Sawney was the first to try to step between them, but the giant swatted him aside with a thrust of his left arm—the one that held the club. Sawney sprawled among his fellow grey men, whose alarm was increased by his flailing limbs. They began to rise to their feet.

Ned was slightly glad that he was flat on his back, in no position to intervene even had he wanted to—but his gladness vanished when he saw Jeanie Bird step between the two fighters, with her back to the ci-devant Comte. She looked up into the giant's crazed eyes.

"No, John," she said, speaking to him as a friend might. "That's not your way. Leave him be."

For one awful moment, Ned thought that the dead-alive giant might sweep Jeanie aside as dismissively as Sawney—but with the other hand, perhaps slicing her head in two if she should happen to catch her with the blade. Instead, the giant stopped, as if frozen by the sound of her voice. He looked down at the tiny woman—who did not seem as tiny as she was, now that she had struck a pose that Ned had seen a hundred times before, on the stage at Jenny Paddock's. She looked magnificent, even in the presence of such a colossal leading man.

The giant slowly relaxed his pose, and let his head nod forward, becoming as meek as any of his peers—any, that is, except the one who stepped through the open door behind him, who held a pistol in each hand.

These pistols, Ned had to suppose, were still loaded.

"She's right, John," said General Mortdieu. "In life, that was never your way, and no good can come of finding a new identity while you have not yet recovered the old. I, on the other hand, know exactly what I was when I was alive, and this was my way—far more than it was ever yours, Monsieur de Belcamp."

John Devil had recovered his balance and his poise now. "I brought you back to life," he said. "I made you what you are."

"So you did," said the grey man. "But you do not own me. I am my own man, and these are my people. We are not your slaves, nor the instruments of your future glory. Our destiny is for us to discover and choose, mon ami—and if I must shoot my redeemer in order to achieve that end, I shall not hesitate. You have five seconds to decide."

"You were a better man that that in your former life, Mortdieu," the ci-devant Comte replied, without letting a single second go by. "You were a man of pride and principle. Let us settle this like men of honor, up on deck. Single combat, with weapons of your choice. Let us settle it once and for all, each agreeing to accept the judgment of destiny."

"A generous offer, since I have two loaded guns and you have none." Mortdieu replied. "Exactly what I would have expected from a gentleman of your sort. Destiny has already judged; the matter is already settled. It only remains for you to accept that judgment—or die."

Ned Knob had clambered to his feet while this exchange was taking place, deciding that his turn had come to take center-stage and play deus ex machina. He stood beside John Devil, and said: "A few minutes ago, this man put a pistol to the head of Gregory Temple, who would not back down. Temple told Monsieur le Comte to shoot him dead. If you knew this man, you would know that he cannot possibly show more weakness than his arch-adversary, his other half. He will invite you to shoot him, just as Temple invited him—but I beg you not to do it, no matter what kind of man you were in your first life. If you're to be the founder of a new race, you must set a better example now than you were ever able to do as a mere man."

"Damn you, Ned!" John Devil murmured. "This is not your scene. How dare you try to steal it!"

"No," said a new voice, speaking from behind the emperor of the grey men and over his head. This scene is mine. Give me one of those pistols, sir, and I shall shoot him dead, if only to show that I can hate longer and harder than he."

Mortdieu had to change his position then, so that he could point the pistol in his left hand at Gregory Temple, and the one in his right at the ci-devant Comte Henri de Belcamp. Ned took note of the fact that the corridor through which all the new arrivals must have come seemed quiet now, and concluded that the fight for possession of the *Outremort* must have been suspended, if not concluded.

"Who the Devil are you?" Mortdieu asked Gregory Temple.

"I am English law and order," Gregory Temple informed him. "Intolerant of grave-robbers and of brawling... although Master Knob informs me that I might soon have to change my opinion as to the ethics of grave-robbing. My forces will increase as the day wears on, and my men can have an army here by dusk if the need arises. If you shoot me, the necessity will be obvious—we'll see then how the dead-alive will fare in the hangman's noose."

"It would certainly be best," Ned Knob observed, "if no one shot anyone, whatever our habits might formerly have been."

"Spoken like a true Republican, Ned," said the ci-devant Comte. "Alas, you are forgetting the lessons of history. There are deep differences of opinion here, and they cannot be settled without violence."

"I cannot believe that," Ned said, "any more than my darling Jeanie could believe that the giant would hurt her, wounded and wrathful as he was. Monsieur le Comte, you and your men must quit the *Outremort*, and retire with the only prizes that you really need, and which Monsieur Mortdieu cannot steal from you unless he shoots you—your knowledge and your intelligence. You must also give your word that any other persons you might raise from the dead in future will be free, not instruments of any of your schemes. Monsieur Mortdieu, you must allow Germain Patou to choose for himself where, and in whose company, he will pursue his own researches—and Sawney too. Mr. Temple, you must leave your army unsummoned and withdraw, allowing the *Outremort* to depart unhindered when she is fully provisioned. All this is obvious—no good can come of any other eventuality. Why should it require a fool like me to explain something so simple?"

"There is nothing obvious about it," said Gregory Temple and John Devil, speaking in unison, as if they really were two halves of the same paradoxical person.

"I have won the battle," General Mortdieu pointed out, "and I hold the loaded guns. It is for me to make the terms."

"We are not talking about a battle," Ned insisted, "or even a war. There should never have been a battle, and there is nothing to be gained by a war. We are talking about how best to make progress, how best to move into the future with intelligent purpose and good heart. That is surely the one cause and the one course to which we can all commit ourselves, and the only one that intelligent men need consider."

Mortdieu had already hesitated far longer than the five seconds he had originally conceded his adversary, and Ned no longer feared that he was about to blast any-one's face away, but he went on regardless. "What you must see," he said "is that things are different now. The future will unfold more rapidly if you do the sensible thing—which is to make a record of all your discoveries and experiments, sending copies to Humphry Davy and Michael Faraday in England, and to the heirs of Benjamin Franklin in America and Antoine Lavoisier in France, so that a thousand men might take up your work of raising and educating the recently-dead—but it will not matter in the long run how long, or how successfully, you try to hoard your secret away for your use alone. The thing can be done, and will be done, even if the thousand have to labor long and hard to figure out the first steps for themselves. I have no idea what each of you hopes or plans to do, but I do know that your achievements will be dissolved soon enough by the tide of history, and that if you desire to be remembered fondly for what you have achieved so far, you will all put away your weapons, now and forever, and return to your real work."

He was speaking to everyone, but Mortdieu was the one who had the guns, at present, and it was into his remarkable eyes that Ned had looked while he delivered his speech. There, despite their alien quality, he read the record of his success.

Mortdieu lowered his hands, and pointed both his pistols at the floor.

"If we ever have occasion to play this scene on the stage, Ned," Sam Hopkey put in, "I shall be proud to speak those lines."

Ned was still anxious lest anyone take advantage of Mortdieu's inaction to start the fight all over again, but no one did.

"It is a compromise I can accept," the grey general said, "for the sake of peace—provided that you will both agree to it."

"I will if Temple will," the ci-devant Comte was quick to say. "Ned's right—if a fool like him can see it, so should we all."

"There is a matter of my duty to the Crown..." Gregory Temple began—but then he stopped, perhaps remembering the head on which the Crown of England was resting just at present, and what he had suffered at the whim of the former Prince Regent. "And England, I suppose," he resumed, "will be grateful to me for help-ing to remove the grey men from its shores, at least for a little while. I'll give you 24 hours. Go, all of you, and good riddance—but woe betide any of you who are still here on Wednesday."

Ned observed, though, that Temple shot a venom-ous glance at the ci-devant Comte, which said as clearly as if the words had been spoken aloud: especially you. It was impossible to tell whether the policeman was more regretful of not having had a pistol to shoot his arch-adversary dead, or of being contemptuously spared by his arch-adversary when the pistol had been in the other hand.

Jeanie Bird took Ned's left hand in hers, and squeezed it gratefully. Ned looked around—not at her, but at the restless dead-alive who were as yet unknown to themselves. Their agitation had calmed somewhat while everyone was standing still. Their black-pointed eyes were very intent, and their ears were pricked. Ned felt free to be hopeful that they were all a little closer to finding the power of intelligence and motive for a sec-ond time.

Ned reached out to Sawney with his right hand, and Sawney clasped it. "Thank you for coming to see us, Sawney," he said. "I wish I had been there when you came back last night, so that we could all have made a proper farewell—but Sam and Jeanie have a performance tonight, and you always told us that the audience must not be disappointed." He remembered, as he said that, that Sawney had always told him something else—that if a playwright puts a gun into a scene, the gun must eventually go off—but he decided that it would be best to disregard that maxim at this particular juncture.

He made as if to go, taking his protégés with him—for his first duty was, after all, to them. Someone had to set an example. The others seemed grateful for his lead, and he was confident that they would follow him into the wings.

"We'll meet again, *mon ami*," said the ci-devant Comte, his posture suggesting that he was speaking to Ned, although his heavy-lidded eyes were fixed on Gregory Temple.

That was yet another thing that Sawney had always said, Ned remembered, in the days when he had played the puppet judge in the mock tribunal. On the stage, where everything is pretense and everything is possible, old friends and old enemies alike must always meet again, until their differences were settled for good and all.

PART TWO: THE CHILD-STEALERS

Chapter One
Gregory Temple's Sleeplessness

Gregory Temple had never been a sound sleeper, and his restlessness had not decreased with the years. There had been many a night when he had tossed and turned for hours on end without ever seeming to sleep at all, even without the excuse that he presently had for the return of his most disturbing obsession.

It seemed to him now that he had not slept for a single minute in the previous 72 hours, since he had first renewed his acquaintance with that ridiculous little man, Ned Knob. Master Knob had brought his obsession back to life, by leading him to his nemesis, John Devil—who had come back from the dead without the seemingly-dire inconvenience of becoming a grey man.

Master Knob had added vile insult to cruel injury by claiming that he was intimately acquainted with Suzanne and her new family, but that should have been a minor irritant by comparison with the news that Comte Henri de Belcamp had not, after all, splattered his brains all over the gloomy walls of the Château de Belcamp. Alas, once lack of sleep began to bring delirium into Temple's waking life, even minor irritants could be temporarily blown up out of all proportion, augmenting his fundamental distress.

It should have been the monstrous thought of John Devil's continued freedom that was keeping Temple awake now, as it had for two nights before, but it was not. He should have been cudgelling his brain in the attempt to figure out a way of finding the bandit again, or at least berating himself for not having succeeded in capturing the bandit at Greenhithe when they had been forced to quit the *Outremort*. Instead, he was berating himself for something else entirely, and calling himself a monster worse than any mindless grey giant or any phantom in a Quaker hat. He was drowning in regret for his own foolishness in somehow having contrived to put it completely out of is mind that he had a daughter, and that his daughter had a husband and a son.

He had been ill, of course, and mad too—but what kind of excuse was that, for a man like him? He was no more than slightly ill now, nor was he much more than slightly mad. He was a trusted agent in the King's secret police, charged with maintaining the peace and security of the realm—but how could he trust himself to do that, when he had not even been able to maintain the peace and security of his own family?

I am a man of great intellect, he told himself, repeatedly. *I am a diehard enemy of evil. How can I be such a stupid wreck of a human being?*

He would have sworn on the Bible, sincerely, that he had not slept for an instant—but he had closed his eyes in the attempt to rest, and he must also have muffled his ears, else he would surely have heard the door of his room open and close. How else could he explain the fact that he had no inkling that anything was wrong until the point of a rapier actually touched his throat?

"Be still, Mr. Temple," a voice advised him. "I am very anxious not to hurt you."

A phosphorus match spluttered then, and a flame lit up. It was applied to the candle on his night-stand, which lit in its turn."

"A miracle of scientific enlightenment," John Devil commented, as he blew out the match. "So much more effective than flint and German tinder. We are living in exciting times, Mr. Temple, when anything and everything seems possible." He looked around the room as he spoke; although he said nothing, Temple knew what he must be thinking: that this was a direly shabby apartment for a man who had once lived in a good house, with a wife and daughter and servants.

Temple could not raise his head from his pillow without endangering his throat. "If you are so very anxious not to hurt me, John Devil," he said, bitterly, "why do you come into my room with a naked blade?"

"Because I am equally anxious to ensure that you do not hurt me, Mr. Temple. I did not shoot you when I held a gun to your head at Greenhithe, even when you refused to obey my instructions. I'm not so sure that you'd have done me the same courtesy, had the roles been reversed. I need you to sit quietly for a little while, so that I can explain to you why we must make a truce—and more than that, become allies for a little while."

"Because of the challenge of the dead-alive?" Temple said, with a sneer. "The protectors of His Majesty's government do not need your advice to make policy on that issue."

"I am not even certain that this concerns the dead-alive, Mr. Temple—although it would be a bizarre coincidence if it did not. I am certain, however, that it does not concern your stupid secret police. This is personal, Mr. Temple. Will you read this letter, please?"

John Devil, who was not wearing his Quaker hat, held out a single sheet of paper, folded in two. Temple took it. It was not until he had opened it and read the name of the addressee and the signature that the blond man withdrew the point of the rapier, allowing Temple to raise his head.

Temple was able to look his persecutor in the face then—and was astonished to see that the handsome features were contorted by anxiety and dread. When John Devil had been James Davy, he had occasionally feigned anxiety, but dread had seemed to be beyond his emotional range, even then.

There was a pistol in the drawer of the night-stand, but Temple made no attempt to reach for it. The letter was addressed to "My Dear Ned", and it was signed "Suzanne"—in the context of his recent delirium, those words seemed unusually pregnant with horror and distress. Temple blinked twice to clear his eyes, and then he read the body of the letter.

My dear Ned, the letter said. *We are in desperate trouble, and we need your help. We also need my father's help, if he is alive and sane and willing to offer it. I do not know whether you will know how to find him, or whether he will see you if you go to him, but I beg you with all my heart to try. My darling Richard—my son, that is—has been kidnapped from the garden at the Château de Belcamp, and two younger children with him: Jeanne's son, and the son of Sarah, Countess Boehm. Since Count Boehm's death, Sarah has returned to live at the new château, and the children very often play together; they were all playing in the garden this morning, watched over by their nurse and Pierre Louchet, when a number of armed men wearing masks came in and took them away. Pierre tried to stop them, but was struck down—he is not badly hurt, thankfully, save for his pride. One of the masked men told the nurse that we should gather gold to pay a ransom, that we would be given instructions for its delivery in due course, and that we must not contact the police. No communication has come as yet, but Jeanne and Sarah are both making efforts to assemble as much gold as they can. We do not know how large the demand will be. We dare not contact the Prefecture of Police in Paris, but we desperately need the advice of someone who knows about such matters. If you can get this letter to my father, I beg you to do so. Please try as hard as you can. Your loyal friend, Suzanne.*

Temple looked up at John Devil, feeling the wrath build inside him. "How do you come to have this letter, Monsieur de Belcamp?" he asked, seething with anger.

"Because Ned brought it to me," John Devil replied, "and entrusted it to me so that I might bring it to you, while he set off for the château without delay. You will understand the logic of the situation, of course—had he brought it to you first, you would not have known where to find me, even if you had consented to show it to me."

"So far as any of the mothers knows," Temple said, sourly, "neither one of us is alive, else they would doubtless have written to us directly. Are you prepared to let your wife know, now, that she is not a widow after all?"

"She is a widow," John Devil said. "But we have learned of late that the dead can no longer be relied on to be as quiet as they used to be. Dead or not, I will help my son if I can, just as you will help your grandson. Together, Mr. Temple, we might be a force to be reckoned with. We are allies in this, whether it pleases us or not, and we must put our differences aside."

Temple let the sheet of paper fall on to the coverlet. He did not doubt that his own features were contorted, probably more hideously than his interlocutor's "Is Mortdieu behind this?" he demanded, hoarsely. "Is he trying to raise funds to defend his empire of the dead-alive?"

"It's possible, but not likely. He cannot be everywhere at once, and he needed all his forces to destroy the *Prometheus* and steal my apparatus. It might well be someone else anxious to acquire the secret in a hurry, who imagines that I know even more than I do—but we must not neglect the possibility that this is the work of perfectly ordinary men possessed of a perfectly ordinary greed."

"Jeanne and Sarah Boehm are both rich," Temple said, thoughtfully. "Either of their children might have been a prime target—to catch both at once would be a rare coup for any gang of kidnappers. It's a pity, though, that my poor grandson should chance to be with them when they were seized. Suzanne and Richard haven't a farthing, alas—I don't know what their exact status is at the Château de Belcamp, but they must be servants in all but name. Friedrich Boehm told me once that he was mixed up with a relic of the *vehmgerichte*—might this be an extension of the feud that killed his brothers, and would doubtless have procured his own assassination had he not been condemned to death by tuberculosis?"

"It's possible," John Devil repeated, "but again, not likely. I knew several self-styled knights of the *vehm* when I was studying in Germany, although I was not supposed to be privy to their secret lives. They all prided themselves on being men of strict honor, and even though there was a measure of self-delusion in their pose, I doubt they'd stoop so low as to imitate Corsican bandits."

"Corsican, you say? Do you suspect the *Veste Nere* then? It's rumoured that a nest of them has lately taken up residence in Paris."

The former James Davy smiled, grimly. "I believe that it was me who whispered that rumor in your ear, in happier times," he said. "And it was Tom Brown who whispered it in James Davy's. Again, it's possible—but not likely. We're wasting time, Mr. Temple. We have plans to make, and must be under way by dawn. We have a long journey ahead of us. I did it once in less than a day, when I was Percy Balcomb, but I had to make careful preparations. We'll be lucky to arrive in two— and I do not know whether or not to pray that nothing will happen before we do."

Temple caught the implication of that remark easily enough. If nothing happened until he and the late Comte de Belcamp arrived, that might be because they were expected and awaited—in which case, the affair might be more complicated than any simple demand for ransom. He looked down at the letter again.

John Devil anticipated his question. "The messenger who brought it came with all possible speed," he said, "but it required 48 hours to get it into Ned Knob's hands. There is every possibility that the man was followed, and it is not impossible that the letter itself has been read. Ned says that he was not followed when he brought it to me, and he is usually trustworthy in such matters, but your intervention might be expected. For that reason, we must make our way to Dover separately—you must take the early morning coach from the Post Office—and we must be careful aboard the packet-boat. I dared not take the risk of our being unable to obtain a seat on the mail-coach from Calais to Paris, so I instructed Ned to reserve two when he passed through, in the names of Gideon Markwick and Henri Moreau—you are, of course, Markwick, and I have taken the liberty of making up false papers in that name."

John Devil took a sheaf of papers from his pocket and threw them on to the coverlet beside the abandoned letter, but he did not pause in his discourse longer than was needed to draw breath. "If you are followed," he went on, "they are bound to suspect that we are traveling together, even if we do not speak to one another—but that will not matter, provided that we are discreet. In Paris, we will separate. I will slip away from anyone who follows me, while you need take no such precaution in going on to Miremont. What you do when you get there will depend on the situation you find; I will contact you as and when I can, but you may be sure that I shall be busy. Given your status, you might be tempted to make contact with the Prefecture of Police in Paris, but I assure you that such a move can only make matters worse—Monsieur Vidocq's so-called *Sûreté* would be far more interested in the gold than the children, and we undoubtedly have enough enemies to deal with already."

"By what right do you expect me to follow your orders meekly?" Temple demanded.

"We have set that game aside, Mr. Temple. We are united now, while we have a common purpose. I have had a little time to think about this; you have not. I have applied the same reasoning to the problem as you would yourself, and we must both follow its dictates. You must get dressed now, and pack in haste. You must be at the Post Office in time to catch that coach—and if you must travel on top, at the risk of freezing to death, you must do it. I must go now, to complete my own arrangements.

I shall see you on the packet-boat, but if we find an opportunity to talk during the crossing, we must be very careful."

John Devil did not prolong his farewell. He opened and closed Temple's bedroom door as quietly as he must have done when he came in, and Temple could not help envying the steadiness and delicacy of his enemy's hand. He got dressed as rapidly as he could, and then packed a bag. The first thing he put in it was his revolver. He hesitated over his makeup kit, but left it aside; his own face was no longer as recognizable as it had been four years ago, and no one in Calais was likely to challenge the supposition that he was Gideon Markwick, provided that the papers made out in that name were in order.

He checked the sheets of paper that John Devil had casually thrown on the bed, and found them to be as expertly forged as the stock of false identities he maintained on his own behalf. He tried to find some consolation in the thought that this was one name John Devil would never have the opportunity to adopt for himself.

He managed to find a cab to take him to the Post Office, and got there in time to buy a ticket for the coach. Had it been high summer, he would not have been able to obtain a seat so shortly before departure even on the rotunda, but it was November, and he was able to secure an inside berth. Fortunately, the roads had not yet been so badly churned-up by autumnal rains as to cause any substantial delay en route; he was reasonably confident that he would arrive in time to catch the packet-boat.

It was during the few minutes that he had to wait before the coach's departure that it struck Temple, with forceful impact, that he would be forced to confront his daughter, and all the bitterness that had somehow accumulated between them. He not only had an excuse for doing so, but a golden opportunity to make amends. Compared with that, the necessity of calling a truce in his eternal feud with John Devil seemed far less important than it might have.

But what if I fail? Temple thought, as the vehicle drew away, its harness jangling. *What if I fail?*

It was not warm, even inside the vehicle, and Temple kept his overcoat buttoned to the neck and his scarf wound tight. He pulled his old felt hat down so that the lining protected the tips of his ears while the scarf warmed the lobes, even though he knew that the combination must make him look as furtive and sinister as any chapbook villain. None of the other passengers did anything different, even though two of them appeared to be the kind of dandy who would normally place the priorities of appearance far above those of comfort. The others were all men of business—as might be expected given the season.

By the time they had reached Dartford, Temple had ascertained that the apparent dandies were, in fact, literary men rather than true gentlemen, following the sartorial example of Lord Byron as best they could on a meager budget. They were speaking in low tones because there appeared to be some dispute between them, regarding an item of fiction one of them—or perhaps his wife—had published anonymously, based on a manuscript provided by the other. There was mention of the North-West Passage and a ship becalmed in ice, and some unusually-vituperative discussion of the necessity of providing an aesthetically-satisfactory ending in a published story, even if it required some bending of the truth. Temple tried as hard as he could not to listen, so that he could concentrate on more urgent matters.

It was even easier to ignore the desultory conversation of the businessmen, who felt compelled to maintain near-silence apart from a desultory flow of conventional inquiries, acknowledgements and apologies, even though some of them clearly knew one another by sight. Thirty years before, it was rumored, mail-coaches had been rich sources of wit and gossip, but that was before the etiquette of English travel had been brought to its full maturity. Things might have been different had there been one or more ladies aboard, but there was no cause for effusive gallantry here, and Temple judged that he was not the only one grateful for the fact.

Temple did not even attempt to sleep, in spite of his success in shutting out his surroundings because he needed to catch up with the reasoning that had put him on the coach. By the time he reached Dover, he had to be sure that John Devil was no longer one step ahead of him in matters of calculation.

In his days as a detective at Scotland Yard, Temple had been involved in more than a dozen kidnapping cases, and had been the senior officer on more than half of them. The tactics of handling such cases were always the same; the first priority was to secure the release of the victim, even if that meant paying a ransom—but every effort was made to follow the kidnappers from the point at which they collected the ransom, with a view to recovering it as soon as possible and apprehending the guilty parties. Sometimes, the bandits were captured; sometimes they got away. More often than not the victim was returned unharmed, but in the minority of cases...

This case would not be an easy one to manage, Temple knew, because it would be on foreign ground. Although he had played the part of Comte Henri de Belcamp more assiduously than any other, John Devil had probably spent less time at the château than Temple had, as a guest of the late Marquis, so it was unfamiliar territory to him too. On the other hand, John Devil might have forces to draw upon in Paris, and it appeared that Pierre Louchet, who had lived most of his life in the forest near Miremont, was now part of the Comtesse de Belcamp's household staff. Then, there was Ned Knob, who seemed to have grown devilishly clever as well as devilishly bold since he had been recruited to Tom Brown's gang four years before, and Richard Thompson, who had shown promise as a detective when he had been in Scotland Yard's employ. When he arrived at the château, he would not be entirely without resources—but everything would depend on the timing of the ransom demand and the instructions it contained.

If the kidnap had taken place three days ago, Temple reasoned, then the mysterious General Mortdieu, the would-be emperor of the dead-alive, could not possibly have been directly involved. He had been in London, planning and executing a very different criminal project. Nor could the masked men who had carried out the abduction have been grey men, else their condition would have been noticed by Louchet or the nurse. On the other hand, the coincidence of timing was so striking that it was difficult to believe that there was no connection at all between the parallel events in Miremont and London. How long, he wondered, had John Devil and Germain Patou been in London? More to the point, how long had they been working in Portugal before that? How had the two of them acquired the secret of resurrecting the dead? How many other people knew that secret, or knew that there *was* a secret?

The last question, he decided, was the vital one. Mortdieu had known that Patou and John Devil could resurrect the dead because they had resurrected him. At the house in Purfleet and aboard the *Prometheus*, they must have had at least 40 hirelings, many of whom must have known what their business was and all of whom would have been able to find out without taking overmuch trouble—and to that number would have to be added Jack Hanrahan and the other body-snatchers who supplied their raw materials.

Even if Patou and John Devil were the only two who knew what the secret was, there must be dozens, if not hundreds, of people who knew that they possessed it. One of the reasons that Mortdieu had been so desperate to make his own play was he knew full well that time was of the essence. There might be only a handful of men apart from Patou and John Devil who knew how to bring the dead back to life, but there must be many more who were determined to possess the secret with all possible speed.

On the other hand, Temple thought, anyone who believed that kidnapping the Comtesse de Belcamp's son might provide a way to acquire the secret of resurrection would have to know that the man who had it was, in fact, the Comte de Belcamp—and even Jeanne de Belcamp did not know that her husband was alive, let alone that he had somehow acquired the secret of a strange immortality. Was it not far more likely that Jeanne's own fortune, which was no secret at all, had been a lure attracting common criminals? Would not that natural magnetism have been redoubled by the fact that Sarah Boehm, whose inheritance must also be common knowledge, had recently moved into the new château, literally next door, with a child of almost exactly the same age as Jeanne's?

He needed to know far more. He needed to know, at the very least, what John Devil knew—and he was determined to find out, no matter how careful and discreet he had been commanded to be on the ferry that would take them both to Calais. Alas, John Devil was not waiting in Dover when the mail-coach arrived, nor had he put in an appearance by the time the packet-boat was due to set out. When the boat left the harbor—without a moment's delay, for it was a brand-new steamboat, which had no need of any generosity from the wind or the tide—Temple had not caught a glimpse of his supposed ally.

Two possibilities sprang to the detective's mind: firstly, that the other man was on board but in hiding, having found a means to keep out of his way; secondly, that the other man had always intended to travel by a different route, at least to Calais, and perhaps all the way to Paris. The second alternative seemed more likely, if only because it fit in with the man's essentially devious character. The combination of the Dover coach and the packet-boat was not necessarily the best or the fastest way to get to the French shore from London; John Devil might as easily have gone to London Bridge to pick up a ship that would sail—or, more likely, steam—all the way around Kent. If the other had taken that route, he might get to Calais first—or he might not go to Calais at all, preferring some other port of entry.

Damn the man! Temple thought, as the ferry began to rock and lurch in the choppy autumnal sea. *Even as an ally, he's the most treacherous snake an honest man could ever dread to encounter.*

Chapter Two
John Devil's Lateness

Temple cursed John Devil a hundred times more while the steamboat made its way across the Channel, across a relatively calm sea. Even as he cursed, though, he recognized the possible logic of the course of action. If there was more to the kidnap than simple banditry, the child-stealers would probably know that Suzanne had written to Ned Knob, and would therefore be expecting Temple's arrival in Calais. If so, it might be unwise to let them know that Henri de Belcamp had also been alerted by the same missive, and had entered into an alliance with his old enemy. But why, if John Devil had never intended to travel with him even for part of the journey, had he implied that he would? Why had he not simply told the truth? Perhaps he was incapable of it, even in—or especially in—circumstances that compelled him to work in association with his old adversary.

It occurred to Temple to wonder whether the letter might have been a carefully-fabricated contrivance to get him out of England—that there might not have been any kidnap at all—but he could not believe it. John Devil was more than capable of playing such a foul trick, but, had he wanted to get Temple out of the way for any considerable length of time, he would surely have chosen a deception that would not be so soon uncovered.

Temple did not go up on deck during the crossing, but contented himself with searching the crowd of passengers below decks with his eyes. He was satisfied soon enough that John Devil was not among them—and was not disguised as a crewman either, unless he was the kind of crewman who spent his time at sea confined to the engine-room. He was also in search of any indication that he was being followed. Five of his fellow passengers from the mail-coach had taken the ferry—including the two literary men—but none of them had shown the least flicker of interest in him since they had got down from the coach. If anyone else on board had been looking out for him, they gave no sign of it.

He was able to take a late breakfast on the packet-boat, and to drink a pot of coffee, but he arrived in Calais neither satiated nor fully alert. Once his papers had been inspected, and handed back to him without hesitation, he made his way to the booking office for the Paris coach and asked whether there was a ticket waiting for Gideon Markwick. There was, and he only had to show his documents again to claim it.

"Has Monsieur Henri Moreau collected his ticket yet?" he asked, in French.

"Non, Monsieur," was the reply.

"But you do have a ticket awaiting collection by the gentleman in question?"

"Oui, Monsieur."

Temple checked his watch. If "Henri Moreau" was going to catch the Paris coach, he had only a quarter of an hour left to pick up his ticket. He stayed close to the booking office while he waited, but no one came. When the coach got under way, there was an empty seat inside.

"This is a rare stroke of luck," one of Temple's fellow passengers said to him, in faintly-accented English, as they settled in to their places. "For once, we may be comfortable. They cannot take on an extra passenger before we reach Amiens, you see, in case the missing man is waiting at one of the stops where we change horses. My name is Giuseppe Balsamo, Monsieur—I'm pleased to make your acquaintance."

Temple suppressed a sigh; he was in France now and the etiquette of English travel no longer applied. He shook the hand that had been offered to him, and said; "Gideon Markwick. Your English is very good, sir—far better than my Italian, I fear."

"I have been away from my native land for a very long time," Balsamo told him, with a slightly theatrical sigh. Temple was sure that the man had not been on the packet-boat, but that might only mean that he had arrived in Calais on another vessel, or that he had been there on business. Balsamo seemed to be some 20 years younger than Temple—certainly no more than 40 years old, and probably less—so his reference to "a very long" time seemed slightly odd.

"We have been living in turbulent times," Temple commented, in a neutral tone. "Many men have been displaced from their homelands, only to find them unrecognizable on their eventual return."

"That is always the fate of the wanderer," the other man agreed—and then withdrew slightly, as if to end the conversation. Temple was not at all displeased by that—except that he suddenly realized, as the man took a French newspaper from his overcoat pocket and began to unfold it, that he had heard the name Balsamo before, coupled with the forename Joseph—which was, of course, the English form of Giuseppe. He had to rack his brains for several minutes before he dredged up the memory, but it came to him in due course.

Many years before, when he had been one of the earliest recruits to the Metropolitan Police's detective division, the complex entanglement between politics and crime had had a very different complexion, more concerned with foreign espionage than domestic radicalism. The new division had inherited a stock of dossiers compiled on hundreds of foreign nationals reputed to operate as spies, including many of wide repute. One of those dossiers had concerned a poseur named Count Cagliostro—whose real name, the reports alleged, had been Joseph Balsamo.

Temple had never had the slightest involvement with the man, but he had read the dossier because of its melodramatic quality, as a kind of modern legend. He recalled now that Cagliostro had cultivated a reputation as a magician, and had been exiled from France after his alleged involvement in the scandal of a necklace supposedly commissioned by Queen Marie-Antoinette, but actually obtained on false pretenses by a band of tricksters. Cagliostro had spent some time in England thereafter, and had been briefly imprisoned in the Fleet—but this could not possibly be the same person, who must have been 50 or thereabouts when he was in England then, and would therefore be 80 now. It might, perhaps, be the other Balsamo's son... or the name might be a pure coincidence.

On another occasion, Temple would have let the matter go—but he was, at present, very sensitive to the potential significance of coincidences. When the other man finally put his newspaper away, and Temple was able to meet his eye again, he took the opportunity to say: "I believe I knew a man named Balsamo once, in London—but he was quite old and I was very young. Perhaps he was your father?"

"My father never left Italy," the other said, mildly, "and Balsamo is not an uncommon name there. Your man might, I suppose, have been a distant relative. I have visited London myself on many an occasion. Things go well there, I hope?"

"Tolerably well," Temple replied. "The war was costly, of course, and we are still paying the price in social unrest, but we are making progress."

"Progress?" Balsamo echoed. "A French idea, is it not? Did you not fight the war to prevent progress?"

"In England," Temple told him, only a trifle stiffly, "we did not consider the Revolution or the Napoleonic Empire to constitute political progress—but when I used the word, I was thinking of an altogether different sort of progress than the merely political."

"Perhaps I am mistaken," Balsamo said, "but I was under the impression that the core of the philosophy was that there is only one sort of progress—that technical progress and social progress march hand-in-hand, each nourishing the other. Or were you thinking of the doughty puritan's *Pilgrim's Progress*?"

"No," said Temple, suppressing a surge of annoyance at what seemed to him a deliberate misunderstanding of his meaning. "I meant that the nation is making progress in returning to normal—to harmony and prosperity."

"Indeed?" Balsamo queried, cocking an eyebrow. "I never had the impression that harmony was normal in England—nor prosperity, for all but the favored few. On the other hand, I believe that your country is in the forefront of technical progress. You have nurtured several important pioneers of the new science of electricity, have you not? Humphry Davy and Michael Faraday are famous throughout Europe. My own compatriots, Luigi Galvani and Alessandro Volta, have made considerable contributions to the same great work, which I find very exciting. It will favor social progress too, I think—it has the potential to bring about a social revolution far more profound than the one wrought by France's Jacobins. It was most unfortunate that they sent their own native genius, Monsieur Lavoisier, to the guillotine."

Temple was slightly surprised by the turn the conversation had taken, but not disturbed. Perhaps it was significant, and perhaps not—but it was, at any rate, not uninteresting. "What kind of social revolution do you mean, Signor Balsamo?" he asked, curiously.

"The second wave of the industrial revolution, of course," Balsamo told him. "Steam is supplying the power to a vast new generation of machines, including traveling engines of various kinds. It is already revolutionizing manufacturing processes, and will surely increase our mobility tremendously. Mechanics is only the beginning—when the capabilities of electricity are added to the skill of new machinery, there will be a further increase in its ingenuity. What a future we would have to look forward to, Mr. Markwick, if only we were not fated to pass on to another world at a mere threescore years and ten!"

"It is certainly becoming easier to clothe ourselves," Temple agreed, judiciously, "but there is only so much land, which can only yield so much wheat to make bread. There are limits to ambition, Signor Balsamo."

"Ah!" said Balsamo. "You are a Malthusian, of course, Mr. Markwick. You find it difficult to believe in my kind of progress because you find it easy to believe in the inevitability of the Malthusian checks: war, famine and disease. The horsemen of the apocalypse, who never rest—with Death himself as their constant companion. Are you so sure, then, that there is so little prospect of progress in diplomacy, agriculture and medicine... or even the fight against Death itself?"

By now, Temple was perfectly certain that the conversation was significant, although none of their fellow passengers could have guessed it, no matter how carefully they were eavesdropping. "The Balsamo I knew in London," he said, casually stretching the truth, "thought something similar. He was an alchemist of sorts, in quest of the philosopher's stone."

"In that case, I do know the Balsamo to whom you refer," the other man said, mildly, "perhaps rather better than you do. He is not a relative. If there were a philosopher's stone, it would probably be electrical in its nature and effects, don't you think? A distillate of the fire of Heaven, which Prometheus stole for the benefit of humankind. His work goes on, of course, despite its early interruption and his cruel punishment. By a curious coincidence, I believe I saw an English poet in Calais today who recently published a wonderful celebration of *Prometheus Unbound*. It came out just a few months ago—have you had a chance to read it?"

"I have not read it," Temple confessed. He only hesitated briefly before adding: "I did notice, though, that there was a ship named *Prometheus* that was burned in Purfleet Harbour only two days ago."

"Was there, indeed? The idea is in the air, you see. We live in a Promethean age. There was another literary work in English, I think, titled *The Modern Prometheus*—an account, disguised as fiction, of work done in Switzerland a few years ago. That was based on a different version of the myth, I think—or perhaps a gloss on Shakespeare. You remember Othello's lament, no doubt, when he contemplates poor Desdemona's corpse, and plaintively regrets the want of some *Promethean heat* to restore its warmth?"

"I have never been much of a playgoer," Temple said, with a slight hint of resentment at the manner in which the other man seemed to be teasing him for a lack of erudition. "I'm a practical man, alas, with little time for literary flights of fancy."

"Now, there you have the advantage of me," Balsamo said. "I, alas, am a rather impractical man, with far too much time for flights of fancy. My father always told me that it was a curse, although I have always insisted, perversely, on reckoning it a gift. If you do not know Shakespeare and Shelley, you will certainly be unfamiliar with Ludovico Ariosto and Torquato Tasso, but I would like to think that theirs is the spirit that flows in my veins—epic, magical and boundless. That is why I am so glad to have some extra space on the journey, thanks to the man who reserved a seat but never arrived to take it. I do hope, though, that no misfortune has overtaken him. I would not like to think of a man suffering serious inconvenience merely to reward me with a little elbow-room."

"We have lived in turbulent times these last 30 years, as I said," Temple observed, with a slight hint of acid in his voice. "Misfortune has been all too common. The blood in my veins is more prosaic in its inspiration. To me, Signor Balsamo, the establishment of peace and prosperity is progress—the only true progress that there is."

"That's an old man's opinion, Mr. Markwick, if you don't mind me saying so—and I mean no insult by it, because you don't appear to me to be a man who is ready to settle for retirement and a graceful fade into oblivion. If you had the chance of a second lease of life,

I believe you'd take it, no matter how turbulent the times might be in which you'd have to make use of it."

"Would you take such a chance, Signor?" Temple asked, point blank. "If there were some risk about it, that is."

Balsamo laughed. "Oh yes," he said. "Once, twice, and as many times as I might, regardless of risk. I have no fear of eternity in *this* life." He left it unstated as to whether he had any cause for anxiety regarding eternity in the other, but Temple took the inference that he might.

"Have you some message for me, Signor Balsamo?" Temple asked. "Or some demand to make, perhaps?"

"Why, no," Balsamo said. "I am merely making conversation, to while away the time. I am impatient for the advent of the steam-powered coach, which will hurtle along the road at 20 or 25 miles an hour—although the road might have to be remade to accommodate such reckless progress."

"Do you really believe that you or I might one day have the opportunity of a second lease of life?" Temple asked.

The Italian shrugged. His round face was configured to accommodate an unusually capacious smile, and now he smiled as broadly as he could. "I don't know, Mr. Markwick," he said, "but I would certainly count it as progress—and I can understand the appetite of those men who are ardently desirous of finding the secret of vital force in the mysteries of electricity. Men who have lived through turbulent times, and have borne witness to so much death and destruction, cannot help but be hasty in trying to seize such opportunities. Peace and prosperity are shallow goals, if they can only be attained briefly, by men long past the vigor of youth."

"Haste is one thing," Temple said. "Crime is another."

"Not all men think so," Balsamo said, his gaze suddenly fixing itself on the narrow empty space where Henri Moreau would have taken up far more room than the actual passengers had left.

Temple did his level best to give nothing away, but his heart sank as he guessed that the cat must already be out of the bag. The mere fact that Ned Knob had reserved two seats had given the game away. He tried to take what comfort he could from the thought that Giuseppe Balsamo must be even more troubled than he was by the fact that Comte Henri de Belcamp, resurrector of the dead, had not arrived to claim his ticket.

Because the journey from Calais to Paris was more than twice that between London and Dover, most passengers on the route made an overnight stop. The coach that Temple had boarded was scheduled to make that stop in Amiens—where it arrived shortly before midnight, according to local time. Those travelers with a greater sense of urgency had the option, however, of transferring to another vehicle in order to continue their journey with less delay that was routinely incurred in changing horses. By exercising that option, Temple knew, it ought to be possible to reach Paris not long after dawn, where he could either hire a carriage or take the local *patache* to Miremont. That was what he did—and honestly did not know whether to be glad or anxious when the mysterious Giuseppe Balsamo declined the opportunity.

"I fear that I need to sleep in a bed nowadays," the Italian explained, when they parted company. "In a lifetime of traveling, I have already spent too many nights attempting to sleep in carts and carriages. French highways are in better condition now than they once were, but the long summer's traffic has left a dire legacy of ruts and potholes, and such repairs as were carried out in the early autumn were superficial. I hope we meet again, Mr. Markwick—you have been an uncommonly entertaining traveling companion."

"That ought to be unlikely, Signor," Temples said, dryly, "unless fate has somehow contrived to tangle the threads of our lives together."

"Who knows what the future might hold?" was Balsamo's reply to that. "As a man of science, and a visionary, I'm bound to say that fate has nothing to do with such things—it's motive and circumstance that tangle men's lives together. We may well meet again, Mr. Markwick, if it transpires that we have goals in common."

Balsamo was right, of course, about the difficulty of trying to sleep on the coach that carried Temple forward in his journey—which had no empty seats, as Monsieur Moreau's reservation was not transferable. He wedged himself into a corner, giving himself the option of leaning his head on the wall beside the *portière*, but the temporary comfort offered by that option was an illusion; as soon as either front wheel hit a pothole, the resultant bump was likely to cause a severe headache and a swelling bruise.

Starved of sleep as he was, Temple was used to falling into a state halfway between a daze and waking delirium, so he contrived to remain relatively still and relatively calm, but the obsessive worries that mingled with his fragmentary dreams were alarming.

Whether John Devil had always planned to let him make the journey alone or not made little difference to the reality of his situation; even the plan that he had stated aloud required Temple to arrive at the Château de Belcamp alone, in advance of any rendezvous. He had been faced all along by the prospect of a painful meeting with Suzanne, and a difficult meeting with Jeanne, both of which he would have to negotiate unaided. While he had still been in England—and even more so while he had been conversing with Balsamo between Calais and Amiens—he had been able to distract himself with other concerns. Now, the question of what he might and ought to say to the two young women was becoming increasingly urgent.

To Suzanne, he owed a thousand apologies, whose profuse offering would at least give him time to think—but what was he to say to Jeanne? Must he tell her that her husband was alive, or should he—could he—procrastinate until the former Henri de Belcamp chose to make his own entrance? What would Ned Knob have told her, given that he was bound to arrive in Miremont first?

The situation was not improved when the journey—which had been pleasantly untroubled until then—was suddenly interrupted by one of those frequent accidents that were the bane of carriage travel. It was only a broken wheel, not a broken axle, but the wheel broke suddenly rather than giving due warning, and the subsequent upset injured two of the horses. Because it happened an hour before dawn, some distance from the nearest stop, there was no prospect of getting immediate help. The postillion dutifully rode off on one of the uninjured animals, but Temple knew that the vehicle would not be back on the road for several hours. He decided that he would probably get to Paris sooner if he hitched a ride to a coaching inn on one of the carts that were passing along the road, heading for the Parisian markets with all the velocity their plodding dray-horses could muster.

He had no difficulty in buying a cheap passage before dawn broke, but the morning was bitterly cold and there was no protection on the cart from the wind. The journey to the next coach-stop was not long, measured in miles, but it was not rapid either, and it dragged on for two hours. When he reached the inn, there was no carriage immediately available for hire, and another hour passed before he was able to resume his journey. By the time he finally reached Paris, it was afternoon, and by the time he had found another vehicle that would take him as far as Miremont, the Sun was sinking rapidly in the western sky. The increasing unease he felt as he drew closer to Miremont was further amplified by the fact that the carriage was being followed, not very discreetly, by a lone rider in hooded traveling-cloak.

The twilight was not quite gone when Temple dismounted at the *étoile* crossroad, but the rider was no longer visible. He must have turned off the road a minute or two before Temple got down. Temple watched the carriage rumble on, bound for Pontoise, then pulled himself together. It would be dark by the time he had climbed the hill to the château, whether he went through the village or risked one of the smaller paths that followed a more direct route, and he had no lantern with him.

Fortunately, he did not have to make a decision. Almost as soon as he had picked up his bag again, the silhouette of a man materialized at the entrance of one of the smaller paths leading away from the signpost.

"Wait a moment, Mr. Temple!" a voice called. "I'll light my lantern."

It was a voice that Temple remembered—that of Pierre Louchet, who once had worked for him briefly in London, after being stranded there, having served as a messenger. In those days, he had been a woodcutter, but now he was evidently employed at the château.

Lighting the lantern took time; Louchet was still dependent on flint and amadou to strike a light.

"How long have you been waiting for me, Pierre?" Temple asked.

"Not long, sir," Louchet assured him—although Temple deduced that he must have been loitering nearby for several hours, at least, if Ned Knob had assumed that his journey from Calais would go without a hitch.

"Is there any news?" Temple asked, as they fell into step.

"None, sir," Louchet told him. "No communication has been made as yet. Madame la Comtesse has raised 15,000 *livres* in gold and silver, and Madame Boehm has probably been able to gather a similar amount, but we do not know whether that will be enough. The waiting is the worst of it, sir. Mr. Richard and Madame Thompson have been out of their minds. They'll be very glad to see you."

"There's very little I can do, Pierre—at least until the ransom demand arrives. Even then..."

"I understand, sir—but your being here will make a big difference, at least to Madame Thompson. Did you know that their son was once confined to my care for a while, when he was a babe in arms? I was in my cottage then, and the circumstances were strange, but I learned to love him as if he were my own. I never knew, sir, when I worked for you in London, that he was your grandson, or..."

"I know, Pierre. I didn't know of his existence then, let alone his whereabouts. I've been the very worst of grandfathers ever since, and have not known how to set about repairing that fault. Now..."

"It's not too late, sir," Louchet said, as he hurried along the narrow bridle-path that provided the most direct route to the château. "She has longed to see you, sir, but... she had no news, no address. I think she would have asked Master Ned to find you long ago, if she could have thought of a good reason."

"She did, once," Temple said. "I came while the old Marquis was still alive—but I did not see her then. She was not yet in residence—I think she was in Paris, with Jeanne. I could have... but no matter. Tell me—is there any information at all regarding the kidnappers? You've questioned the villagers, I dare say?"

"Nothing's known in Miremont, sir—and nothing escapes the eyes of those gossips unless it's truly invisible. Whoever they were, they came across country and not by road. They knew the terrain well, and they picked the season well enough—there was no one abroad in the fields that day, for the weather was too cold. The livestock has been gathered in for the winter. I saw four, but there must have been more. I couldn't see their faces but they were strongly-built and purposeful—former soldiers, I'd judge. But who isn't a former soldier nowadays? They weren't the Emperor's men, I hope—but who can tell to what depths the poorer remnants of a humiliated army might sink? I never thought to cry *à l'avantage*, but it would have made me weep to receive a reply. Madame Boehm asked me whether they might have been Germans, but the one who spoke seemed French—Belgian French, mayhap, but French nevertheless. Mr. Knob asked me whether their skin was at all discolored, but I have no memory of any such thing. They were pale, not bronzed like southerners, but I couldn't tell whether they were Normans."

"They were mere mercenaries, Pierre. Even if we knew such details, it wouldn't tell us who sent them, or why. Until we know exactly what they want, we shall have no real idea what we are up against. If it's only the money..."

"Madame la Comtesse says that she is willing to pay. Madame Sarah is very angry, but she has agreed. If it's just the money they want, they'll release the children, won't they, sir?"

"I believe so. The children are too young to identify them in court, or give information that might lead to their capture; there's no profit in hurting them, and it always make good business sense to keep such vile bargains, for it encourages cooperation on the part of future victims."

"Madame Thompson is afraid that they might hurt young Richard, merely to put pressure on the Comtesse and Madame Boehm."

"That's unnecessary, and hence unlikely," Temple assured him—although he was far from certain that he was right in that estimation. If little Richard really were surplus to their requirements, the kidnappers might well think him useful for demonstrative purposes—and he had to be surplus, had he not? It was surely unthinkable that the real target of this whole insidious plan might be Gregory Temple, and not the Comtesse or late Comte Henri de Belcamp at all."

Louchet had the key to the main gate of the château in his pocket, and he locked it behind him when they had gone in. They went into the house by the main door, which the servant also locked behind them. Another Pierre—the Marquis de Belcamp's old manservant—hurried to meet them.

"Madame Thompson has fallen asleep," he said, in a whisper. "Mr. Thompson is with her, but Madame la Comtesse asked that you be taken in to see her before you see anyone else. Is that agreeable?"

"Of course," Temple said. "Lead on."

Chapter Three
The Comtesse de Belcamp's Distress

The drawing-room was lit by two candelabras, one of which was on the mantelpiece while the other stood on a small table set beside the armchair in which Jeanne, Comtesse de Belcamp, was waiting. She got up when Gregory Temple was shown in, and came towards him. He bowed politely.

His eyes darted around the room, taking its appearance in at a single glance. The décor was much as he remembered it, although the portraits had been rearranged. The late Marquis now had pride of place above the mantel, while his miscreant wife's portrait had been added to a recess beside the chimney-breast.

Temple was tempted to pause and study the portrait of Helen Brown at his leisure. When he had had been confronted by John Devil in the cell in Newgate where he had expected to find Richard Thompson, John Devil had told him a fantastic story concerning the locket he sometimes wore around his neck, claiming that the woman whose portrait was within it had been Helen Brown, and that the outlaw Tom Brown had been the result of her brief pseudonymous affair with Temple. The latter part was nonsense, of course—but as to the former, Temple had never been entirely sure. He resisted the temptation, knowing that contemplation would only add to his uncertainty, and hence to his torment.

"It's good to see you, Mr. Temple," the Comtesse said, a little hoarsely. "Last time we met, circumstance made us adversaries, but things are very different now. You are welcome in my home. Please sit down."

Temple waited until the Comtesse had taken her own armchair again before sitting in the one facing it. Once she was seated again, the light from the candles shone directly on the Comtesse's face. The last time Temple had seen her, in 1817, Jeanne had seemed an exceedingly young woman, little more than a child. In the intervening four years, she had aged a great deal. She was a woman in her prime now, and a mother; she was very beautiful, but her beauty was sorely distressed by pain, some of it recent and acute but some of longer duration and chronic. She seemed ten years older than she really was.

"I never considered you as an enemy, my lady," Temple assured her. "You may rely on my friendship now, if there is any way I can be of service."

"I'm glad to hear that," Jeanne said. "You'll forgive me, I hope, if I don't ask my servants to wake Suzanne immediately, but I wanted to see you alone first."

"I have not had any contact with Suzanne in four years," Temple said, grimly. "Another hour will make no difference."

"I have always thought that your refusal to communicate with Suzanne must have much to do with her intimate friendship with me," the Comtesse said. She did not phrase it as a question, but it was a question, and Temple knew that it demanded an explanation—one that he was unready to give.

"No, milady," he said. "That was not the reason. Have you any more news to add to what Pierre Louchet has told me?"

"Alas, no. Do you think that you will be able to help us, Mr. Temple?"

"I don't know," Temple confessed, frankly. "Until the kidnappers make contact, we shall not know exactly what they want, and even when we know what their demands are, it will be difficult to estimate whether they intend to play fair. Unless you intend to involve the Prefecture of Police, we have no alternative but to do as we are instructed and hand over the ransom. If we can get the children returned safely, we might then be able to make plans for its possible recovery, but I cannot be optimistic on that score. I shall act as your intermediary in the negotiations, if I may, and will do my utmost to make sure that the children are returned safely. In all probability, the best we can hope to achieve is that we shall be able to set someone to follow the money once it is handed over—but the kidnappers will expect that, and it will not be easy. Ned Knob is, I'm told, an accomplished bloodhound; I'm sure that he will do his best."

"And is Ned Knob the only assistant you have, Mr. Temple?" the Comtesse asked, with brutal directness.

Temple hesitated a moment, then sighed. "Madame la Comtesse," he said, "I am an honest man, although I am sometimes required by the necessities of my employment to practice deceit and dissimulation. I do not know what Ned had told you, or has refrained from telling you, but I must make my own judgment in any case. To be perfectly frank, milady, I do not know whether I am alone in having rushed to your aid. Another man was supposed to travel with me from Dover to Paris, but he did not appear to be on the packet-boat. Perhaps he was merely delayed, or perhaps he always intended to make his own way here—in which case, given that I was delayed on the road, he might have arrived in Miremont ahead of me. I dare not call him my assistant, and he has no right to think of me as his, but in this instance, if in no other, we are working to the same end. I do not know what resources he has to deploy, but I am forced to admit that he is a more ingenious man than I am, with a far greater capacity for working apparent miracles. Whatever little I can do to assure a successful outcome to this tragic business, he will more than double—but exactly what he will do, and how, I cannot tell."

"Who is this man?" the Comtesse asked.

"Your husband, milady," Temple told her. "Comte Henri de Belcamp, alias Percy Balcomb."

She did not show any obvious sign of shock or disbelief, but Temple judged that she had not had the news already from Ned Knob. The little man seemed more inclined to honesty now than he had been in 1817, but it seemed that his first loyalty was still to John Devil. It was, after all, to John Devil that he had taken Suzanne's letter in the first instance.

There was a long pause before the Comtesse spoke again, but when she broke the silence, her voice was almost steady. "I would be a liar if I said that I had always known," she said, softly, "but I had always felt *something* that would make such news, if and when it came, seem reasonable and expectable. I would be a liar, too, if I said that I had hoped—for how could I hope that the man I loved was withholding himself deliberately, refusing even to let me know that he was still alive? And yet... strangely, I do not feel betrayed. I think I came to understand what kind of man he is during our few precious days together. He warned me often enough that things might go badly awry—that he would be called murderer, traitor, madman—and that the path of our love might run anything but smooth. I do not know how he

163

could bear to be alive and not to see his wife or his son, but I do believe that he has not found it easy, and must have thought it a necessity. But he will come now, will he not? Nothing will prevent him but actual death."

"He believes it to be possible, milady," Temple told her, thinking it best to put everything out into the open, "that he may be the real objective of this vile affair—that what the kidnappers want might not be limited to money. He has a secret, which might be reckoned valuable."

"He has a secret!" Jeanne de Belcamp echoed. "How can I be surprised by that? Secrets have always been his chief stock-in-trade. How could it be otherwise?" Her eyes flickered sideways, towards the portrait of the late Marquis, from whom the young Henri had had to keep the terrible secrets of his own identity, and his mother's fate.

"As yet, we have no way of knowing for sure whether he might be right," Temple went on. "It may be, though, that the reason he did not catch the packet-boat from Dover to Calais is that he was certain that I would be followed and did not want to be seen with me. I *was* followed—and something more insidious than that occurred on the coach between Calais and Amiens, where I believe that I may well have made contact with one of the people behind the kidnapping."

This time, the Comtesse did seem startled. "Morbleu!" she exclaimed, in a fashion that was not entirely ladylike. "Who?"

"He called himself Giuseppe Balsamo, but I think that was a teasing lie, intended to be suggestive. He judged that I would recognize the name as that of the self-styled Count Cagliostro, who made such an impact in pre-Revolutionary France as an alleged magician and alchemist."

"Magic and alchemy? Does he think that Henri has the secret of the philosopher's stone, then?"

"No, milady—but he may well believe that your husband has the secret of resurrecting the dead. The Comte de Belcamp certainly convinced Ned Knob that he has that secret, and, no matter how much I would like to doubt it, I have to admit that he almost certainly does. I have seen the results of his work. They are more horrible than hopeful, at present, but it seems that he and his associate—a Parisian physician named Germain Patou—had barely begun their research. Reanimating the body is, it seems, far easier than reanimating the mind. Most of his reanimated corpses were mindless idiots—but some were not, and he seems to have been exploring means to help the others remember who and what they had been, with some limited success. His work in London was cut short—but not, it seems, before attracting attention from more than one interested party."

"I do not want to be indelicate, Mr. Temple," the Comtesse said, "but there have been persistent rumors since the beginning of 1817 that you had gone mad. This story is not likely to dissuade its hearers from wondering whether the rumors might be true."

"The rumors may well be true," Temple said, flatly, "but my madness is an obsessive one, not a delusional one. If I am forced to believe and say things that are incredible, it is not because I have lost touch with reality but because the reality that has caught me in its web is one that presents a stern challenge to the imagination of ordinary people. No matter what you think of me, and no matter how this unfortunate business develops, you will discover before very long that the dead *can* be reanimated, after a fashion—and that the world of the future will be very different from the world of the past, no matter what the limitations of the process eventually prove to be. Ned Knob can tell you more about it than I can, for he has seen a resurrection accomplished, and has talked to a close friend who had been hanged. Your husband can tell you far, far more... if he will deign to show himself and dare to face you."

"My husband never lacked daring, Mr. Temple," Jeanne de Belcamp said. "No matter what you think of him, you cannot deny that. Whatever his reasons have been for letting me think that he was dead these last four years, a lack of daring was not among them."

"No," Temple conceded, "it was not. His madness is a more reckless sort than mine. Young Ned is not mad, though. I do not like the man, or his politics, but I cannot call him mad. With his sanity to support us, our history compels belief."

"You think, therefore, that when the ransom demand comes, it will not demand money?"

"Oh no, milady—I'm perfectly certain that it will demand money. I doubt that it will mention anything else, at least to begin with. On the other hand, I think it quite possible—and perhaps likely—that a snare is being set. While your husband works to recapture your children and the money, Signor Balsamo's friends may be working to capture him—which raises, I think, an important question.

"For myself, I am only concerned with the children. I confess that any money you and Sarah O'Brien might lose in consequence of their safe recovery is a matter of scant importance to me, although I always do what I can to see justice served and criminal enterprise thwarted. As for your husband, I do not care in the least what may happen to him. If the true price of recovering the three children were to hand him over, in order that his secret might be extracted from him—by whatever means—then I would do it without a moment's hesitation. You might think otherwise. If so, I need to know. I make no promises, but I will take your opinion into account."

The Comtesse de Belcamp frowned slightly as she considered the question. Temple was interested to know what her reply would be—but he had no chance to find out immediately, for the drawing-room door opened at that moment and Suzanne Thompson raced in, followed by her husband. Evidently, Suzanne had awoken without being roused, and her very first thought had been to ask whether her father had arrived.

Temple had expected some stiffness, some reproach, some reserve—but there was none. His daughter hurled herself upon him, and threw her arms around him. She was sobbing, but she contrived nevertheless to say: "Daddy, oh Daddy, I'm *so* glad you're here."

Temple hesitated, but then he returned the embrace, leaning over to kiss his daughter on the top of her head. "I'm sorry, child," he said. "So very sorry—for everything."

There was a long pause then, while the other people in the room had to wait.

Eventually, Temple disengaged himself from the embrace, and stepped towards Richard Thompson, extending his hand. "It's good to see you again, Richard," he said, adding—after only the merest hesitation—"my son."

Thompson gripped his hand gladly, and shook it vigorously. "It's good to see you, sir," he said. "We're in dire need of your quick mind and wise counsel."

Temple pulled himself together. "It might be best," he said, "if we were to assemble all the interested parties in one room, so that we may all know what we're about.

Is it possible to summon Countess Boehm from the new château? And where is Ned Knob?"

It was Richard Thompson who answered. "Ned is watching the gate," he replied. "If any messenger comes, Ned intends to follow him when he departs. Sarah knows that you were coming—she will be waiting to be summoned. Surrisy is with her. Do you remember Surrisy?"

Temple did remember Robert Surrisy, and could not help darting a glance at the Comtesse. Robert Surrisy had been in love with Jeanne Herbet before Comte Henri de Belcamp had made his spectacular entrance on the Miremont scene, and had only dallied thereafter with the woman he knew as Lady Frances Elphinstone because Jeanne had rejected him. Sarah O'Brien—alias Lady Frances—had rejected him too, and Temple had half-expected that Surrisy would renew his suit with Jeanne once Henri had been declared dead. He knew that the two of them had undertaken a voyage on the *Deliverance* with two committed couples—Richard and Suzanne, and Friedrich Boehm and Sarah—but it seemed that their brief alliance had not matured into anything richer. Perhaps that was as well, given that Henri was still alive.

"I'll send Old Pierre to the new château," the Comtesse said. "Sarah and Robert will come. Should I ask him to search for Ned?"

Temple considered the matter briefly, then said: "No. I was followed from Paris by a rider. The kidnappers must know that I'm here. If that's what they've been waiting for, their demand will arrive tonight. Let Ned stay where he is, so that he can follow his plan through."

"Should we wait a little while before holding our council of war, in case the messenger—or someone else—puts in an appearance?" the Comtesse asked.

"No," Temple said without hesitation. "When you, Suzanne and Sarah O'Brien are all gathered together, I shall be able to say what I need to say to the people who need to hear it. We must make our own plans, without regard to anyone else—but if a messenger does come, so much the better, We shall all be together to hear what demands are being made."

The Comtesse de Belcamp picked up a handbell from the table in order to summon the two Pierres, but before she had a chance to ring it, her hand froze. Another, more distant bell had sounded. Temple recognized it immediately as the bell suspended beside the main gate.

"I'll go," he said, immediately—but he was not as quick off the mark as Pierre Louchet, who had already gone out through the front door, with a lantern in his hand, by the time Temple reached it. Nor could Temple match the former woodcutter's stride as they crossed the courtyard. By the time he caught up with the other man, Louchet was already staring through the bars of the gate saying, in a scornful tone: "What do *you* want?"

"Who is it, Pierre?" Temple asked, placing a calming hand on the former woodcutter's shoulder

"It's the Besnard boy, from the village," Louchet said. "The one they call Don Juan—ironically, of course."

In the meantime, the offended individual had stretched out his hand, bearing a sealed envelope. "You should not speak in that fashion to a man who is attempting to do you a service," Besnard said. "I was asked to deliver this note by hand, and generously agreed to do it. I did not expect to be insulted for my trouble."

Temple reached through the bars and took the letter. He did not bother to ask how much the young man had been paid, but merely said: "You have my sincere thanks, sir. Who gave you the message, my friend?"

"I have never seen him before," Besnard replied. "He did not give me his name."

"Please describe him as carefully as you can," Temple said. "It's a matter of some importance."

Besnard shrugged. "He was much older than me," he said, "though not quite as old as either of you. He was a little stout, I suppose, but seemed very healthy. His face was rounded, his hair and eyes dark. Well-dressed, though somewhat travel-stained."

"What about his voice—his accent?" Temple asked.

"He was certainly French, but not local. A southerner, perhaps—there was something of the Languedoc about his pronunciation."

"And where did your encounter take place?" Temple wanted to know.

"At the inn—or, rather, outside its door. He did not come in, but met me as I was coming out. He said that he needed to get a message to the Château de Belcamp urgently, but did not know his way around and was in any case in a hurry to get back on the Pontoise Road. He offered me a *louis* if I would help him out—although it was not the money that made me do it, you understand, but kindness, to the stranger and Madame la Comtesse alike."

"You fool...!" Pierre Louchet began—but Temple silenced him with a curt gesture.

"We're much obliged to you, sir," Temple said. "Thank you, and good night." As he pulled Louchet away, he glanced left and right into the darkness. There was no sign of Ned Knob, but he trusted that the little

170

man had heard every word, and would make every effort to catch up with the mysterious stranger—or at least to discover which way he had really gone.

"Will you run to the new chateau, Pierre, and fetch Countess Boehm?" Temple said. "This is what we have all been waiting for, and we must all know what it contains."

Louchet nodded, and let himself out by the small gate beside the main one. He took his lantern with him. Temple had to carry the letter back to the house to read what was written on the envelope. It was not very revealing, saying only: *To the Comtesse de Belcamp*.

Temple took it into the drawing-room. Instead of waiting for Sarah Boehm, he carefully broke the seal and took out the piece of paper folded within. He scanned its contents quickly, but then raised his hand to prevent the Comtesse from snatching it from his hand. "I will need to examine it more closely," he said, by way of explanation. "I shall read the message. It says: *Bring 10,000 livres to the eastern extremity of Little Switzerland at midnight. The first child will then be released. The money must be delivered by one of the parents, accompanied by no more than one man. If any attempt is made to interfere with us before the exchange, the first child will be killed; if we are pursued or harassed thereafter, the other children will be killed.*"

He paused, so that his listeners would know that he had stopped reading. Then he added: "It appears that the affair is to proceed by stages, and that we have a very short deadline to complete the first phase. The complexity is tiresome, and the short deadline leaves us no time to make preparations. On the other hand, the fact that Little Switzerland is nearby—I believe that is the nickname of the plateau on top of the hill that overlooks the château and the valley—implies that our adversaries must be close at hand, and ought to have at least one of the kidnapped children with them. Do you have 10,000 *livres* in gold ready to hand, my lady?"

"Yes I do," the Comtesse confirmed. "I shall make up a package. Which of us should go to make the exchange?"

"Suzanne will go, with me," Temple said. "I shall do my very best to make certain that the child is handed over before I surrender the money."

He had to repeat the contents of the note then, because the former Sarah O'Brien had just arrived, escorted by Robert Surrisy. He also repeated his assertion that he would go with Suzanne to deliver the money. "Monsieur Surrisy," he said, "you must give us half an hour before following us, if we do not return—but if you hear a gunshot, you must come immediately, as quickly as you can, with Richard and Pierre Louchet—but you must make sure that the château is not left unguarded."

"I wish you would let me go in your stead, sir," Surrisy was quick to say. "I am a lawyer now, and my soldiering days are behind me, but I know how to use a sword and a pistol, and I can ride very well."

"No," said Richard Thompson. "I should be the one to go. Suzanne is my wife."

"If I were not here, either one of you would doubtless make an excellent job of it," Temple said, "but it's me they expect, and it may be that they want me as well as the gold. It was no coincidence that this letter arrived so soon after my arrival. They've been watching out for me since I left London, and have even taken the trouble to sound me out. I was careful to conceal the extent of my knowledge regarding the secret of electrical resurrection, but they undoubtedly know that I am in the employ of His Majesty's secret police, and may imagine that I know far more than I do about the recent events in London. That might work to our advantage—if they are willing to hand over a child in order to persuade me to surrender to their custody, it is an exchange worth making."

Sarah Boehm stepped in front of Surrisy then to say: "What events in London? What secret of electrical resurrection?"

Again Temple had to repeat himself, informing the entire company that Henri de Belcamp was still alive, and had recently been involved in a violent struggle along the banks of the Thames for possession of a company of the dead-alive, and the means to revive more.

"Impossible!" was Sarah Boehm's response. Temple did not know whether she meant the resurrection of the dead, or the fact that her friend and longtime companion had played dead for so long without letting her know that he was still alive and still scheming to turn the world upside-down.

Surrisy, who evidently assumed that she meant the former, said; "There have been rumors abroad in Paris..."

"What rumors, Monsieur Surrisy?" Temple was quick to ask. "Have you heard mention therein of a man named Germain Patou?"

"The little physician? I know of him, yes—but not in connection with these rumors. I paid them little heed, to tell you the truth, for they seemed stale as well as silly. Have you heard of the Comte de Saint-Germain?"

"Yes I have," Temple said. "A poseur—a magician and pretended immortal, of the same stripe as Count Cagliostro, likewise not heard of since the Revolution, or at least since Napoleon's ascent to power. Is he said to have reappeared?"

"So rumor has it—and it's also said that he's on the track of some great secret, as valuable in its way as the elixir of long life that he already possesses. It's said that he's a member of an ancient secret society—but everyone in the world is nowadays said to be a member of some secret society or other, and every such society that is actually formed claims roots in deepest antiquity."

"I can well understand," Temple said, with a sight trace of sarcasm, "that a stalwart of the Brotherhood of the Deliverance would know far better than to pay any heed to silly talk of secret societies. What say you, Sarah O'Brien? Your husband was intricately involved with some relic of the *vehmgerichte*, I understand?"

"I was a very active member of the Deliverance myself, Chief Inspector Temple," the Irishwoman retorted, with more than a hint of vitriol, "under more names than one. Are you bearing grudges still, to speak to me in that tone?"

Temple recalled the night on which he had surprised Sarah O'Brien and Richard Thompson together, riding the Russian Mountains at the Colisée, thus slotting the last piece of James Davy's intricate jigsaw of deception into place—but that belonged to another life now, and another world. "I beg your pardon, Countess Boehm," he said, humbly. "I had no right to be rude—and I bear no grudge. In this matter, we are all on the same side—even John Devil himself. I hope, now that he was able to arrive ahead of me, for I'd be prepared to wager that he would have seen the stranger accost young Besnard in the village, and might even now be watching from the ridge of the hill. We cannot rely on that, though—it is more likely that he is still in Paris, if he is in France at all. We must be prepared to handle this our-selves. I will do my utmost to secure the freedom of whichever child they bring to the meeting-place, if they bring one at all, and I shall not fire on them unless there is some treachery. If I can simply exchange the money for the child, I will. Then, I suppose, we shall have to await a further communication. If things go wrong... well, we shall have to re-evaluate the situation. Are we all agreed on what will happen at midnight? It's not far off, I fear."

"I cannot see why you should automatically assume command, Mr. Temple," said Countess Boehm. "I un-derstand why your daughter sent for you, but it is not your money that is at stake."

"He has assumed command because I have asked him to do so, Sarah," the Comtesse de Belcamp stated, flatly. "Tonight, at least, it is my money that is at stake. Who else should be in command, do you suppose?"

Sarah Boehm did not reply. Robert Surrisy hastened to fill the silence. "Mr. Temple has far more experience in this sort of matter than anyone else, Sarah," he pointed out. "Richard has been a policeman too, but I dare say that he is perfectly willing to follow the advice of his old senior officer. I was a Knight of the Deliver-ance, and am proud to have served in that capacity, but the mothers of kidnapped children surely ought to look to a man like Gregory Temple for expert assistance."

Temple bowed to Surrisy, but Countess Boehm still seemed inclined to rebellion. "That does not mean that Temple's daughter should go with him," she objected. "Why should I not go—or Jeanne since she is deter-mined to part with her money while I hold mine in re-serve?"

"It is precisely because the two of you are the ones with the money that Suzanne should go," Temple said, flatly. "If I am to be trusted to handle the affair, the matter is not negotiable. Now, Monsieur Surrisy, may I question you further regarding these rumors? Was there, by any chance, any reference to a man named Giuseppe Balsamo?"

"That was Cagliostro's real name," Surrisy said, immediately. "No, I have not heard it spoken—but if there were a secret society of magicians that included the Comte de Saint-Germain, how could Cagliostro not be a member of it? He's said to be dead of course—but we know what rumors of *that* sort are worth."

"What about the *Veste Nere*?" Temple asked.

Surrisy's expression shifted. "I've heard that term, and its French equivalent, the *Habits Noirs*, bandied about the Palais de Justice," he admitted, "but that's another matter, somewhat less fanciful in essence. There's a world of difference between bandits who ape gentlemanly dress, and aristocrats who wear it with the entitlement of centuries. The *Veste Nere* are common criminals; these others—if they exist—are more likely to be madmen."

"That seems only too likely," Sarah Boehm put in, acidly, "If we are to discuss rumors while the clock ticks, did I not hear a rumor to the effect that Gregory Temple is now a lunatic, who cannot be trusted in anything?"

"That's a lie!" Suzanne protested.

"I liked your late husband, Madame Boehm," Temple said. "Indeed, I offered to sell you to him once, for the price of a steamboat engine—but I sold the bearskin before I had the bear, and the engine went to a trader who matched my price with slightly greater immediacy.

All that is water under the bridge now, and I have said that I bear no grudges; it would be as well if you could set yours aside, at least for tonight. Even an old lunatic can carry a bag full of gold to the top of a hill and complete the purchase of a child—and if there's some trickery afoot, a madman of my sort might be as useful as a sane man. I am, if nothing else, expendable."

Sarah Boehm hesitated, but then she nodded. "Why not?" she said, presumably meaning: *If someone has to risk his neck, why not you?* Suzanne must have understood that, because she put her arms around her father's neck again, and said: "I'm sorry."

Temple was astonished to find tears in the corners of his own eyes as he replied: "I am the one who should be sorry."

Chapter Four
The Child-Stealers' Enterprise

The route from the Château de Belcamp to "Little Switzerland" and a hunting-path that diverged from the bridle-path that Temple had already followed in company
with Piere Louchet, going uphill instead of down before
looping back to make its separate way to the *étoile*
where the road to Miremont quit the highway. The region's nickname was ironic, because there was nothing
mountainous about the region at all; most of the plateau
was wooded, but at the eastern extremity to which the
ransom note had referred was a small heath, which cul-
minated in a viewpoint from which one could see the
entire valley of the Oise, including the full extremity of
what had once been the Belcamp domain.

Temple assumed that he and Suzanne would be required to cross the heath and stand on the viewpoint itself, fully exposed beneath the Moon and stars to anyone
watching from a semicircular arc of woodland that
measured at least 200 paces from end to end. They
would be watched from some covert there, and someone
would eventually come to meet them. With this prospect
in mind, they set out from the château some 25 minutes
before the appointed time.

"You have not really been mad, have you, Father?"
Suzanne asked, as they trudged through the grounds to
the commencement of the path. The gold, packed into a

single satchel, was weighing very heavily on his right arm.

"Have I not?" Temple replied. "I believe I was, at least for a while—but I am making progress." His mouth twisted into a grimace as he used the word—by which he meant, yet again, the restoration of normality and harmony—but Suzanne was holding her lantern in such a way as to light their path, and she could not have seen the expression.

"Is that why you did not write to me?" she asked. "I thought that you were angry with me—that I had betrayed you in so many ways. Richard... the baby. When I helped Henri de Belcamp, I was acting under duress, but I know that's no excuse... not what you would expect of your daughter."

"I should never have made the stupid declaration that Richard was no fit husband for you," Temple said. "I was to blame, not you. As for your being here when Henri de Belcamp came home, and being caught up in his machinations—I understand how desperate you were, and how helpless you felt. It was none of your doing that prevented me from writing to you, but my own shame. I was angry with myself; it was I that felt unworthy of contact with you. I was a fool. I had put it completely out of my mind until Ned Knob reminded you—and I immediately became angry with him, and called him all manner of ugly names, for which he was right to chide me. I should have done everything I could to clear Richard's name and open the way for the two of you—I mean the three of you—to return to England, but I did not, because I could not face him. If only I had got to his cell in Newgate before John Devil, instead of after... but that, again, was my fault, not his."

There was a pause while she digested this, and then she said: "Did you mean what you said about the kidnappers wanting you as well as the gold?"

"It's possible," he said. "They've been dogging my footsteps since Calais, at least, and could have seized me by force at any time, but they know that if they want my full cooperation, they'll have to play a craftier game. It's Henri they really want—he's the one with the secret—but they must be afraid by now that he'll stay away, or at least in hiding, for exactly that reason. They might regard me as a mere morsel to give them something on which to chew until Henri is prepared to show his hand."

On the other hand, Temple thought, but dared not say aloud, *they might need someone to kill, in order that John Devil may be challenged to bring him back alive.*

"Sarah and Jeanne are at odds," Suzanne told him, after another brief pause. "They were never the best of friends, for they began as rivals, but this business has driven them much further apart."

"So I observed," Temple said. "It will not matter. Circumstances will force them to work together, to the same end."

"If all the children were all released together, that would be true," Suzanne agreed. "But that is not the case. If Sarah's boy were the one returned tonight... I'm not so sure that she'd be ready to give her money for the release of the others."

"I think you underestimate her," Temple said. "In any case, it will be little Richard who's released tonight. He's the least valuable of the three."

"Do you really think so, Daddy?"

"I'm almost certain—but hush now. We're getting close to the rendezvous, and we're almost certainly under close observation."

Suzanne obeyed immediately, falling silent and lifting the lantern higher. Not for the first time, Temple shifted his satchel from one hand to the other, bring temporary relief to one of his overstressed arms. He had not anticipated, although he should have, the state of extreme exhaustion that he would be in when he had climbed the hill. He had not rested properly since he set off from London, nor for three days before. No matter how little resemblance the hill above Miremont bore to a Swiss Alp, the steep climb was as hard on his tired legs as the gold he carried was on his shoulder muscles.

By the time they reached the bare land at the eastern extremity of the ridge, Temple was very glad of an opportunity to pause and draw breath. The sky was hazy and such moonlight as there was seemed quite impotent, but it was possible to see that the patch of heath was utterly deserted. No one was waiting there.

Suzanne looked at him fearfully, and he put his spare hand on her shoulder in what he hoped would pass for a gesture of reassurance.

"They'll be watching from cover," he assured her. "We must go to the edge, where the drop is sheerest, so that they can see that we're alone and have nowhere to run." He stepped forward again, taking a deep breath as he did so. The night air was cold enough to slice into his lungs like a razor, but it carried the oxygen he needed to replenish him.

When he and Suzanne had reached the limit of the ridge, where the ground fell away almost vertically, Temple set the bag that contained the gold down on the ground, positioning it carefully. He instructed Suzanne to keep the lantern elevated, displaying their faces plainly to any watchers in the bushes on the edge of the forested section of the ridge.

He was fully prepared to wait, if it should prove necessary—but they did not have to wait long. A lone man came out of the bushes, just about visible although he had no lantern in his hand. He did not have a child with him either.

"Step away from the gold, if you please, Mr. Temple," a voice said, in very good English, spoken with a mild continental accent. "Then take your pistol out of your pocket, very carefully, and throw it over the edge, hard enough to ensure that it will fall for ten or twelve times a man's height before it hits the ground."

"I will do nothing until we see the child," Temple said. "Indeed, I want the child safe in Suzanne's care before I step away from the gold. I shall keep my revolver, but you may watch us depart in company with the child, leaving the gold behind. That way, we shall both be sure of getting what we want."

"How do we know that the bag contains gold?" the other asked.

"You still have two children captive," Temple pointed out. "We would not put them at risk by playing false. Shall I throw you a coin or two by way of demonstration?"

"What would that prove?" the kidnapper asked—but he had the luxury of sounding amused, knowing that he had the upper hand.

"As much as your returning one child proves regarding the well-being of the others," Temple retorted. "Next time, I shall insist on seeing both before I hand over any money—and before you waste time in pointing out that you could shoot us down from ambush and simply take the gold, may I point out that the slightest nudge from my foot will send the bag skidding down the slope, scattering its contents far and wide. No one will disturb us if no shots are fired—but if you fire on us, you will not have time to gather your plunder before others come running."

"The brave soldier of Napoleon, the former apprentice detective and the old woodcutter?" the other countered. "We are men of peace, who abhor violence, but I think we could take care of them were the need to arise. Your midget, by the way, is off on a wild goose chase just now. Your other friend has not shown up at all—which is a deep disappointment to us, though not entirely a surprise. Do you know how to contact him?"

"Who?" Temple asked. The other man was close enough now for his face to catch a glimmer of lamplight. It was not the man who had called himself Giuseppe Balsamo, nor did he fit the description given by young Besnard. This was a tall and slender man with a goatee beard. He was wearing a black coat beneath his traveling-cloak, but he seemed no more reminiscent of a member of the *Veste Nere* than a medieval alchemist who had outlived his natural span. The cloak was hooded, but the hood was not up.

"Don't play games, Mr. Temple," the kidnapper said. "You know the stakes we are playing for—but we do need the money; this promises to be a very expensive campaign. We are honest brokers, though, and not averse to sensible compromise." He lifted his arm and beckoned.

Temple could hardly see the gesture, and he was much closer to his interlocutor than the bushes from which the bearded man had come, but someone there with good night vision was ready to respond to the summons. Two other people stepped out of the thicket—one of them a little child, perhaps four years old.

Suzanne must have had good night vision herself, or a mother's instinct, for she immediately ran towards them, crying: "Richard! Richard!" The flame of the lantern flickered wildly as she ran, but it did not go out.

Temple bit his lip, wishing that she had waited for the child to come to them but not wanting to call her back.

"We will need proof that the others are alive and well," Temple said, grimly, to the dark shadow confronting him. "This is an earnest of our intent, but we will not hand over any more money unless we are convinced that the younger boys are well."

"Very well, Mr. Temple," said the man with the goatee, with suspicious alacrity. "You are very welcome to come with us, and see for yourself."

Temple had half-expected that, but he was still somewhat uncertain of what he might be letting himself in for. It seemed an opportunity that might be too good to be missed—but he knew that it would also be a dangerous move, and that it would leave Jeanne de Belcamp with no more help and support than she had had before his arrival.

"Suzanne," he said. "Take little Richard with you and go back the way we came. I'll stay here to make sure that you're safely on your way home, and then I shall go with these men, to make sure that... the other children are safe." He stumbled slightly in his discourse when he suddenly realized that he had not asked the name of Jeanne's child, or of Sarah's.

Suzanne opened her mouth to protest, but he cut her off abruptly. "Don't waste time, Suzanne!" he commanded. "Go—take the lantern with you, and hold it up so that I can measure its progress."

She did not hesitate any further. She had her son and the opportunity to make him safe. She hurried him back to the point where the path disappeared into the trees, drawing him along by the hand, and soon vanished from sight. The boy had not looked at Temple, even when he spoke, and presumably had no idea that he had just met his grandfather for the first—and perhaps the last—time.

"You knew, of course, that my grandson was the least valuable of the three," Temple said, in a low voice. "Thus far, you've given away very little and received 10,000 livres. You must not raise the stakes too much— and you ought to play fair with me, for I'm the best hope you have of making everything go smoothly."

This time, the man with the goatee laughed in the near-darkness. "It's not in our interests for anyone to die," he said. "At least, until we can be sure that we can bring them back. I hope you can assist us with that, Mr. Temple—or at least in locating your old adversary. We were hoping to see him on the coach from Calais, and were sorely disappointed when he missed it. Please pick up the gold and step away from the edge."

Temple waited a little while longer, for Suzanne's sake, but as soon as his shadowy interlocutor took another step forward, he did as he as he had been told, and picked up the gold. He stepped forward, and handed it to the bearded man, who fumbled as he took it because he could not see what he was doing.

"Lead on," Temple said. "I'll do my best to follow, in spite of the gloom."

"I think it best if there's no delay," the other said. "Give him the flask, Brother."

Again the darkness made it difficult, but Temple eventually contrived to accept a small stoppered bottle from one of the two men who had brought little Richard out of the bushes.

"Drink it all," the leader instructed.

Temple did not hesitate. He took the stopper from the bottle, raised it to his lips and drained the vessel. He might have tried to tip the contents into his sleeve, or hold them in his mouth in the hope of an opportunity to spit them out, but the advice he had given the kidnappers held good for him too: at this early stage of the game, it was best to attempt no trickery.

He did not even dare to pretend to fall unconscious before the draught actually took effect—which gave him time to consider its taste very carefully. The drug was not one that he recognized. It was not bitter, but it did not seem to have been sugared or mixed with liquor to make it more palatable. It was certainly not laudanum.

"The secret of the philosopher's stone *and* a better sleeping draught," he murmured. "You seem well-supplied with secrets already. I apologize for my awkward size—it won't be easy to carry me to..."

He could not complete the sentence, and was in any case regretting that he had not thought of something wittier to say. He felt his knees buckling as his senses reeled—and was oddly grateful to surrender his effortful grip on consciousness. He had, after all, been extremely tired for a very long time.

Chapter Five
The Alchemists' Masquerade

Gregory Temple woke up gradually and reluctantly, extricating himself by slow degrees from a dream whose joy and comfort were based in lack of meaning, absolute inconsequentiality and a profound sense of well-being. He had not been able to escape himself to such a remarkable degree for many years, and he could not help but struggle against the compulsion to return to himself and put on all his troubles once again.

The physical necessities that finally forced him back to the awful pattern of his life were thirst and a need to urinate. The windowless cell in which he found himself, lit by a single candle that had burned very low on the wooden table set beside his pallet, fortunately provided the means to satisfy both needs. He drank directly from the pitcher set beside the candle, and drained it to the dregs. Otherwise, he felt quite well; there was no trace of the headache he would have expected to feel had he been rendered unconscious by any conventional means.

The cell was small—when he stood in the center he only had to lean slightly to one side or another to touch all four walls, three of which were made in grey brick and one of solid stone—but it was not unfurnished. In addition to the bed and the small table, there was a writing-desk bolted to the wall, with a long-legged chair. There was paper on the desk, and the inkwell was full.

The night-stand had a cupboard, but all it contained was a bundle of candles—perhaps enough to light the cell for a week. There were no matches, however; Temple made a mental note to be sure to light a new candle before the old one burned out.

The door of the cell was made of wood, without any cast-iron reinforcements, and the inspection hole set at head-height had a wooden shutter rather than a wrought-iron grille. There was no flap at the bottom through which trays of food could be passed without the necessity of unlocking the door. It was, in consequence, more reminiscent of a monk's cell than a dungeon—but the door *was* locked, presumably by means of an external bar. Temple estimated that it would only be the work of ten or twelve minutes to break it down—but he could not do that without making a good deal of noise.

It was easy enough to push the shutter back and look out, but the corridor beyond was unlit.

"Hello!" he shouted. "Is anyone there?"

His ears—which were still keen, despite his age and his failure to hear John Devil enter his bedroom in London—caught the sound of movement from what he guessed to be a cell next to his own, but no one replied.

"Hello!" he called again. "My name is Gregory Temple. My daughter Suzanne is the wife of Richard Thompson, and the mother of another Richard, who was returned to his home last night."

There was no evident reply from the next cell, but his raised voice had attracted attention from elsewhere. The radiance of a flickering candle-flame, approaching from some distance away, shed some little light on the wall opposite his cell, which was grey stone, as solid as the opposite wall of his cell. The reflections brightened as the candle came nearer, until the flame was held up so close to the hole in the door that he could not see through it, at first, to the man who was holding it. Eventually, though, it was moved aside, deliberately displaying the carrier.

The man's face was invisible, completely hidden by a ornate mask carefully molded in the form of a death's-head. There must have been real eyes within what appeared to be empty sockets, but they were not visible; they must have been obscured by something resembling smoked glass—although it must have been very difficult for the masked man to see by feeble candlelight with his eyes screened in that fashion.

"You have slept for a long time, Monsieur," said a voice he did not recognize, in French. "You must have been in dire need of it. You owe us a debt for your healing, as well our generosity in granting your request."

"My request has not been granted," Temple replied, in the same language. "I have not seen the children yet." It occurred to him then that he had called out before in English—a language in which neither the three-year-old Marquis de Belcamp, nor the three-year-old Count Boehm, could be expected to regard as their first. Even the four-year-old Richard Thompson probably spoke French far more often than English, although he must be fluent enough in both languages.

"That is easily remedied," the masked man said. "But you must swear an oath that you will be peaceful and obedient. This is a convent, after all."

"Is it?" Temple countered. "To judge by the cold and the quality of the air, we are underground. Are we in a crypt, then? Or are we in the catacombs beneath Paris, where the bones of past generations are stored for want of burial-grounds?"

"The Council will be glad to find you in an inquisitive mood," the masked man said. "I do need your solemn oath, sworn on the name of almighty God, that you will obey the instructions given to you, and that you will do no violence to anyone while you are here."

"I swear by almighty God," Temple said, speaking in English so that he would not fall victim to any careless or inept expression, "that I will do no violence to anyone while I am here unless I am compelled to defend myself or the children you have stolen. I similarly swear that I will obey the instructions I am given to the best of my ability, so long as they are not in conflict with previous oaths I have sworn and the duties that I fulfill as a servant of His Majesty King George of England."

The masked man laughed. "We have nothing against King George, at present," he said, continuing to speak in the tongue with which he was more comfortable, although he seemed to understand English well enough. "We have not been in sharp conflict with an English King since the 16th century—but more than one of England's recent enemies has been our adversary."

"Times change rapidly nowadays," Temple reported. "Yesterday's enemy of England may be today's ally. May I see the children now?"

"You may." Temple heard the sound of the bar being withdrawn, and then had to step back as the door opened inwards. The masked man stood aside, and bowed slightly as he let his prisoner out.

Temple immediately went along the corridor to the next cell, and removed the bar blocking its door. He pushed the door carefully, in case the children were huddled behind it listening—but they were both sitting on the bed, huddled close for mutual comfort but without either one placing his arm around the other's shoulder.

They seemed very small, although Temple did not know what height a three-year-old boy might be expected to attain. They were very similar in stature and in appearance, although one had dark hair and one was blond.

"Am I in the presence of the Marquis de Belcamp and Count Boehm?" Temple asked, speaking slowly, in French. "I am here on behalf of your mothers, who asked me to make sure that you are well."

The blond boy relied first, saying "I am Armand de Belcamp, monsieur."

"I am Friedrich Boehm," the other said, also in French. He added: "Have you come to take us home?"

"Now that I have met your captors," Temple said, "I am convinced that they mean you no harm, in spite of their attempts to seem fearful. They seem to think themselves a cut above the ordinary run of bandits, and will doubtless treat you politely in consequence. You must stay here for a little longer, but I will talk to them, and will try to work out a means of getting you both safely home." He was not certain that boys so small could follow the logic of this overly florid speech—which was intended as much for his captor's ears as for theirs—but the blond boy nodded, and said: "Thank you, sir," in English.

Temple reached out a hesitant hand to touch Armand de Belcamp on the top of the head, and the young Marquis reached up to grip his wrist, almost as if he were the one doing the reassuring rather than the one being reassured.

"You're brave boys," Temple said. "Your fathers would be proud of you."

Friedrich Boehm's dark eyes—his mother's eyes—welled with tears then, but the little boy hastened to wipe them way. He had obviously been old enough to be conscious of what was happening while his father died. Armand de Belcamp released Temple's wrist and put his arm round his friend. There was no reflection here of the tension that had sprung up between their mothers.

Temple stepped back, and allowed the masked man to secure the door. "Very well," Temple said, in French, when the task was complete. "Let us proceed to my audience with the Comtes de Saint-Germain and Cagliostro. I am eager to hear what your brotherhood of alchemists and magicians has to say to me."

"You are a fortunate man, Monsieur Temple," the other replied. "It has been 40 years and more since such a council as the one which will interrogate you has been summoned. I hope that you are sensible of the privilege. The world has changed a great deal in the interim—but that is nothing compared with the changes that the next 40 years will bring, if we cannot contain this demon electricity."

"A demon, is it?" Temple retorted. "Your friend Balsamo spoke of it quite affectionately. I do hope that he was not misrepresenting his ideas in the hope of teasing some indiscretion from me—that would not be a gentlemanly way to behave."

"After you, Monsieur Secret Policeman," the masked man said, in English, pointing the way that his prisoner should go.

Temple was as obedient as he had promised to be. He judged by the condition of the corridors along which they walked that they were most certainly underground, and that they were not about to return to the surface. The chamber to which he was taken was a rounded cavern some 30 paces in diameter whose ceiling was a vault of grey rock. The walls were lined with a series of elaborately carved wooden compartments, many of which were equipped with benches and some with writing-desks, while the humblest had the kind of half-seats that were called *misericordia* by the Romanists—mercy seats, to which the weak might go to the wall for support when the long masses of Medieval times became too burdensome. Temple, not much to his surprise, was shown to an individual chair placed in the center of the near-circle, at the focus of everyone's attention.

Less than half the seats were occupied when he was ushered in, but that was because the council had not yet gathered in full. While he sat patiently in the center, a dozen more came in one by one, making 31 in all. Every one of them was wearing a black monk's habit and a carefully-made death's-head mask. Had they raised their hoods and taken up scythes, they could have passed for Death himself, multiplied 30 times over—as Death must surely be nowadays, in order to cope with the incessant demands of the present population of Christendom.

Temple waited until he was spoken to, observing as much as he could his self-appointed judges—which was, for the most part, their hands. It was difficult to be sure, but he suspected that at least five of the 31 were women. There was not a single pair of hands in the entire ominous circle that was as gnarled and wrinkled as his own—but he was reluctant to take that as good evidence that no one else here was as old as he was. Indeed, he had begun to suspect the opposite. If the scene was reminiscent of the Inquisition of the 17th century, he thought, that was probably not entirely by coincidence, nor the result of the careful mimicry of some ancient woodcut.

Eventually, his examination began. The acoustics of the chamber were odd, making it difficult to determine exactly which death's-head was speaking. Without the sight of moving lips to prompt him, he could only determine the approximate direction from which each voice came.

"Thank you for the oaths that you have given, Mr. Temple," said a voice which might have been that of Giuseppe Balsamo, in English. "We have taken due note of their exactitude, and we are as acutely aware as you are that some of our questions will touch on information that you must have learned in your capacity as a policeman. I repeat, however, that we are not enemies of England, and have nothing against you personally."

"As to whether you are enemies of England or not, I cannot judge as yet," Temple replied, "but there is certainly a matter of personal enmity between us. You have kidnapped my grandson, and two other children who are his closest friends, and have offered them for ransom. That is a despicable criminal act, and no amount of mummery will dignify it. If I can do so, I shall deliver you all to the judgment of the law—but first, I must see the children safe, and it is for that reason that I am here. Let us discuss the terms for the ransom of the two remaining boys."

"The matter is not so simple, as you well know," another voice said, also in English, but more heavily accented. "The most important issue of personal enmity at stake here is that between you and the man who once styled himself the Comte de Belcamp."

"That is irrelevant," Temple said, flatly. "I am here as the representative of the widowed Comtesse Jeanne de Belcamp."

"But she is not a widow," another voice put in. "Let us not waste time with pretense. You were expecting the Comte to join you on the coach from Calais. He did not. Where is he now?"

194

"I have no idea," Temple said. "I can only suppose that he is making his own arrangements, probably in Paris, to hunt you down."

"He has no army to bring to bear," said a voice from the left, again speaking English, seemingly not as a native tongue. "He has no claim on the Deliverance now, and could not muster them if he had." There seemed to be no president or appointed spokesman in the circle, but neither was there any apparent contest as to who should speak next, nor any obvious system determining the pattern according to which they took turns.

"I had not seen the man for more than four years, until three days ago or thereabouts," Temple said. "I know nothing of his resources."

"You know his work."

"Do I? I have been presented with a bizarre patch-work of evidence and rumor, but I know nothing for sure. He claims to know how to restore the dead to life—but from what I've seen, it's a futile pursuit even if the claim is true. Nor is he the only one who knows the se-cret. If, as it's claimed, the method is a matter of science and not of magic, it will be common knowledge soon enough. Even if that were not the case, kidnapping his son in the hope of making him surrender it is a foolish as well as a vile thing to do. If, as rumor has it, you repre-sent yourselves as alchemists and magicians, you are doubtless long practiced in deceit, but I would have thought you capable of greater wisdom. Since you obvi-ously cannot make gold, but must steal it like any other bandit troop, why can we not discuss *that* business, in-stead of wasting time with idle fancies."

"You have not sworn an oath to tell the truth, Mr. Temple," said yet another voice, "but it will save us all time if you do. The longer you seek to delay us with your policeman's tricks, the longer it will be before those two children are returned to their anxious mothers. As a matter of fact, we *can* make gold—but the process is expensive as well as troublesome. Magic is not wish-fulfillment, Mr. Temple, but labor as hard as any other. Nothing is free—especially the ability to live longer than the normal human span. The resurrection of the dead cannot be expected to be different; it will doubtless be a difficult and tiresome business, requiring hard-won skills and carefully-stored wisdom."

"So it seems," Temple agreed, softly. "You might have done better not to wait for my arrival. Had you sent your note a little earlier, you might have snared a man who knows far more about the dead-alive than I do."

"Don't lie to us, Mr. Temple." This voice was as calm as all the rest, but it had an edge of exasperation in it. "Edward Knob knows only what he saw. You have access to everything that King George's police forces know."

Temple felt a slight sinking feeling, as he realized that these masqueraders really did think that he knew far more than he actually did. They had assumed that King George's police forces had been watching the mysterious Arthur Pevensey since the *Prometheus* had first docked at Purfleet, and that they had kept close watch on the *Outremort* too. Perhaps there were European nations where foreign ships were monitored as closely as that, but England had too may radicals of her own to deal with, and was obsessed with the danger that her own people might revolt as the French and Americans had.

Temple and his fellows had been far too busy hunting Tom Paine and suppressing *The Rights of Man* to take any note of the likes of Pevensey and Mortdieu, whose adventure would have been written off as a mere ghost story had any word of it reached the ears of Temple' fellow agents. Not a word had been committed to any official dossier until Temple had made his own report of his official interrogation of Ned Knob and the subsequent events at Greenhithe. If his calculatedly-tentative statements concerning Mortdieu had been believed by his superiors, their only response would have been relief that the *Outremort* had sailed, thus taking the problem away from the troubled English shore. Unless and until he returned to London—or more grey men began to appear in evident profusion—no clerical functionary working for the English government would inscribe a single line to ensure that the matter would be pursued.

"There may be men in England who would be intensely interested in Ned Knob's story," Temple said, dully, "but they are not working for His Majesty's Government. From the viewpoint of Lord Liverpool, and everyone working in his administration, it would qualify as Jacobin science, to be parodied and suppressed. No Parliamentarian in England has the imagination to see what difference the resurrection of the dead might make to the condition of the world, and none would sympathize if they could. Their response to the notion would be to condemn anyone who espoused it as an enemy of the state, to be pilloried, imprisoned or transported."

"Do you have the imagination, Mr. Temple?" someone—who might have been Balsamo—asked.

"I doubt it—and if I had, it would be better for my career were I to suppress it rigorously," Temple replied.

"You're too modest, Mr. Temple. Were you a man who put his career before his principles, you would not be here."

"The reward for such meager imagination as I have," Temple told them, "is I am considered a madman, tolerated but not trusted. My past achievements, and the skills that forged them, are grudgingly respected, but I have no friends among those in power, or even positions of petty authority. But that is not the issue. I repeat: I had no idea that the former Comte Henri de Belcamp, alias Tom Brown, was still alive until three days ago. The first conversation I had with him lasted no more than a few minutes, and mostly consisted of threats uttered while he held a gun to my head. The second was solely concerned with the matter of the kidnapped children, which forced us to set aside our differences and make an alliance. I did expect to meet him on the packet-boat from Dover, and to travel with him to Paris thereafter. I do not know why he did not follow his own plan—assuming that plan was any more than a device to manipulate me. All I *can* do, gentlemen, is to negotiate the release of the two children. That is the only reason why I am here. I strongly suspect that you know far more about this business of resurrection than I do. I am sorry that I cannot tell you more, but it is not my duty to the crown that prevents me from doing so—it is simple ignorance."

There was no interval in the séance, nor any whispered conference— merely a few moments of silence while each of the people in the death's-head masks decided whether they ought to believe him. The one who eventually spoke was not Balsamo, nor the man with the beard he glimpsed in Little Switzerland. It was a voice that spoke with a measure of natural authority.

"Your achievements and the skill that forged them are respected here, Mr. Temple, and not grudgingly. We have always thought of you as an ally of our cause, even though you probably had no idea we existed, or what our cause might be. You have called us common bandits, and we are certainly outlaws, although we could never concede that we are common; even so, we are entirely in sympathy with the campaigns you have waged against men like Tom Brown—and, for that matter, Tom Paine. We preferred Napoleon to the National Convention, but only as the lesser of two evils, and we had no love for the *Ancien Régime*, although we thought it the least of the three evils. We do not like Napoleon any better *now that the Deliverance has done its belated work*, and we are urgently desirous of acquiring the secret of resurrection in order that we might begin to use it in a manner that befits its delicacy as well as its power. We would like you to help us, if you will."

There were two important revelations contained in that speech, which Temple was both astonished and glad to learn. He closed his eyes momentarily, trying to summon up the image of a grey face, and cursed himself roundly for not having realized immediately *who* General Mortdieu must have been when he was alive. Even Ned Knob had guessed, it seemed—although he had kept the information to himself, save for one teasing hint. Temple understood, too, why men like these might be consternated by the former Comte de Belcamp's choice of resurrectees. Apart from the self-styled Mortdieu, formerly Napoleon Bonaparte, the only one who had so far recovered a significant portion of his former identity was Alexander Ross, popularly known as Sawney, the master of a "puppet tribunal" that had made mock of English justice, and the leader of a troupe of false witnesses, ever-ready to provide alibis at the Assize Court on payment of a fee.

"You say that you have the philosopher's stone," Temple said, slowly, ignoring the question that he had been asked. "You can make gold, and live far longer than common men—but not without cost. The gold you make is too expensive, and the longevity you have falls far short of immortality. You want the secret that Belcamp has so that you might reincarnate yourselves, and further increase your superiority to the common men to whom you concede no rights—and you want to reserve it for yourselves, if you possibly can. Will you assassinate men like Michael Faraday and Luigi Galvani, or will you try instead to recruit them to your pantomime?"

"We have never had to persuade men of that sort to join us," someone told him. "They have always done their utmost to beat a path to our door, as soon as they suspected that we might exist."

"And those who have not succeeded have done their very best to imitate us," another supplied. "The Rosicrucians are only the sincerest of our flatterers."

"And now, Mr. Temple," the man with the authoritative voice said, "you know that we exist, even if you only suspect who and what we are. What is your answer to our question? Are you prepared to help us obtain the secret that we seek?"

"I'm not even prepared to consider the matter until the two children you have stolen have been returned to their homes," Temple retorted, immediately.

"Yes, of course," the other countered. "But you are not such a prisoner of obsession as to be unable to think of the day after tomorrow. You know exactly what I am offering in return for your loyalty. Are you determined to die, or are you prepared to seek a better redemption that faith has to offer? If the latter is the case, will you curry favor with your former enemy, in the presently-frail hope that he might bring you back from the dead as something better than an imbecile—or would you rather ally yourself with wiser men? Men, that is, who have means of preserving you much as you are while you wait for the most disciplined scientists in the world to perfect the process of resurrection, and will do their utmost to guarantee you an afterlife in which your faculties will not be diminished in the least. You and I both know that it is possible, do we not? And it is, as you have remarked, a matter of science, not of magic."

"I'm flattered by the invitation," Temple said. "Will I be a full member of the brotherhood, or merely an employee, like your methodical kidnappers?"

"We are not offering membership," the authoritative voice replied, frankly. "We very rarely issue invitations of that sort, and you have done nothing to deserve one. We are merely pointing out the logic of the situation—which is that your wisest course of action by far would be to commit yourself to our cause."

Gregory Temple nodded his head slowly, to imply that he could indeed see the logic of the situation. He wondered if John Devil would see it as clearly, if he were sitting here—and how John Devil might react to that logic, when the time came for him to do so. "First," he said aloud, "the children. When the children are both safe, there will be time to consider other matters. Until then—and afterwards too, if you have sold them for three satchels full of gold—you are merely common criminals, too despicable to warrant the consideration of an honest man. My answer is no."

He thought that he heard the slightest of sighs disturb the silence that followed but it might have been a draught of air from one of the corridors disturbed by some obstruction.

I'm a fool, he thought. *I should have lied, and played along—but at least I'm still an honest man.*

"English stubbornness," said a voice from the left, in an accent more heavily accented than most. "We've met *that* before. We still need the other—and we need him now."

There was a sound then—not of a sigh but of a muffled hiss of disapproval.

"Take him back to his cell and tell him what to do," instructed the commanding voice. "We proceed with the plan."

Chapter Six
Giuseppe Balsamo's Overtures

After eating a meagre meal, Gregory Temple began to write a letter that he had been asked to produce on his captors' behalf.

My dear Suzanne, it read, *I have seen both Armand and Friedrich, and can attest that they are both well and are being cared for with all possible diligence. I am convinced that their captors have no intention of harming them, provided that the remaining two thirds of the ransom are paid. Tonight, at midnight, the Comtesse de Belcamp must take a further 10,000 livres to the bridge by the mill, where the Comte de Belcamp once saved her life. She may take Pierre Louchet with her, but no one else. The second child will then be surrendered. I will write again to give instructions for the third exchange. I too am quite safe and well, and will return to you when this business has been completed.*

He signed it *Your loving father, Gregory Temple*, and gave it to the masked man who was waiting to read it. When it was given back to him, he sealed it in an envelope, which he addressed *To Madame Suzanne Thompson, Château de Belcamp*. Before handing it over to the man who was waiting for it, he said: "When you have taken the second child away, the third may be afraid. Might he be allowed to share a cell with me so that I can reassure him?"

"Perhaps," was the only reply he got.

He surrendered the envelope, and went to lie down on his bed while the bar was replaced on the door of his cell. He did not feel tired; indeed, he felt quite well. He had no idea how long he had been unconscious, or to what particular day the "tonight" written in his letter might refer, but even if he had slept for 24 hours, it seemed to him that his current feeling of well-being was unexpected. The meal he had been given had satisfied his hunger despite its simplicity—which supported the hypothesis that he had not, in fact, slept around the clock—but he had only been given water to drink, so he had not been dosed with any obvious medicine since waking up. Whatever the kidnappers had given him to make him fall unconscious in Little Switzerland had not done him any harm, and apparently quite the reverse. Was that, he wondered, supposed to be a subtle demonstration of the extent and efficacy of their esoteric knowledge?

He wondered whether the fact that he had been asked to instruct the Comtesse de Belcamp to make the second ransom delivery meant that her son would be the second to be surrendered. If the conspirators' chief objective was to lure Henri de Belcamp out of hiding, they must be hoping that it would bring him hurrying to the bridge by the mill. It seemed a risky strategy, though. If he had not reached Miremont yet, the second exchange would doubtless proceed as ostensibly planned. What then?

It occurred to Temple that the demand that Jeanne de Belcamp should make the second exchange might be a feint, and that the child she would obtain in return would be Friedrich Boehm. But that seemed an unnecessary complication. Perhaps the alchemists believed that the order in which the children were returned would make no difference to Henri's inclination to intervene. They might well expect—and rightly so, in Temple's view—that pride would compel him to make just as much effort on behalf of Sarah O'Brien's child as Jeanne's. Sarah had, after all, been his close companion—and presumably his mistress—for far longer than Jeanne Herbet.

On the other hand, Temple thought, the kidnappers might have some way of knowing that the first installment of the gold had been provided by Jeanne, and were anxious that Sarah might hold back her share if her son was released before Armand. Was that likely? Temple had only met Sarah O'Brien while she was playing other parts—Sarah O'Neil in London, then Lady Frances Elphinstone in Miremont—and he could not claim to have the measure of her, but if she and Jeanne really had fallen out, despite the fact that Sarah must have moved back to the new château following her husband's death in order to be near her, her response to an appeal for help might be difficult to predict.

Temple was conscious of the fact that he was concentrating very narrowly on the immediate matter in hand, and ought perhaps to be devoting more thought to the question of exactly who his captors were and what their grander plan might be. He was first and foremost a policeman, though. He was no longer attached to Scotland Yard, because the King and Lord Liverpool apparently thought that his talents as a detective were more useful in another context, but he was still, in his heart of hearts, a diehard opponent of crime. His vocation was to catch robbers and murderers, coiners and cut-throats, kidnappers and fraudsters—anyone, in fact, who threatened to disturb the peace of law-abiding citizens.

Many attempts had been made to bribe him, and he had rejected them all, because his was a calling that could not be corrupted without being utterly betrayed. He had been accused of breaking the law himself—and had done it, too, most of all when he cheated his way into Newgate Prison with the intention of liberating a wrongly-condemned man—but he had never betrayed his calling, always acting in favor of innocents and against malefactors. That was his duty and his sole purpose now, no matter what fantastic lures might be laid out for him.

For that reason, he maintained the concentration of his thoughts on his future course of action in respect of the captive children—or, in a matter of hours, the captured child. His only objective, for now, was to keep that child safe. If there was a possibility that he and the child might escape safely, then he must try to do so—but in order for that possibility to come about, he would need to find out a great deal more about where he was being held and exactly how it was guarded. Might his captors consent to their prisoners taking a little exercise in the open air? Probably not—but he would ask anyway. If no escape proved possible, then he must think instead in terms of protection and defense—but he no longer had his revolver, or his knife. Both had been taken from his person while he slept, along with his watch, his pocketbook and most of his other trivial possessions. He had no weapons but his hands and his wits

No matter how insistently he told himself that he was not impotent, while he was sound in brain and limb, his opportunities for action seemed direly limited.

After what seemed like two hours, he heard noises in the corridor. He went to the door of his cell, opened the hatch and tried to see what was happening, but the angle was too narrow. It was his ears that told him that one of the two boys was being taken from the cell next door. Their youthful voices, raised in distress, told him that it was indeed Armand, not Friedrich, who was being taken away to be sold. He called out to Friedrich in very poor German to tell the boy not to be afraid, and then renewed his pleas in French to be allowed to have the boy in his own cell, so that he might soothe the child's fears—but the only reply he got was: "Later, perhaps."

He inferred from this that his captors had something else in mind for the interim, and so it proved. After the lapse of a further half hour or so, his cell door was opened and an unmasked man came in. It was the man with whom he had conversed on the coach between Calais and Amiens. The door was closed and barred behind him by someone in the corridor.

"Have your 30 comrades delegated you to make a further appeal, Signor Balsamo?" Temple asked. "There is no point, you know, until all three children are safe at home."

"There will be no further appeals, Mr. Temple," the other said. "We are satisfied that if you know any more than you were prepared to tell us in the star chamber, you will not yield it voluntarily. Personally, I believe you, and I made no secret of my confidence."

"Have you come to gossip about the wonders of electricity and the meaning of progress, then? I thought we had exhausted those topics on the coach. Shall I continue to address you as Signor Balsamo, by the way, even though that is not your name?"

"It would be convenient," the pretended Italian told him. "Are you so certain that I am not who I claim to be?"

"Perfectly certain. I saw the logic of the situation when your comrade mentioned the Rosicrucians and other flattering imitators. It is a matter of cryptic coloration. In pretending to be members of your brotherhood, poseurs like Cagliostro and the Comte de Saint-Germain provide you with a series of perfect disguises. By offering yourselves as defunct poseurs, layering folly upon folly, you augment the impression that there is no reality behind the sham. What better disguise could there be for a true secret society than to masquerade as a false one? The devil's greatest asset, it is said, is the inability of people to believe in him."

"We are not the Devil's men, Mr. Temple," the false Balsamo said. "You have encountered us in strange circumstances—but that too is a kind of imposture."

"I disagree," Temple said. "I, a policeman, have disguised myself on occasion as a criminal, in order to eavesdrop on other criminals—but I have never gone so far as to collaborate in their crimes. Had I done so, I would have ceased to be a policeman in disguise, and become a common criminal myself."

"I take your point. We have honest ways of making gold, of course, which were adequate to our limited needs for centuries—but times are moving much more swiftly nowadays, and our needs have increased. Our worst misfortunes are far behind us, but we have had our difficulties during the recent wars, just like everyone else. We have always been firm adherents of the principle that the end justifies the means—including means like hostage-taking, and others of which you would disapprove wholeheartedly. It was once a common form of bargaining between powerful men, and we are great adherents of tradition. Are you so sure of your own moral ground, when your own upholders of the law hang so many men, woman and children, and transport so many others to hell-holes in Australia, in futile support of your own less-than-ideal ends? Your friend Ned Knob would not agree with you, I think."

"He's not my friend."

"He's a better friend than you imagine, Mr. Temple. He has confirmed your testimony and proclaimed your innocence loudly."

"Is he here, then? How did you capture him?"

"As my friend told you last night, he went chasing wild geese—and they caught him. He seems a good deal more interested in our temptations than you did, Mr. Temple. He offered to work for us with great alacrity, and swore to be our loyal servant for as long as we might need him."

"Then you would be well advised to make full use of him," Temple said. "He's a man of many talents, despite his size. If anyone can discover where Mortdieu went, he's the one."

"I don't doubt it. He probably swore eternal allegiance to Mortdieu with the same alacrity that he swore it to us, not to mention Henri de Belcamp. Still, such a man might be useful to us—more useful, it appears at present, than a man like you."

"Agreed," Temple said. "And yet, here you are, talking to me like a man in need of friends. Would it be possible, do you think, for me to take young Friedrich outside for a breath of fresh air? It's not good for a child of his age to be locked away underground for days on end. The air down here is terribly stale."

"On the contrary," the false Balsamo replied, calmly. "The corridor is uncommonly well ventilated, for a convent whose bowels have been slotted into natural fissures in the rock. Monks have ever been an ingenious breed, you know."

"Apparently, some monks have been more ingenious that anyone knows," Temple retorted. "That's where your secret society must have begun, I suppose, in the days when monasteries were havens of peace in a turbulent world, and the sole custodians of learning. There's an unmistakable Catholicism about your procedures and philosophies—the whole idea of a covert elite deciding what the multitude might be allowed to know, and hence to do, is Romanist through and through."

"We have a few ostensible protestants in our ranks," the other told him. "We have attempted to transcend the squabbles of the Reformation as we transcended other schisms, with a measure of success. You are correct, of course, to judge that we have long been formulated as a monastic order, but we have never taken our orders from Rome—not, at least, from the papal throne. In better times we were sometimes able to put our own people on the papal throne, but that was never easy. The college of Cardinals was always a difficult institution to influence, let alone control. Fortunately, its habitual introspection makes it easy to avoid."

"And I suppose that you have sometimes been able to put your people on other thrones?"

"No, Mr. Temple—that is one aspect of the game that we have let well alone, although we have sometimes had occasion to ensure that secular thrones fell vacant. It is a fundamental aspect of our philosophy that the quarrels of petty barons and their armies are irrelevant to the true pattern of history, which is the growth of knowledge and its careful application to the cause of progress—in the meaning that *we* attach to the word."

"You spent a good deal of time criticizing my use of the term," Temple told him, "but I confess that I still do not know exactly what you mean by it. Somehow, having sat through your star chamber as well as your subtle interrogation on the coach, I cannot see you as Godwinian Utopians committed to the ideals of universal liberty, equality and fraternity."

"No, Mr. Temple, we are not Utopians. We are, I suppose, dedicated Malthusians—although we have less affection for the negative checks than you might have supposed, on seeing our costumes. We believe in liberty and fraternity for the few and discipline for the many, and in a strictly ordered social hierarchy."

"Did you tell Radical Ned Knob that before he swore eternal loyalty to your cause?"

"I was not present, but I dare say that my comrades mentioned immortality for the few and mortality for the many, and pointed out the logic that would lead any other situation to hellish chaos."

"I would have to give that matter a great deal of thought," Temple said. "Even Ned Knob, I think, might hesitate to jump to that conclusion too readily."

"I agree entirely that you should give the matter a great deal of thought, Mr. Temple—and I trust your logic to reach the right conclusion in the end. We really are men of science nowadays, you know, even though we retain certain attitudes and rituals that were more appropriate to the alchemists, astrologers and diviners we once were. There was a time our organization included the only true men of science in Europe—but that was before the invention of the printing press. We underestimated its danger—perhaps the worst of all our many miscalculations, the Great Catastrophe notwithstanding.

Attempting to manage history is a direly difficult business, as you can imagine."

"If history was ever manageable," Temple retorted, "it is no longer. Any attempts you have made in recent times must have demonstrated the hopelessness of the task."

"A fair comment," the other admitted, equably. "Even if one sets aside such irrelevancies as wars, empires and nations, we have not done well. We kept the telescope, the microscope and the principles of optics secret for 300 years, but they escaped us in the end. Steam we thought unlikely to make a vast social impact, for want of fuel, but we failed to anticipate the extent of the coal measures waiting to be excavated. The real tragedy, though, has been our failure to usurp the secrets of electricity. That genie was out of the bottle before we even had a chance to attempt its containment. No matter how many Faradays we might be able to draw into the fold, there will be many more—and the reanimators are already proliferating in their wake. This is our final challenge, Mr. Temple—our last throw of the dice. You may be able to understand our desperation."

"May I?" Temple counted. "You're talking to me face-to-face now, but you're hardly less a phantom than your 30 comrades. I don't know who you are, and don't expect to find out. I can't see the least reason to think that the secret of resurrecting the dead would be any safer in your hands than anyone else's, or that you have any moral claim to it whatsoever."

"It would be safer in our hands—especially if it could remain our monopoly for a while—because we would not use it to make slaves or soldiers. It would be safer in our hands because we would use it to preserve intellect and creativity, not brute force and greed. It would be safer in our hands because we would be deaf to the wailing of the multitude who want their *loved ones* restored but cannot see beyond the horizons of their own petty affections and lusts. It would be safer in our hands, Mr. Temple, because we are not radicals but conservationists, enthusiastic to maintain the order of the world irrespective of the ambitions and bloodthirst of empire-builders. Yes, we are a self-selected and self-appointed elite who believe that we have the right to determine the fates of our fellow men, irrespective of what they may think or believe—and we are proud of that fact, just as we are proud of the fact that our order began within the confines of monachism, not on a battlefield. Whether you will support our cause or not is up to you, Mr. Temple—but if you set yourself against us, you will be taking the side of violent and brutal men, of tyrants and terrorists, of the avaricious and the envious. You cannot begin to think about that, of course, until young Friedrich is safe once again in the bosom of the *vehmgerichte*, who are searching for him as we speak and will doubtless storm the convent without a second thought, with guns blazing and swords red-tipped, if they contrive to locate us and think us too weak to resist. But when you *can* think of it, Mr. Temple, think about the kind of world that is nowadays in the making, and whether you believe the message that General Mortdieu asked Ned Knob to deliver on his behalf, forswearing any desire to make war upon the living."

Temple no longer had any retorts ready for delivery, and fell silent for a while. Eventually, he said: "Who are you, really?"

"I cannot tell you any more than I have already told you," the false Balsamo replied. "Should we ever meet again, in the outer world, you will recognize me, and will doubtless discover the name by which I am more generally known—but even then, Mr. Temple, you will know no more about who I *really* am than you know at this moment. I will have Friedrich Boehm brought into your cell, so that he might feel a little safer—but his best guarantee of safety is not your presence but his mother's temperance, Suzanne Thompson did no harm by appealing to you for help, but Sarah Boehm was unwise in the extreme to turn to her husband's former comrades for assistance. Whether they achieve anything or not, she is theirs now, and always will be—they will have her child far more securely and permanently in their grip than he is now in ours, and they will not make him the kind of man that you or I could admire."

"What do you want from me, Signor Balsamo?" Temple demanded.

"Nothing, at present," Balsamo replied, "since you have made it abundantly clear that you are unwilling to give anything. You know as well as I, though, that this will not be over when the last child is exchanged, no matter what we obtain in return. *The Empire of the Necromancers is only just begun*, and there will be a titanic struggle to determine the form of its hegemony. You are caught up in that struggle whether you like it or not, and you will have to take sides in situations far more complex than this one. You have met Mortdieu and you know Henri de Belcamp of old. It is for you to decide which of the players so far engaged offers the least of several evils. Personally, I still think that you are a natural ally rather than our enemy—but only you can decide. That is what I came to say to you. Goodbye, Mr. Temple—I am leaving the convent now, and it may be some time before we meet again."

After finishing this farewell speech, the false Balsamo rapped on the door, to signal the masked man outside to remove the bar. Then he went to Friedrich Boehm's cell, and brought the boy to Temple's, as he had promised.

It was not until the bar had fallen back into place, and the corridor was silent again, that Temple realized that he had not the slightest idea how to hold a conversation with a three-year-old boy—especially one whose first language was German.

"You must not be afraid," he hazarded, in limping German. "You must be strong."

The child drew himself up to his full height—which was unimpressive, even for a child of his age—and said: "I am a Boehm. I am not afraid."

Temple could imagine the other Friedrich—the recently-dead father—saying exactly the same thing, in exactly the same fashion, in frank defiance of his own lack of height and health.

"You are a Boehm," Temple agreed. "You and I shall befriend and protect one another, as good men should."

The little boy nodded his head, and Temple turned away from him, in order not to see his tears.

Chapter Seven
The **Vehmgerichte***'s Rescue*

When Friedrich Boehm had gone to sleep, lying on the bed and wrapped in a blanket, Gregory Temple sat down on the floor of the cell with his back against the wall, facing the door. He became gradually drowsy, but did not go to sleep. He drew up his knees and folded his arms upon them in order to let his head slump forward, but he lifted his head again whenever his ears caught muffled sounds from the side or above—which they often did, as the convent's inhabitants went about their mysterious business.

Because his watch had been removed and he had been unable to observe the alternation of day and night Temple had no reliable means of knowing what time it was, but suspected that it must be the early hours of the morning when he heard the bar being removed from the outside of the door, in what seemed to him to be a stealthy fashion. The peephole had not been opened.

Temple came to his feet, ready to act. He was poised for action by the time the door swung inwards to reveal a man in the customary black habit—with the hood up—and death's-head mask. The only unusual thing about him was that he was holding a sabre in his right hand. Temple could not possibly recognize the man—but he started as he recognized the weapon as a German duelling-blade. The newcomer raised the upraised forefinger of his left hand to his lips; Temple nodded his head to signify that he understood.

The newcomer looked down at the dark-haired boy on the bed, and nodded his head slightly in apparent satisfaction. Then he knelt down, and pushed the mask on to the top of his head before putting out a gnarled hand to wake the child. Temple did not recognize the man, but he was unsurprised to see duelling-scars on his cheek and forehead.

When the boy opened his eyes, the knight of the *vehm* whispered to him in German, so rapidly that Temple could not catch the full significance of what was said. It included a reassurance, and an instruction to be very quiet.

The child seemed reassured to hear his native tongue. Although there must have been some among his captors who spoke it fluently, this was obviously a different sort of man, more closely akin to the servants who had looked after him in his infancy.

When the child had signified his consent, the rescuer brought him to his feet and wrapped the blanket more tightly around him. Then he signaled to Temple, indicating that he must pick the boy up. Temple nodded to signify that he understood, and assented to the request. Friedrich Boehm made no objection to being picked up, and seemed perfectly ready to play the game required of him.

The German readjusted his disguise. He had not brought a light of his own, but he picked up the candle from the night-stand to light his way back along the corridor. He moved through the bowels of the convent confidently, apparently having no doubt as to the route he must take. The way was tortuous, involving three flights of stone stairs and numerous turnings, but in the end they came to a small door that let them out into a small chapel. From there, they made their way into the nave of a larger church. There were other men waiting in the shadows of the church, all of them wearing death's-head masks—but they were obviously allied with Temple's companion, for they returned his silent salute—which must have included a private signal of some sort—and moved off into the chapel from which he had come. They were not dressed in the same fashion as Temple's earlier interrogators—they wore ordinary traveling-cloaks over secular costumes—but Temple supposed that the convent's residents must dress is a similar fashion when they went abroad, and that the death's-heads would protect them from instant recognition as invaders,

The rescuer and his two charges made their exit from the church through the vestry, and continued to move very carefully until they were clear of its sur-rounding buildings. The German blew out the candle then, although the moonlight and starlight were very hazy and it was difficult to see their way in the neat-total darkness. They went forward carefully, eventually reaching a clump of trees 200 paces further on, beyond a fallow meadow. There were at least a dozen horses teth-ered in the gloom within the copse. So far as Temple could tell, there was only one man guarding the horses, who uttered a whispered challenge in German, and was immediately satisfied by the password their guide re-turned.

"Is that Friedrich?" the sentry asked, suggesting to Temple that the agents of the *vehmergichte* had not been certain until now which child had been taken to the sec-ond exchange.

"It's Count Boehm, alive and well," the other re-plied, again pushing his mask up to the top of his head so that he might see a little better. Temple's German was not good enough to follow exactly what the man went on to say, but it was something along the lines of: "Herr Temple and I will take him to the meeting-point and guard him until dawn. We'll gather then to take the Pontoise Road as a company, whether we have the gold or not. Is that understood?"

The sentry nodded.

"Are you able to ride with the boy?" the German asked Temple, in slurred English.

"I can hold him securely enough," Temple replied, in the same language, "and keep him warm—but we'd best proceed slowly."

The other nodded, and they did indeed proceed very slowly across open country, for two miles or more, until they reached a wall of thorn-bushes. Their rescuer led Temple and Friedrich Boehm into a clearing within the bushes, to which the crag formed a rear wall, and where there was a small hut. There was smoke belching from the chimney, promising a good fire within.

"You will be safe here," the German said, still speaking English. "I will stand guard outside."

"You'd be warmer inside," Temple said—but a knight of the *vehm* was too proud to be intimidated by mere autumnal cold.

Temple carried the boy indoors. There was a candle already lit within, and a man sitting on a stool beside the hearth.

"I'm delighted to see you, Mr. Temple," John Devil said, in English. "I wanted to rescue you myself, of course, to seal our new alliance, but our friends would not hear of it. It's not so much that they don't trust me, but they have their own priorities. They would never have found you without my help, mind—I knew the country well enough to set them on the trail, although not as well as I imagined. Who would have imagined that it might be possible, in 1821, to find not one but two priories of the *Civitas Solis* so close to Pontoise? Is that my son you're carrying?"

"Temple answered the last question first. "It's Friedrich Boehm," he said. "Armand was taken to Miremont some hours ago. The second exchange should be complete by now, and your son should be safe at home."

John Devil frowned, perhaps in disappointment that he was not to meet his son, and perhaps partly in puzzlement, having expected a different order of exchange.

"I suppose that I would have been less surprised had you appeared in my cell yourself than I am to find you sitting out the action here," Temple said, setting his burden down with great care. "Would it not be better if our entire company were to set off immediately, without waiting for dawn?"

"It might," John Devil agreed, "but it's difficult and exceedingly uncomfortable traveling by night in weather like this, and it's less than an hour till dawn. I'm not in a position to give orders—my position is slightly delicate, as you'll readily understand—and my friends were determined to search for the gold while the convent was so lightly defended, even though that very fact suggested that it had been removed in the course of the general exodus."

"I'm afraid that I don't understand your position at all," Temple told him, as he persuaded Friedrich to lie down on the hearth, still wrapped in the blanket. "I have no idea what is going on. Your German is presumably far better than mine—can you explain to Friedrich that he is safe?"

John Devil knelt down to talk to the boy, and did so in such a soothing fashion that the child seemed completely reassured. When he stood up again, he turned to face Temple and said: "I'm sorry that I didn't join you in Dover as we arranged, Mr. Temple, but an opportunity turned up that seemed too good to miss. It led me into unexpected trouble, but I've always had a knack of turning trouble to my advantage. The situation remains delicate, as I say, but it seems that all three children are safe now—which was our primary objective. I assume that Jeanne will be able to produce the required ransom?"

"I believe so," Temple confirmed.

John Devil nodded, and sat down on his stool again, pointing Temple towards an identical one. "I'll tell you my story, in brief," the blond man said. "When Ned Knob brought me Suzanne's letter, I was in company with a few old friends—Tom Brown's friends, I fear—who immediately volunteered to help. I sent one to the river shore to inquire as to the disposition and sailing plans of any vessels that might be useful, and another to procure horses for a ride to Dover. When I returned, I discovered that there was a vessel moored not far from Southwark Bridge which intended to sail for Antwerp via Ostend before dawn. She had no engine, but the weather reports promised a favorable tide and a brisk northerly wind. It seemed likely to be the safer course, given the difficulties that might arise in riding to Dover on winter ground, so I hastened to beg a passage, along with two of my friends.

"The tide and the wind were exactly as anticipated, and the captain of the vessel assured me that I would have no trouble making my way from Ostend to Calais by sea or land—or, if it seemed preferable, going directly from there to Paris. Because my friends were so obviously English, I thought it best not to travel as Henri Moreau, and it happened that I had papers on me that I had used several years before, when I traveled regularly via Ostend and Antwerp on my way to and from the university where I studied in Germany. They were in the name of George Palmer—which is, of course, familiar to you, although I recklessly assumed that everyone else would have forgotten it. Not so—there were Germans in the crew who had exotic connections and long memories. George Palmer, it seems, was wanted for questioning in Germany—not by the authorities, but by one of the relics of the old *vehms*, which refused to die when Napoleon's minion was supposed to have killed them off."

"So the murder of Maurice O'Brien has not been entirely forgotten," Temple observed.

"That was hardly a crime, in the reckoning of the *vehms*," John Devil told him. "No matter how much favor he had accumulated, O'Brien had been a mercenary officer in Napoleon's army, and was not considered a man of honor. What had not been forgotten was the abduction of his daughter, Sarah O'Brien, who was a ward of the Emperor Francis I, and thus had a significantly different status. In itself, that might not have been afforded any great importance, but the efforts made by Count Boehm to trace her—in advance of his fateful meeting with you in London—had not only placed the members of his own society on the alert but had sent signals to every port from Le Havre to Copenhagen. The police and customs knew nothing of it, but George Palmer has been a hunted man since 1814. The fact that George Palmer had ceased to exist in 1813 confounded the search—but the years that had elapsed before his abrupt resurrection was not time enough for the name to be forgotten, and Count Boehm had never thought to call it off when he found the object of his desire.

"At any rate, I was ambushed and seized before the ship put in at Ostend, and compelled to complete the journey to Antwerp as a prisoner. My friends could do nothing, and were left behind. From Antwerp, I was taken overland to Brussels, and then to Liège—with all due haste, thank God. Liège is not a city where a *vehm* could normally be convened, but the word had already gone out from Central Westphalia bidding members of the society from Maastricht, Aachen and Bonn to make their way there with all possible speed for a special convention. That was no coincidence, of course—the reason for the command was a message received from the widowed Sarah Boehm, appealing for help in the recovery of her kidnapped son.

"The convoluted politics of the *vehmgerichte* are of little relevance to outsiders, but you will understand that a certain tension existed between the *vehm*—which had seen two of its strongest and bravest members assassinated in the persons of Friedrich Boehm's older brothers—and the Irish widow of the enfeebled heir to their fortune. There was no evident enmity, but relations had been a trifle cold. Her appeal for help was, in its way, a small godsend, promising that the relationship would be much warmer in future—and, more importantly, ensuring that young Friedrich would be committed to the society from his earliest youth, to be educated in its traditions and ambitions.

"As you will imagine, the assembly was not grateful to be interrupted by the delivery of a prisoner it had not time to try, but when I explained to them that I was not George Palmer at present, but the similarly dead

Comte Henri de Belcamp, and thus intimately familiar with Miremont and its surroundings—I might have stretched the truth slightly in that regard—and also the father of one of the other kidnapped children, their attitude changed dramatically. I was immediately recruited to their cause.

"We had already wasted too much time to be able to reach Miremont ahead of you, so we did not arrive in time to discover what was happening on Little Switzerland, but we did contrive to pick up the trail of Ned Knob, who was attempting to follow the tracks of the man who had given the message to that poltroon Besnard. Ned had picked up the trail—and was in too much of a hurry to cover up his own. We were able to track him, and were close behind him when he walked into the trap that had been set for him. We followed his captors easily enough to an ancient convent in the middle of nowhere. At first, I thought it a mere shell serving as a temporary refuge for common bandits, but as we watched it I guessed—much to my astonishment—that we might actually be dealing with something far more exotic. Although there were no documents of any kind, I was amazed to discover evidence once we got inside that we really were dealing with an echo of the *Civitas Solis*."

"Of which I have never heard," Temple put in.

"That's not surprising, even for a secret policeman—Scotland Yard's records can hardly go back *that* far. The society has rarely had much success in its dealings in England since it recruited Roger Bacon, and the dissolution of the monasteries by Henry VIII was greatly to its disadvantage. Rumor has it that it was prevented from recruiting Leonard Digges thereafter, despite Mary's accession to the throne, and failed to recruit his colleague John Dee—although it punished him for it, and would not forgive him when he begged for reconsideration during his journey to the heart of the Empire. How they would have loved to snare Isaac Newton! I dare say they feel the same now about Faraday—but that's by the by. The significant point is that, although they used to consider themselves above the Papal Throne, they always operated more far comfortably in Catholic countries than Protestant ones—including France, despite what they call the Great Catastrophe."

"The man who called himself Giuseppe Balsamo mentioned that," Temple remembered.

"Balsamo? You meant Count Cagliostro?"

"No—that was merely the name he gave me. They seem to imagine themselves to be real alchemists, cleverly hiding themselves by masquerading as charlatans—but they might well be charlatans themselves."

"They might—but the alternative is the more exciting prospect, wouldn't you agree? Everything I knew about them until today is ancient hearsay, implying that they no longer exist—but if they *are* still active, even as bandits, that would be a wonder of sorts."

"*Civitas Solis* means *city of the sun*," Temple said. "Was that really the name of their society?"

"Societies of that sort always have several names," John Devil replied. "But yes—that is the one by which it is most commonly known to those who have heard of it. It was formed at much the same time as Augustine published his *Civitas Dei*, which argued that Christendom need not regret the fall of Rome too much, because the city of God was an idea contained in the hearts of men, not a mere place. The *Civitas Solis* aspired to be a city in the same sense: a city of enlightenment, located in the hearts and minds of scholar monks."

"And the Great Catastrophe?" Temple queried.

"Pride goeth before destruction, the Bible warns," John Devil observed. "The *Civitas* should have heeded that warning, no matter how much of the scriptures it had set aside. When the organization was at the very height of its power and wealth, its militant and commercial arm—almost the whole of its corporate body, in fact—was rudely and brutally excised by Philippe le Bel of France, who was in dire need of its money."

"*The Knights Templar?*" Temple said, incredulously. "You're saying that these clowns in death's-head masks are the relic of the Templars."

"No, I'm telling you that the Templars were an extension of the *Civitas Solis*, whose humbled brain survived the murder of its extended body for a while—longer than a while, it seems. They struggled afterwards, of course—such stored wealth as they contrived to save was gradually expended in order to secure the remnants of the order. They must have sunk to a very low level—almost as low, perhaps, as the relics of the *vehms*—but if they still have secrets to keep... did they interrogate you?"

"Yes," Temple replied, "but not brutally."

"But they believed you when you explained that you knew less that they had hoped?"

"Yes," Temple repeated. "They seemed particularly bitter about my inability to tell them where they might find you."

"Did they, indeed? Well, to resume my story, we thought at first that the children must be held in the convent to which they took Ned Knob. While my tempestuous allies were making plans to attack it, though, we saw a substantial number of men ride out, mostly leaving in ones and twos at intervals of several minutes. I had not confided my suspicions regarding the *Civitas Solis* to my companions, but they deduced immediately that the monks must be heading for a conventicle at some other abbey.

"When the exodus was complete it was a much simpler business to invade the building and release Ned Knob. There was little resistance, and no one was badly hurt. As I told you, I took the opportunity to look for evidence as to the true nature of the convent's tenants, and found enough to interest me. When Ned had told us what he could, we sent him back to Miremont to tell Sarah that we would do what we could to rescue the remaining children. He wanted to go with us, but my new friends were suspicious enough of me and did not want a second outsider in their midst.

"The convent where you were held seemed a much tougher nut to crack, and we had not even begun to conceive a sensible plan of campaign when a company rode out—keeping tightly together, this time—with a child in their midst. The boy was wrapped up too well to be identifiable, but what Ned had told me allowed me to deduce that the three children must now be in three different places—one in Miremont, one on the road to Miremont and one still in the convent.

"Our company was not large enough to split into two, and it seemed best to let the second exchange take place while we secured the child who remained in the convent, if that were possible. Again, the task became much easier in short order as the pattern of the first exodus was reversed; monks again began to leave in ones and twos, presumably dispersing before returning to the base we had already sacked.

"My inclination was to forsake the ransom payments, but my companions were differently minded.

They wanted to seize the one already paid, and then make plans to ambush the men returning with the second. I suppose that I shall be given no alternative but to join them in the second project—but they will take due care to make sure that you and young Friedrich are not exposed to any risk. They will return you to Miremont with an escort of two or three riders. If I can, I shall rejoin you there in a matter of hours, and face the various accusations and resentments that are my just desserts. You have, I suppose, informed my widow that my death was more apparent than physical?"

"I could not lie to her, even by omission," Temple said.

"Of course not. I did not ask you to do so. You have always been an honest man."

"Unlike you, Mr. Brown," Temple pointed out.

"Unlike Tom Brown, and unlike Henri de Belcamp," John Devil agreed, readily enough. "But they are dead and gone now—one hanged, one shot. I have made a fresh start, not for the first time. I suppose that I should not have brought George Palmer back to life, even as a temporary flag of convenience—but it worked out for the best, I think... and it was, after all, Tom Brown, not George Palmer, who murdered Maurice O'Brien and Constance Bartolozzi."

"I can see why the members of the *Civitas Solis* are so interested in you," Temple observed. "That one mere body can contain so many different persons, alive and dead, is a remarkable natural phenomenon."

"So it is," John Devil, agreed. "I should not have been tempted to wear a Quaker hat in London, either—but the weather was so cold and the hat so warm! I wish I had it now. Does it seem to you to be getting darker outside rather than light?"

The hut's only window was shuttered, but the shutters were as ill-fitting as the door, and the texture of the darkness was evident through the cracks."

"The Moon has set and the mist is getting thicker," Temple judged. "The starlight is so feeble now that one would need to be a cat to make much of it. I think there may be hint of twilight in the east, though—dawn surely can't be more than a few minutes away."

"Let's hope that it illuminates more than freezing fog," John Devil said. "I suppose our alliance is almost at an end. That's a pity, in a way."

"Is it?" Temple queried, archly. Then, suddenly recalling the portrait hanging in the drawing-room at the Chateau de Belcamp, he said: "How did you know, in Newgate, about the locket I wore around my neck? Did Suzanne tell you?"

John Devil was sitting in such a fashion as to keep his facial expression shadowed from the candlelight, but the voice that answered seemed surprised. "Is that what you thought?" the bandit asked. "If I were you, I'd have had more faith in the loyalty of a daughter such as her, even though I had succeeded in blackmailing her for lesser favors. No, I saw it when I was James Davy, and took a closer look when I once found you asleep, after an exceedingly hard night's work. I was struck by the lady's resemblance to my mother, and the coincidence of the initials. Indeed, I half-convinced myself that the lady must actually have been my mother, and took such great amusement in the thought that she might once have seduced you, while you were a married man... but I never had the chance to ask her, and I doubt that it was possible. It was a fine story, though, was it not? My hidden ace... almost, but not quite, good enough to complete the slam. I knew when I left you, though, that you wouldn't

229

die, and wouldn't be driven permanently mad. It's strange, I know, but I couldn't entirely regret it. I had always admired you, Mr. Temple—I wanted to believe that you could endure the worst that John Devil could do to you, and survive to fight another day, even against me. Is that odd, do you think?"

"Insane," Temple judged.

"Perhaps, Mr. Temple, ours is a *folie à deux*," John Devil said. "We bring out the worst in one another... or the most bizarre, at least. You were wrong to think that Suzanne might be to blame, though, and I hope you'll beg her pardon for entertaining the suspicion."

"If it's James Davy I must blame," Temple said, "then it's James Davy I shall hunt down. Or is he dead too?"

"As a doornail, I fear. A pity, in a way—he'd have been well-placed to intercept the news when Lord Liverpool's agents figure out where Mortdieu took the *Outremort*. A ship and company of that sort can't escape the eagle eyes of the ruler of the seven seas for long, can she?"

"You'll never bring your reanimated Napoleon to heel," Temple opined. "Nor would you ever have been able to use him as you hoped had you actually succeeded in freeing him from St. Helena before he died."

"Perhaps not," John Devil agreed. "But he has grey men with him who might have far more in common with me than with him, if they only had a choice of tutors. Sawney Ross and poor re-embodied John are not his kind at all—nor is Germain Patou, in spite of his desertion at Greenhithe."

"What do you mean, exactly, by *re-embodied* John?" Temple wanted to know.

"Exactly what I say," was John Devil's infuriating reply. "As the *Civitas Solis* must have discovered, life can be hard for a sound brain in an irreparably damaged body—but as my Swiss predecessor found out, the vital principle contained in electricity can do more than renew life in pre-existent corpses. I was only at the beginning of my studies, you know—there was so much more to discover, so much more too attempt. Germain is brilliant, but he lacks my imagination. He and Mortdieu do not realize how much they need me...

"You were right about that hint of twilight, I think—but the Sun isn't making much impact on the mist as yet, and I don't hear any riders approaching, singing German drinking-songs as they come—as they would be, if they'd won a victory with their swords and seized a fortune in gold."

"It wasn't such a vast fortune," Temple said, almost absent-mindedly, as his eyes followed John Devil's to the cracks in the shutters. It was definitely brighter now, but there seemed to be a wall of mist surrounding the hut, which would reduce visibility to a matter of a few yards even though the Sun had unmistakably risen.

John Devil did not reply to Temple's remark. Instead, he went to the door and opened it. He looked out, and cursed. He called out in German, but received no reply. He drew his rapier.

"I'm sorry, Mr. Temple," John Devil said, softly. "It seems that the sequence of traps had one more layer than I anticipated."

Temple cursed himself for not having taken time to think about that possibility, even though he knew that it was Comte Henri de Belcamp, and not the not-so-vast ransom, who had been the true objective of the tangled plot.

First, Temple moved instinctively to stand astride the sleeping boy. Then unable to tolerate the thought of not being able to see what was happening, he picked him up and went to the door,

Black figures were appearing in the mist, on every side of the hut but the one backed by the wall of rock. It was not obvious, at first, that their hoods were the hoods of monastic habits rather than traveling cloaks, but their faces stood out more clearly in the grey mist than anything else: the faces of leering, fleshless skulls. There were at least eight of them, all on foot and all armed—some with swords, and some with pistols. The horse on which Temple had arrived was still tethered to a tree nearby, but there was no sign of the German sentry.

"They read the *vehm* more accurately than I did," John Devil murmured, mournfully. "Whether the brave knights were taken prisoner or whether they've simply sold us out, the result's the same—but we're not taken yet."

Chapter Eight
Friedrich Boehm's Return

"Put down your sword, Monsieur de Belcamp," a soft voice said, in French. "We mean you no harm." As in the council meeting, it was difficult to determined which of the masked men had spoken.

"Why, there do not seem to be more than a dozen of you," John Devil retorted, lightly. "Cyrano de Bergerac put a hundred to flight, so legend has it—and they were authentic bravos, while you are mere scholars in fancy dress. You might shoot me, of course—but what use would I be to you dead or mortally wounded? I, on the other hand, do not care in the least how many of you I hurt." While he spoke he placed himself *en garde*, taking up a protective position in front of Gregory Temple, which the detective did not like at all.

"Don't be a fool, man," he murmured. "Drop your weapon."

"I'm delighted that it will distress you to see me killed, Mr. Temple," John Devil said, in a voice far louder than a murmur, which must have been audible to everyone present. "Please don't worry too much about the fate of my soul,"

"There is no need for anyone to be hurt, Monsieur de Belcamp," said the soft voice. "None of your German friends has been killed, nor any of our people. We have no wish to harm you, and you have no reason to wish harm to us. Would it not be best to bring this matter to a peaceful conclusion?"

Temple was strongly reminded of the awkward situation that had developed aboard the *Outremort*, when little Ned Knob had made John Devil and Mortdieu see sense—but Ned Knob was not here now.

"That's not my way," John Devil said. "I was born reckless—sired by Satan, I wrote in my autobiography, although I'll allow that there was a certain satirical self-aggrandisement in that. I'll make you a bargain, though, if you wish it—I've always had a fondness for diabolical pacts."

"You're in no position to make terms, Monsieur," the voice told him.

"Am I not? Damn me, I'll make them anyway. Let Gregory Temple mount up and take the child safely back to his mother, and I'll not only drop my sword but swear to tell you everything I know about the means to reverse death. You'll get no more ransom money—but my friend was telling me just a moment ago that the ransom wasn't such a vast fortune anyway, so I deduce that you're at least as interested in me as you are in the gold. If I fight, you know, I'll be a very difficult opponent to put down, given that there are far less than a hundred of you. Which of you will take the lead, by the way?"

Temple knew that the other was playing a game, and putting on a show—but the men in masks did not seem so sure.

"Temple can go," the voice of the death's-head conceded, as if it were a matter of no importance whatsoever. "He may take the child. Now, please drop your sword."

"Wake the boy and mount up, Mr. Temple," John Devil said. "If you travel a few points north of east, orientating yourself by the dawn, you'll come to the Pontoise road eventually. Turn left. From Pontoise, the way to Miremont is signposted, if you don't know it. Go now, before I'm tempted to fight them anyway."

Temple knew that for an empty boast, but he thought that he understood why John Devil was putting on his show of reluctance and recklessness. Meekly, he did as he was told. "This does not make us better friends, Monsieur de Belcamp," he said, as he set the dazed child carefully in position before climbing into the saddle, bidding him to be silent with a warning hiss.

"Of course not," John Devil replied. "But you won't find it nearly so easy to hunt me down once I'm wearing a death's-head mask and have a thousand convents scattered half across the world in which to hide. Don't worry about who is trapping whom, Mr. Temple—just get Sarah's boy safely home to her, and tell her to be careful of the *vehmgerichte*, which is yet another company of fools uneasily ignorant of the redundancy of their cause."

Temple did not reply to that, but he moved his horse towards the gap between two thorn bushes that marked the exit from the clearing. The two masked men blocking the path moved aside to let him through, and no one else tried to stop him once he was on the open heath again.

He found the Pontoise Road easily enough, and had no difficulty then finding the route back to Miremont. No one came after him, and he soon allowed the horse to relax into a safe and steady pace.

"Nearly home," he said to his tiny companion, in English.

"*Danke*," the boy replied, as if to chide him for his lapse.

The mist lingered long into the morning, but the cloak in which Friedrich was swaddled kept the cold at bay. The boy seemed uncommonly patient and quiet; whether that was because he had been brought up in a disciplined fashion, or because he was in shock after all that had happened to him, or whether he simply had no confidence in his protector's German, Temple could not tell.

By the time they reached the gate of the château, Temple knew that the effects of the drug that had been used to render him unconscious had completely worn off. His limbs and face were numb with cold, and his aggravating exhaustion had returned in full force. He rang the bell, and waited for help to come.

At least a dozen people came rushing out. As soon as Pierre Louchet had opened the gate, Sarah Boehm rushed forward to collect her son. She showered Temple with effusive thanks as he got down from the horse, but he shrugged them off, telling her that the friends she had summoned from Germany had actually contrived the rescue, and advising her to take the boy home and get him warm without delay. Her carriage was reharnessed in a matter of minutes, and she set off in company with Robert Surrisy and her servants before Temple had had time to go inside the château, flanked by Suzanne and Richard Thompson.

"I'm all right," he assured them, "and I don't deserve any congratulations. I didn't free the boy; I merely brought him home."

He was ushered into one of the smaller reception-rooms, where a fire was blazing and an assortment of chairs had been arranged about the hearth. This must have been the room in which they had all been waiting, for there were more seats than people now. Ned Knob—

who seemed to be avoiding Temple's eye—took it upon himself to effect the necessary rearrangement.

"Thank you, Mr. Temple," said Jeanne de Belcamp, when he had slumped into an armchair as close to the burning logs as he could, "for whatever part you played. My son was returned at midnight last night, exactly as specified in your letter."

"I doubt that you will see your money again, milady," he replied. "I don't know what happened when Sarah's pocket army of obsolete knights went in search of the first consignment of gold, but the kidnappers were well-prepared. Reinforcements must have arrived in force as soon as they discovered what had happened at the second convent—the one where Master Knob was being held, after walking into their trap. Either the knights were trapped and disarmed, or they made a bargain to sell us out. Fortunately, the kidnappers were more interested in securing Henri de Belcamp's peaceful co-operation than holding on to Friedrich—when he threatened them, they let us go."

"I was a fool to be taken so easily," Ned Knob put in. "But you must admit, Mr. Temple, that neither of us suspected the sheer numbers we were up against. I was thinking in terms of eight or ten adversaries skulking in a cottage or a barn, not a hundred false monks with more than one priory at their disposal." He was still not meeting Temple's eye, doubtless expecting a stinging rebuke for having passed Suzanne's letter to John Devil rather than delivering it himself.

All Temple said was: "They weren't false monks—not, at least, in the sense that they were merely pretending to be monks. If they and Monsieur de Belcamp are to be believed, their organization might date back further than the days of St. Benedict and the cenobites of the

237

Thebaid. There might well be documents stored in Whitehall that refer to them, but they're probably rotting in a vault with other produce of Tudor and Jacobean spies. They obviously don't consider themselves a spent force, though, in spite of their intense interest in resurrection."

"You have seen Monsieur de Belcamp?" Jeanne de Belcamp asked, keeping her voice quite level. It was a simple prompt; she knew that he had

"I parted from him a little while ago, milady," Temple told her. "He traded his freedom for Friedrich Boehm's—or, at least, made a great pantomime of doing so. My guess is that he was delighted to discover who the convent's proprietors were, and was very enthusiastic to join them. I dare say that he will do his utmost to use his supposed captors for his own ends, just as he tried to use the Brotherhood of the Deliverance. At this very moment, if I read him right, he thinks himself their potential master, and is planning how to deploy their resources in his own cause. He does not change.

"In all fairness, though, it might well have been your husband's ability to manage the *vehmgerichte* that got Friedrich safely out. I don't believe that the kidnappers ever intended to harm the boy, and they will presumably be well satisfied with the trade they made, but things could have gone badly awry had the agents of the *vehm* taken matters into their own reckless hands. If word of this gets around, milady—as it surely will, thanks to the involvement of the *vehm*'s self-styled knights—you will have to pay more attention to your son's protection. You need better fences and a larger staff. Pierre Louchet is a good and loyal man, but he cannot defend a château."

"Did Henri see his son?" was all the Comtesse said by way of reply. "Armand has no memory of seeing him, but..."

"No, milady," Temple said. "He could not get close to him. I do not think he will try again, at least for a while. I do not pretend to understand why he has not contacted you during these last three years, when there were abundant opportunities, but now that the boy is safe, I suspect that he will continue to consider you a widow—and himself, I suppose, a ghost."

There were no tears in Jeanne de Belcamp's eyes, although Suzanne's were moist.

"I know that you hate him, sir," Richard Thompson said, "but he is not entirely a bad man."

"He put the noose around your neck from which he eventually condescended to save you," Temple said, harshly. "With more than a little help from Ned Knob. You owe him nothing, Richard."

"But I owe him everything," the Comtesse de Belcamp said. "He really did save my life, and he really did love me, with all his heart. He still does—and that, however perverse it may seem, is why he believes that he must remain dead."

Suzanne got up from the settee where she was sitting with Richard. "I must go to my son," she said. "I'm sorry—I know that it's absurd, but I am too anxious when he is out of my sight even for a few minutes. Will you come and see us, father, before you go?"

"Go?" Richard echoed. "You're surely not intending to go, sir? Not today."

"You are very welcome to stay for as long as you want, Mr. Temple," the Comtesse said—although Temple could see that she understood well enough why he would not linger long.

Temple did not answer Richard, who only hesitated momentarily before following his wife.

"Will you leave us alone for a few moments, Ned?" Jeanne de Belcamp asked. Ned hopped down from his chair, bowed and left the room.

"Is he well?" the Comtesse asked, when the door had closed.

"Yes, milady," Temple said. "I never saw a dead man looking so well, and there was a real fire in his eye at the end. He's still very young, and his dreams have not abated in the least. If he no longer plans to conquer India, it's because he cannot think of anything less, now, than the conquest of death itself. He pretended to be somewhat dismissive of the society into whose custody he has delivered himself, but he is highly delighted with the notion of resuming his work with their collaboration. They will be a hundred times more useful to him than Germain Patou—and I suspect that he is more than capable of taking control of the organization that considers him its prisoner and its instrument."

"He will not be coming home for quite some time, then."

"He has no home, milady. He came here once because he wanted to make use of his father. He was astonished to find you here—and was thrown completely off balance by the discovery, as headstrong and purposive men often are by the unexpected. He might as easily have killed you as fall in love with you, but he's a man of very powerful passions, however perverse they may be."

"And now that your alliance is over, you'll resume the business of hunting him down."

"Until five days ago," Temple said, grimly, "I had had no business with him for three long years. I have a

240

job to do, and a duty to perform, which have nothing to do with him—or had not. It will be very difficult indeed to persuade my blinkered superiors that the grey men are the seed of a revolution in human affairs far more powerful than the one envisaged by the poor fellows in St. Peter's Fields, who are merely asking for the right to vote for the government that rules their lives—but I shall have to try. What they will command me to do about it, I have no idea. I am not even certain in my own mind what I ought to suggest. They may well be interested in the society that he has joined, though, if not in him. Secret police are jealous folk by nature, intolerant of any rivalry."

"Who are they?" the comtesse asked, at last.

"Like the *vehmgerichte*, they appear to be the residue of a reality that ought to have dwindled away to mere legend—but there are a great many men in today's world who are trying to live out the legends of the past. The account their representative gave me and the one that your husband subsequently supplied are doubtless shot through with illusions and impostures, but they are men of flesh and blood, who do more than hold meetings in fancy dress. They have a mission now, and will pursue it with all the gladness of men who have been without a clear and achievable purpose for far too long. When I explain that in London... yes, milady, I dare say that I shall be set to hunt your husband again, if only as a first step in a much broader campaign."

"I'm glad of that," the Comtesse de Belcamp said. "I cannot expect you to violate the trust of your profession, of course—but I hope that I might learn something of your progress, and hence of his. You will maintain contact with your daughter now, I presume—unlike my husband, you will not continue, perversely, to play dead?"

"I have been a unforgiving fool," Temple admitted. "My own cardinal fault is stubbornness—but you're right. I shall maintain contact with my daughter, if only by letter, and it's not impossible that you might learn something of my progress, insofar as my duty will permit me to let it be known."

"Would you like to see my son?" she asked, out of the blue.

He only had to meet her eyes to understand. She did not expect to see her husband in the foreseeable future, but she hoped that Gregory Temple might—and she wanted Temple to be able to tell the late Comte de Belcamp that he had seen his son, the rightful Marquis de Belcamp.

"Yes, milady," Temple said. "But I should like to see my grandson first, and my daughter. There is an order of priority that ought to be observed—and enough warmth has now returned to my ancient bones to permit me to follow it."

He stood up, and she stood too. He bowed, but she was not content wth that and offered him her hand.

"I would like to be your friend, Mr. Temple," she said. "I hope that will be possible, given that my husband, your former enemy, is dead. I would like to think that you and I could start afresh, with nothing between us but the gratitude I owe you for coming so promptly to our assistance when you were called. Can we do that?"

Temple took the proffered hand, and kissed it. "Yes, milady," he said. "I will be your friend, and a friend to young Armand, if I can."

"And Sarah?" the Comtesse de Belcamp ventured to ask.

"That might be more difficult," Temple admitted, "especially now that she is inextricably tangled with the *vehm*. But I will certainly go to see her and Surrisy before I leave, and build what bridges I can."

"Good," the Comtesse said. "Now, I must follow your daughter's good example. I shall expect to see you in Armand's room when you are able to come."

On the way to Suzanne's apartment, Temple met Ned Knob, who was loitering in a corridor in the obvious expectation of such a meeting. The little man still seemed anxious.

"I did what seemed best, Mr. Temple," the little man said, defiantly.

"You did right," Temple conceded, grudgingly. "Just as you did at Greenhithe. I know better than to ask a loyal radical like yourself whether he would be interested in a position with Lord Liverpool's secret police, but will you at least condescend to travel back to England in my company?"

Ned seemed startled by that, and then suspicious—perhaps fearful that Temple only wanted to pump him for information about his radical acquaintances—but in the end he nodded. It was Temple who offered to shake hands.

Then he went in to meet his grandson, and to make amends for his desertion of his daughter. The fault was not mended in a minute, or even an hour, but he found the time eventually to meet Armand de Belcamp too, and memorize as many details of his existence as a paternal ghost might justly find interesting. By the time he went to the new château, night was falling again, so he had no alternative to postpone his journey plans until the next day.

Sarah O'Brien, as he had expected, was not much interested in counting him a friend, but she was still grateful for what he had done for her son. She had received a letter from the men she had begged for help, which assured her that Temple had, in fact, done nothing, and that it was they who had saved her the necessity of paying any ransom, but Friedrich had apparently told her a different story.

Surrisy was suspicious of Temple too, simply because the former lieutenant had spent so much of his precious youth in fighting the English, but Surrisy had always respected him, and was perfectly ready to renew that respect. It was, in fact, Surrisy who eventually took him aside and said: "What is your opinion of this magical means of restoring life to the dead, Mr. Temple? What kind of upheaval is it likely to cause in the affairs of men?"

"In my affairs, very little," Temple told him. "In yours, perhaps, a good deal more. In the lives of Friedrich, Armand and little Richard... no one can tell, as yet. Everything depends on matters not yet ascertained by trial and error. If a reliable means can be found to make all the grey men as mindful and competent as General Mortdieu, then the world will be changed out of all recognition within a generation. If, as John Devil supposes, the brains of dead men can be relocated in new and sturdier bodies, the change will be even greater. If, as Ned Knob once proposed, the grey people will eventually be able to produce children of their own who were never alive in the usual sense... but all of that remains to be discovered.

"When the contest to discover such things was a hole-in-the-corner affair involving lone men of dubious soundness of mind, it was bound to progress slowly— but that is no longer the case. Now there is a t that is no longer the case. Now there is a considerable organization involved, which is already party to uncommon knowledge, and has first-rate scientific minds among its ranks. It is not so very improbable that Michael Faraday, and every other student of electricity in England, will be working on the question within a year, and that the British Empire—like every other in Europe and the world—will be a Empire of Necromancers within a decade."

Surrisy had gone quite white. "I had not realized..." he stammered.

"Given the innate conservatism of the European aristocracies," Temple added, "and the authority of the Church, diehard opposition might slow that timetable by a factor of ten—but it can only be slowed, not stopped. We passed the point of no return some time ago. The world as you and I knew it is already ended. Even if the existing grey men were to be exterminated, and the means of reanimating more were prohibited by law, that would only drive the necromancers underground—where many of them have been well used to living for centuries. If the world is not to become a Gothic nightmare, it will have to discipline its dreams."

"I see," Surrisy said, and paused for a moment before adding: "My mother is not long dead..."

"Exactly," Temple agreed. "Mothers, fathers, brothers, sisters, sons and daughters are dying daily, very few of them unloved. Humankind has been the helpless victim of grief and tragedy since the dawn of consciousness and conscience. Now, the war has begun in earnest. You might try to make your government see that, as I shall try to do in England. It will not be easy."

"No," Surrisy conceded. "It will not."

The next day was the first of December, but the cold relented somewhat as clouds came in from the Atlantic, bringing a steady rain to harass the roads. It did not deter Gregory Temple and Ned Knob from waiting at Miremont crossroads for the *patache* to Paris.

"Since you have forgiven me for giving Suzanne's letter to Henri, and for being on friendly terms with your daughter while you were not," Ned Knob announced, portentously. "I shall forgive you for having me knocked over the head on the quay near London Bridge and arresting me in Jenny Paddock's. You will remain my enemy, of course, while you remain Lord Liverpool's lackey and spy, but you shall have my respect."

Temple shook his head wearily. "That is very civil of you, Mr. Knob," he said, in a voice that sounded very unlike his own, in tone and sentiment alike. "I, in my turn, shall hope that I am not forced by circumstance to have you arrested or hit over the head again."

"You might be forced to do something of the sort," Ned Knob conceded. "Some things never change, despite the fact that everything does. I suppose we ought to be grateful for that, or there would be no sense to life at all."

There was no denying it, so Temple contented himself with saying "True" as the *patache* rolled up—no more than ten minutes behind its stated time—to start them on the long journey home.

www.ingramcontent.com/pod-product-compliance
Lightning Source LLC
Chambersburg PA
CBHW060352030726
47497CB00003B/683